Beware a Pale Horse

Also by Ron Schwab

The Lockes

Last Will

Medicine Wheel

Hell's Fire

The Law Wranglers

Deal with the Devil

Mouth of Hell

The Last Hunt

Summer's Child

Adam's First Wife

Escape from El Gato

Peyote Spirits

The Coyote Saga

Night of the Coyote

Return of the Coyote

Twilight of the Coyote

The Blood Hounds

The Blood Hounds

No Man's Land

Looking for Trouble

Snapp vs. Snapp

Lucky Five

Old Dogs

Day of the Dog

Lockwood

The Accidental Sheriff

Beware a Pale Horse

Sioux Sunrise

Paint the Hills Red

Grit

Cut Nose

The Long Walk

Coldsmith

Beware a Pale Horse

Ron Schwab

Uplands Press

OMAHA, NEBRASKA

Uplands Press
1401 S 64th Avenue
Omaha, NE 68106
www.uplandspress.com

Publisher's Note: This is a work of fiction. Names, characters, places, and incidents are a product of the author's imagination. Locales and public names are sometimes used for atmospheric purposes. Any resemblance to actual people, living or dead, or to businesses, companies, events, institutions, or locales is completely coincidental.

Ordering Information:
Quantity sales. Special discounts are available on quantity purchases by corporations, associations, and others. For details, contact the "Special Sales Department" at the address above.

Uplands Press / Ron Schwab -- 1st ed.

ISBN 978-1-943421-64-0

Chapter 1

EIGHT MOUNTED MEN dressed in black rode silently in single file over the snow-crusted, valley grasslands. A near full moon cast its glow over the white landscape, illuminating the night like a giant lantern, creating a small army of shadows that joined the riders on their journey. Their forms were varied, some appearing short and stocky and others long and lean, and, of course, those in between. Their faces could not be distinguished, however, since each wore a black hood beneath the wide brim of his black, low-crowned hat.

The leader, a man who had adopted the name "Reaper" some years earlier, was a tall, skeletal visage in the saddle, and he raised his hand, signaling a halt. The other riders reined in their horses and gathered within hearing distance. "We should be at the homestead in fifteen minutes," Reaper said in a voice that sounded like a low growl, devoid of emotion. "You know your jobs. Three of us will roust the pair out of the house. We'll torch the place to smoke them out if need be. The two hangmen will find suitable gallows. Check the big cottonwood in the front yard. It's the only tree on the place. A perfect warning sign to those who find the bodies. If that won't work, we'll use beams in the barn and complete our task before we burn it. The rest of you, free any critters in the barn and drive them out. Hold back one horse and halter it for the hangings."

One of the men asked, "Not two?"

"They will hang one at a time. I want the woman to watch her man die before she gets her turn. Just hold off torching the barn till we know the tree will serve our purpose."

He reined his stallion toward their destination, and the riders fell in with nary a whisper in the ranks. The stallion was a large, muscular beast, a claybank, light yellowish in color. Reaper insisted he was a pale horse and had named him Lucifer when he stole the critter some years earlier. Does not the Book of Revelation state that Death rode a pale horse? And, of course, Hell followed.

When the riders approached the farm, a 160-acre tract sitting alone in the middle of prime grazing land, their course was diverted by a barbed wire fence separating the tract from surrounding pasture. They rode along the edge of the fence until they came to a sagging wooden gate across a wagon road that led up to the building site. Several of the riders dismounted and dragged the gate open, allowing the visitors to proceed up the rutted drive that led into the farmyard.

They paused at the edge of the farmstead while Reaper studied the pitiful buildings. The residence was a sod and log structure with a board roof likely sealed by mud or clay that was covered by a good six inches of snow now. He could smell the smoke from what he assumed was a woodstove that drifted his way from a pipe that protruded from the roof. It was doubtless a single room home and warm enough for the two occupants, given the small space to be heated. Sod walls were often two or three feet thick.

Aside from the privy behind the house, the barn and a chicken house were the only other buildings on the site. The barn walls were sheathed with what he guessed to be pine, unpainted and starting to warp, no doubt admitting winter drafts at the seams. The tin roof, however, likely kept out the worst of rain and snow. The lonely cottonwood looked promising, but the hangmen would verify its suitability.

"Let's do our work," Reaper said with a wave of his hand, and the men split off to see to their tasks.

The two men assigned to Reaper reined their mounts forward so that one rode on each side of him, and they moved toward the house. The plan was to crash through the door and surprise Kade McDowell and the woman and drag them from the house. Suddenly, however, a big, gray-furred creature burst from the side of the house, barking ferociously and biting at the horses' legs.

Lucifer held his ground, striking at the hound with his front hooves. The other mounts reared and shrieked, fighting to turn away as the two riders struggled to get control. Reaper reached beneath the black cloak that covered his wool jacket, and slipped his .45 Army Colt from its holster, aiming the weapon at the dog. He squeezed the trigger, and the gun's roar echoed across the valley, launching a lead slug into the animal's chest. The dog gave a quick yelp before it dropped. Reaper was not one to waste cartridges, and he knew it was over for the attacker, or would be soon, so he returned the pistol to its holster.

The soddy remained dark, but he knew the plan to surprise the occupants had been aborted. This gave him no concern. Justice would still be rendered.

The front door opened a crack. "Who is it? What do you want?" It was a male voice.

That would be Kade McDowell. Reaper nudged the stallion ahead. "Step outside, McDowell. Leave your guns behind and bring the whore with you."

"Go to hell." A wild rifle shot came from the door opening before it slammed shut.

Fool. McDowell was not going to change the outcome, only delay it. "Danek, unwrap the torches. I guess we'll have to smoke them out."

His two companions dismounted, and a stocky rider removed a bundle anchored behind his saddle. "I got five torches," he said. "Already soaked with kerosene but I got a bottle in my saddlebags, and I can freshen two for the house."

"Do that. Stake your mounts. Each of you take a torch and toss them through the front windows. Head off to the sides of the house. Danek, you do the left window, and Joker, you take the right. I'll draw McDowell's attention."

He pulled his Henry rifle from its saddle scabbard and dismounted. He levered a cartridge into the chamber and readied to fire, confident that Lucifer would not spook. When the men reached the front corners of the house, he aimed at the left window and squeezed the trigger. The instant the rifle cracked, the window shattered. He was surprised when the other window also broke, and fire was returned from both. The woman must be joining the fight. Good. That was even more reason for her to hang with McDowell.

Still, he had second thoughts about hanging a woman. Was it a step too far? Would it scare off support for the cause? Hanging a male rustler was still acceptable in cow country, and he had strung up a few women in Texas. He was unaware of a female hanging in Wyoming, however, and things were different here. The men in the territory had even granted the vote to women.

His two men were striking their matches now, and the torches flared. They inched along the front of the house, and Reaper cut loose with a rain of rifle fire. The instant he stopped, Danek and Joker stepped forward and rammed the flaming torches through the broken windows before retreating. The frantic yelling and screaming from inside the house informed Reaper that they had been successful. Flaming curtains along the edges of the vacant windows confirmed it.

When Danek and Joker reached the horses, Reaper said, "They'll be out. Five minutes, maybe ten. Don't kill them unless you're forced to. Smoke should take the fight out of them."

One of the hangmen edged his mount over to Reaper. "The cottonwood will do fine, boss," he said. "Nice thick branch about ten feet off the ground and plenty long for a couple's dance."

"Toss your noose rope over the branch. We'll do one at a time. The woman can watch McDowell hang before I decide what to do with her. Pass the word. No names mentioned in front of the woman in case I decide to let her go."

He turned his attention back to the soddy. Smoke streamed from the window openings now. The door swung open, and two rifles flew out and landed in the dirt. McDowell yelled, "We're coming out."

The pair broke through the doorway together, stumbling to their knees, coughing and choking as they sucked the cold air into their lungs. McDowell was a small, wiry man, and at first Reaper was uncertain which one was McDowell. Both wore baggy denim britches and clodhoppers with bulky coats and what appeared to be beaver skin caps with earflaps. He led his horse over to the couple, followed by Danek, who had slipped his Colt Peacemaker from its holster and had it aimed threateningly at the coughing, gasping pair on the ground.

"McDowell?" Reaper said.

One of the figures looked up at him. "Yeah, I'm McDowell. What the hell is this about?"

"Justice. We are the Justice Riders."

"You ain't making sense," McDowell struggled to his feet.

"You've been rustling your neighbors' cattle. Justice demands you pay for it. Who is your woman?"

"This lady is my wife, Ginger, and I ain't rustled no cattle. Them in the pen has got my three dots brand. They was unbranded mavericks on open range, free for the taking."

The woman got up now, still coughing. She was only a bit shorter than her husband, who might stand six or seven inches over five feet. The bulky clothes probably covered a slim figure, and she had a pretty face in the moonlight with fair hair cropped short, so she could have passed for a boy-child. Certainly, she could not be more than eighteen or nineteen years old, Reaper figured. Again, it struck him that she was a poor candidate for a hanging. Public opinion would not come down kindly on such a lynching.

"McDowell, you are not a member of the Wyoming Stock Growers Association. Do you know what that means?"

"I tried to join up, but they wouldn't take me. Operation ain't big enough, they said."

"Only association members can harvest mavericks, and that's during set times. Those are the rules, and the Big River County Stock Growers Association has adopted them."

"Association rules, but that ain't the law is what I was told."

"You were told wrong. It's the law of the range."

"Made up by the big ranchers. That don't make it the law. Report me to the sheriff, if you think I'm wrong."

"That won't be necessary. We'll see justice done tonight. Look over there at your cottonwood." He gestured toward the noosed rope anchored to the cottonwood tree.

"Hanging. You are a crazy son-of-a-bitch. I ain't hanging for taking in mavericks."

Danek stepped over and thumped McDowell on the side of the head with his pistol butt, dropping the young homesteader like a sack of flour. "He'll be good to hang in five or ten minutes, but I'm wondering if you might want to think about this," Danek said before the woman slammed into him and toppled the solidly-built man to the ground where he landed on his buttocks.

She began kicking at Danek and screaming. "You animals. Leave Kade alone. He hasn't done anything to harm you. He's entitled to a judge and jury. Get out of here."

At that moment, flames erupted from the barn. She turned toward the light and was met by Reaper's fist driving into her nose, which sent her reeling backwards, where she fell against Danek who was getting up. He grabbed Ginger, tossed her to the earth. "Stay put and shut your mouth, lady, if you know what's good for you."

Reaper stepped over and gave her several rib kicks and more to her face and head until she was nearly senseless. "Now," he said, "let's get about our business and get this man ready to meet his maker."

"What about the woman?" Danek said. "I'd hate to see that happen."

Danek had fighting skills unequalled by any of the Riders and was the smartest of the bunch, but sometimes he was too soft, and his tendency to give an opinion was an annoyance. But often his instincts were right. Reaper said, "I like her gumption, and I'm not inclined to hang a woman just yet."

Joker, who had joined them, said, "We done it in Texas more than once."

"We caught them in the act. And this ain't Texas."

Flames danced on the soddy's roof now, and Reaper thought of the fires of hell, a nice backdrop for a hanging. Reaper called to his hangmen. "Hey, hangmen, get a horse over here and get the rustler ready for his trip to hell." He turned to Joker. "Can you handle this hellcat? I want her to watch."

"She ain't causing no more trouble. I guarantee it." Joker grabbed Ginger McDowell's wrist and drug her to her feet.

Fifteen minutes later, Kade McDowell sat astride a bay gelding bareback, a hangman's noose looped about his neck, hands tied behind his back, his knees tightly gripping the mount's back. One of the hangmen held the horse's halter, and the other waited near the right buttock.

The hooded men silently watched the scene like it was a holy sacrament in a church. Reaper was disappointed that the young man did not cry or beg. Instead, McDowell sat stone-faced as if he were more observer than participant. Strangely, Ginger McDowell was likewise passive now, seemingly accepting her spouse's fate.

"Any last words, McDowell?" Reaper asked.

McDowell turned his head toward his wife. Their eyes met. "I love you, Ginger. Tell our child that Daddy was not a bad man."

"I love you, Kade, and I will."

The woman was with child. Reaper almost backed off, but, no, he had work to do, and this was just the beginning. "Do it," he yelled. The horse's reins were released, and a hand slapped its buttock. The animal lurched forward, leaving its rider, whose body dropped, suspended by the tree branch. The fall did not break Kade McDowell's neck, so he struggled and kicked for some minutes until the noose strangled him and, finally, he was still.

Chapter 2

GINGER MCDOWELL WATCHED the hooded visitors ride away, apparently headed northwest. Before departing, the vigilante raiders had cut the barbed wire fence surrounding the cow lot adjacent to the barn that confined the dozen Three Dot-branded, young steers and heifers Kade had collected this fall.

She turned back toward the corpse hanging from the tree branch. Poor Kade. He was a decent young man dead too soon after twenty-five years on earth. She hoped there was a heaven and that he found his way there. She had liked him a lot. She had professed her love to him but was not sure what love for a man was. In time she might have discovered this thing called love with him. She had just turned eighteen and knew more than most about some things but a lot less about others. Kade always treated her with kindness, though, never laid a hostile hand on her and did his best, albeit unsuccessfully, to satisfy her in their conjugal bed. For that, she would never have faulted him. She just wanted to please him.

Her first instinct was to try to cut him down, but he was out of reach unless she could capture one of the horses that the invaders had chased off. It occurred to her, also, that perhaps the body should remain undisturbed until the law was called in. Would someone be on duty at the sheriff's office at night? She thought that Deputy Ozzie White slept there most nights. He had always appeared a kindly sort. She was a good six miles from town. The nearest house was Grant Coolidge's some three or four miles down the trail toward town, and the lawyer Hannah Locke resided not more than a mile beyond. Ginger had a feeling she would be requiring a lawyer's services. Her life was suddenly becoming very complicated.

She had no choice but to walk to town. She was afraid to stay here in case the vigilantes or whatever the murderers claimed to be had second thoughts about her reprieve and returned. Thank God, she had slipped into her coat and grabbed the beaver cap before they broke from the house.

The crash of the barn roof caving into the fire snatched her attention and she turned to watch the inferno of flames and sparks that lit the sky. She noted that the soddy's roof must have surrendered more silently during the melee, but the walls stood fast, seemingly impervious to the attack. She doubted, however, that there would be anything left to salvage within.

Ginger knelt beside Mazie, the dog that had sounded the alarm and died for it. She had shown up at the place four months back and decided to stay on. She ran her fingers through her friend's thick fur, caressed her nose. Tears rolled down her cheeks, and she felt a moment of guilt that she had not responded more emotionally to Kade's death. Perhaps she had not faced the reality that he was really gone. She had been like that when her father died some five years back. Grief had not appeared for another year.

She got up and circled the burning heap that had been the barn, wondering how many of the animals escaped. There had been two mares, bred this fall, and a mule, in addition to Rebel, the bay gelding that had been pressed into service by the hangmen. The horse had disappeared following the hanging. Maybe the raiders had taken it as a prize. She was fond of Rebel, a gentle creature that Kade claimed could outrun any critter in a quarter-mile sprint.

The cattle apparently triggering the vigilante attack had access to a sectioned-off portion of the barn for shelter but were free to go in and out of the side door to the fenced lot. Since the fence wires had been cut, she guessed that they would be far away by now, but they should not have perished in the fire.

Mazie's pups? There were two of them still sleeping in the barn, about three months old now, having been born with two others that had disappeared shortly after weaning, likely taken by a coyote or wolf or some other predator. A male and a female, they looked like their mother, gray and thick-furred, and showed promise of being just as large if not larger than Mazie. She called their names again and again as she circled the barn, the heat so intense now that she could not get within fifty feet of the burning structure. "Scamp," she called. "Lovey." She could not spend the night looking for them but promised herself she would return to search. She feared they were incinerated in the fire.

Ginger started walking on the snow-blanketed wagon trail that led from the farmstead to the rutted road that was one thread of the spiderweb of pathways that crossed public and private lands to connect ranches and farms of Big River County to Lockwood, the county seat. It was cold, but she thought that the temperature would not be many degrees below freezing, and it was a still night devoid of the vicious wind that would be tearing through the valley as winter came on. She was taking on her second winter in the North Laramie River Valley, but the previous winter had been spent in the relative comforts of town. She had been nervous about the life she faced in the low-roofed soddy where snow might bury their lodging place, forcing them to tunnel their way out, especially since the discovery that she was with child.

A half hour later, Ginger was discouraged. She had underestimated the chill, and her teeth were chattering now. The snow-filled road ruts had tripped her to the ground twice as she tried to maneuver between them. At the present pace, she would not reach the Coolidge house before daylight if she survived that long.

Then she heard the snow crunching behind, and her heart raced at the realization she was being followed. The leader had, indeed, had second thoughts and sent someone for her. She could not outrace a pursuer on this road or across the frozen grassland. She stopped and turned around to face her fate.

Thirty feet in front of her, a horse whinnied. A riderless horse. Rebel. She almost fainted with relief. "Rebel," she said softly. "Come on, fella."

The big bay trotted toward her and seemed grateful when she grabbed its halter and began rubbing its muzzle. The horse's presence warmed her and gave her hope. Without bridle and the bit and reins to control the gelding, she was not certain he would help that much, but she took comfort that she was no longer alone. Rebel, notwithstanding his name, was such a gentle creature, she wondered if she might not be able to grasp his mane and guide the mount with tugs on the halter.

It was worth a try, she decided, but without stirrups or saddle how would she get astride the horse to ride him? Her bulky clothes would not render her more acrobatic. Her eyes scanned the valley around her, and no more than fifty feet distant, she spotted a boulder at the fringe of a cluster of stones. She led Rebel off the road and across the snow-matted grass to the big rock that she figured would give her another two feet above the ground. That would be enough if the horse did not bolt.

She tugged the gelding over beside the boulder and, clutching its mane, scrambled upon the stone, slipping and sliding before getting a foothold. She pulled herself onto the horse's back, landing crossways when the mount decided to move slowly out of position. Neither horse nor rider panicked, however, and soon she was upright. She leaned forward and tugged the halter, pulling Rebel's head toward the road. She turned it again as they approached the road, thinking they would follow the road's course but stay with the grass to avoid the treacherous, invisible ruts.

Chapter 3

GRANT COOLIDGE'S GRAY and black striped tabby cat woke him with his yowling. The tomcat had already rousted Grant out earlier during the night to go outside to relieve himself rather than use the sandbox his human kept in one corner of the room. "Sarge, what is it now? I can't be getting up every few hours to tend to your demands. You sleep all day. We need to get our clocks synchronized."

The cat's use of the box was whimsical. His name had been chosen because of the way he had taken over Grant's life like sergeants had in his Army days. Occasionally, he regretted surrendering to Trouble Yates's pitch to buy the animal. Yates, a sixteen plus-year-old entrepreneur, had his fingers in a half dozen enterprises and raising cats was one of them, a quite profitable one, Grant had learned. There were plenty of puppies around free for the taking, but the West suffered a shortage of felines that sold at a premium because of their utility as ratters.

Sarge had been a twenty-dollar purchase, but so far as Grant knew that cat had no interest in ratting, much preferring to share his human's beef and ham.

Grant swung his legs out of bed, grateful he had surrendered to wearing long underwear for sleeping garb a month ago. It was early October 1885, and he was embarking on his first winter in the Rocky Mountains with initiation by an early snowfall in the North Laramie River Valley.

Sarge was still yowling by the door, but Grant stopped at the fireplace to add a few logs to fading embers before he answered his summons. When he reached the door, he stopped short upon hearing the rapping on the thick oak. He detoured to snatch his old Army Colt from the holster that was suspended from its belt on a peg a few steps from the door.

He could not imagine who would be at his door several hours before sunrise. "Who is it?" he called.

"Ginger McDowell," came a female voice. "Kade has been killed."

He remembered Ginger. He liked her and had been happy for her when she married the young cowhand. Grant unlatched the door and opened it. He was greeted by a red, swollen face and nose that rendered the woman unrecognizable.

"Ginger. My God, what happened? Come in."

"My horse first. His name's Rebel. Can I put him up in your stable for a bit?"

"Of course. Let me tend to him. I'll pull on my boots and grab a coat. You come on in and get warmed up."

"He's just haltered and might not let you get ahold of him. Get your boots on, and I'll wait out here."

He turned away, leaving the door ajar while going back to the side of his bed to slip on boots. Only then did he remember that he was dressed only in his underwear. He plucked his Levis off the nearby chair and pulled them on before sitting down on the bed to put on socks and boots. Snatching up his sheepskin coat, he returned to Ginger and took the horse's halter. "You go on in and get warmed up by the fireplace. I'll see to the horse, brush him down and give him some hay and a bit of grain. I've got some water barrels in the barn that aren't frozen over yet, so I can put a bucket of water out for him."

It was a good half hour before he returned to the house. When he entered, he was surprised to find his visitor asleep in a fetal position on the bearskin rug in front of the fireplace. Sarge, the traitor, was curled up against her back, lucky devil. He decided to let Ginger sleep a spell while he organized his thoughts.

Tossing his coat on his bed at one end of the room, he moved to the opposite side where he had recently installed a cast-iron cookstove, heated by coal. The stove had rendered the fireplace an unnecessary luxury in terms of heating the two-room cabin, but he liked the ambience of flickering flames in the stone fireplace and enjoyed pulling his rocking chair and lamp table nearer to the hearth and reading there some evenings. Sarge preferred the fireplace and a spot on the bearskin rug, and it was nearer Grant's office off the sleeping area of the main room, boosting more heat to his workspace.

With mining in the area, coal was cheap to come by, would burn the entire night, and offered much more control over the temperature. He had already decided that he would use the stacked woodpile conservatively and that he would not be cutting more wood if his current supply ran out sometime during the winter. With the stove and a healthy pile of coal outside, that task could wait till spring.

Grant prepared a pot of coffee to put on the stove, so he could offer a cup to his guest when she awakened. He had picked up some cinnamon sweet rolls at the town's new bakery, and he could warm a few on the stovetop if

Ginger was up to eating. He went into his office which formed an 'L' off the rectangular shape of the log cabin that included kitchen, parlor and sleeping area. Deciding that this day was not likely to be a writing day, he gathered up the scattered handwritten papers, arranged them in sequence, and placed them next to the expensive, unused Remington typewriter that he had purchased on a whim a month earlier.

Ginger McDowell was still sleeping when he returned to the front room. He hated to awaken her, but if her husband had been killed, it was time to discuss the matter. He knelt beside her and spoke barely above a whisper. "Ginger. Ginger, we should talk now."

Her eyes opened slowly, and she looked up at him. "What happened?"

"You fell asleep, but we should talk about why you are here. I have a pot of coffee brewing if you want to come over to the table." He stood up, extended a hand to her and helped her to her feet. "Can I help you get the coat off? I don't think you will need it now with both the cookstove and fireplace heating."

He seated her at the little table and poured a mug of coffee for each of them, noting that a sliver of sunlight was slipping through the curtains. "You're probably not hungry, but I have cinnamon rolls I could warm up a bit."

"I'm starving," she said. "That would be nice."

She did not sound like a bereaved woman who had just lost her husband, but he was glad to warm up the rolls, especially considering he would have been reluctant to eat one if she did not. Also, as a former Union infantry man who had survived Gettysburg, he knew that people reacted differently to death and tragedy. After completing that task and setting a plate with roll and fork at both of their places, he sat down across from her and said, "Now, do you want to tell me what happened and how I can help?"

Ginger nodded but finished chewing a healthy bite of the roll before she spoke. "They lynched Kade. He is still hanging from the cottonwood tree in the front yard." She told him about the hooded men who had appeared at their homestead that night and accused Kade of rustling before they hanged him.

"How many men were there?"

"Eight."

"Anything that would identify them?"

"The leader rode a big stallion, more yellow than white in the moonlight and against the snow. I'm sure he planned to hang me, too, but for some reason changed his mind." She hesitated. "I recognized the leader's voice."

"You know who he was?"

"Not by name, but I would know his face if I saw it. The way he talked told me whose face I would be looking for."

"I don't understand."

"His voice was very, very deep, almost like a bear's growl, the kind folks might listen to if he was giving a speech. It would stand out in any crowd. Scary—terrifying under circumstances like last night."

"So you have met him?"

"Yes. That's all I want to say right now."

Grant reminded himself that he was no longer sheriff of Big River County and certainly had no desire to be after a brief stint in that job last spring. He noticed that she had downed her cinnamon roll during the time he had worked through half of his. "Would you like another roll?" he asked. "I can warm up another."

"Are you sure? I feel like such a pig."

"I have plenty." He got up and warmed another roll. When he turned around to set the plate on the table, he saw that Sarge had sprawled out on the tabletop and was purring loudly while Ginger scratched his ears. "Do you mind this varmint being on the table?"

"Not at all. He's a sweetheart."

"He can be, but he's obviously taken with you."

"Have you thought about what I should do now? About the law and all?" She forked a piece of the roll into her mouth.

She was apparently passing the responsibility to her host. He did not mind, and he had been thinking about the dilemma. "Would you be comfortable staying here while I went to town and brought the sheriff out to speak with you? I thought I would stop by Hannah Locke's place and ask her to come over and visit with you. She is the acting county prosecutor right now, and she will be involved in this at some point anyhow."

"I will be fine staying here with Sarge. Do you have a spare rifle? And I would like to speak with Miss Locke."

"I will tell her that, and, yes, I will leave my Henry and a box of cartridges here. You can handle a rifle?"

"Certainly. Shooting rabbits was the only useful thing my father ever taught me. I'll keep the door latched, but if the vigilante snakes were going to follow me, they would have been here by now. Those aren't the kind to do their work during the light of day."

"All right. I'll head over to Hannah's house in a few minutes. The sheriff's likely going to want you to ride out to your farmstead with him. He will probably bring some help to take care of Kade. Do you want somebody to contact the undertaker . . . to do what must be done?"

"No. I can't afford that. Maybe you could find a blanket, and we can bury him on the place today. He'd like that, I think. Embalming and a coffin only puts off the bugs and worms for a while." She finished her coffee.

"Another cup?" Grant said.

"Not now. Later maybe, if you will leave the pot out. Now, I need to relieve myself."

Grant had wondered about that. "I do have a clean chamber pot under my bed. We could put it in my office for you to use."

"Why not your privy? The sun's up now."

"Well, I do have a path scooped just off the front porch to the privy behind the house."

"Paper?"

"A stack of old newspapers."

"That will be fine. Let me grab my coat, and I'll take care of business there."

When Ginger left, Grant gave a sigh of relief. The young woman seemed much calmer than he felt. He did not know what to make of her, but he had an uneasy feeling that his role in this tragic situation was going to extend beyond his mere turning the problem over to the sheriff. Fortunately, he was ahead of schedule on the six dime novels required annually by his Beadle and Company contract under his pseudonyms P. J. Bowie and Jake West.

That good fortune he owed to his dear friend and lover, Moon Dupree, who rescued his manuscripts before succumbing to the fire in the boarding house she operated and where Grant had resided. His eyes misted at the thought of Moon. She had touched him deeply, and the hurt still flared daily after the passage of over five months.

Chapter 4

HANNAH LOCKE WAS finishing chores in the stable with the help of Primrose, a fifteen-year-old Arapaho girl who had become her ward along with Jasmine Dupree, daughter of Moon, Hannah's best friend, who had died in the tragic fire months earlier. Both girls had been abducted by the slavers responsible for the fire. She was surprised when the stable's side door opened, and Grant Coolidge stepped in.

He was sober faced, which was not all that unusual, but he was also unshaven and unkempt, which was. The forty-year-old Grant was nothing if not fastidious, and the six-footer with chestnut brown hair and hazel eyes was sinfully handsome and seemingly unaware of it, which added to his allure. She consciously kept an invisible barrier between her and the man who was her client as well as the mourning lover of her friend Moon. It had become more difficult as their own friendship grew. She guessed life just was never meant to be simple.

"Good morning," she said, as Grant approached. "What brings you here at this hour of the morning? I thought you were not an early riser, that you worked into the night."

"Usually, but that did not work out last night. I had company."

Company. She had no claim on him, likely never would, but if Grant entertained a woman overnight, he might walk out of the stable with a bloody nose. Disrespect for Moon, she would say.

"I am listening."

"Ginger McDowell came to my cabin several hours before sunrise."

"The Doll House Ginger? The prostitute?"

"Former prostitute, and you know it."

He was scolding her, and she knew she deserved it. "Yes. Ginger helped us recover the girls, and she seems to be a fine young woman. She's married now, but I've never met her husband. Homesteader, isn't he?"

"Was. That's why she came to my house. Her husband was killed last night. Lynched, hanged from a tree in front of their soddy."

"Oh, my God. That poor woman. Why? What is this all about?"

"Rustling, Ginger said. Kade McDowell has been rounding up unbranded cattle and putting his own brand on them."

"Branding mavericks is not necessarily rustling. It's certainly not a capital offense under Wyoming law regardless. The men who did this are murderers and should be brought to account. Does she know who they were?"

"She doesn't have any names. They wore black and were hooded. She thought she would recognize the leader's horse—she heard him refer to it as a pale horse. She claims she could identify him, if she saw him, based upon his voice." He explained the voice connection. "She didn't explain how this came to be."

"That would be shaky evidence in a court of law, but that information could open a door to more solid facts."

Grant said, "She seemed reluctant to talk about how she became acquainted with the leader. I've got a hunch she would be more open with another woman, especially someone like you."

"What do you mean someone like me?"

"It's a compliment. You're a lawyer. You listen. You keep your mouth shut. Anyway, I told her you would go over to my place and talk to her this morning."

"That was a bit presumptuous, wasn't it?"

"Don't get your claws out. I know you've got to get to the office and have girls to boot off to school, but if you could just stop by for ten minutes or so, I know you could give Ginger some comfort."

"You don't even know it's Saturday, do you?"

"It is? My days all run together when I'm writing. I could figure it out on my calendar if I cared."

"Yes. No school. I often go to the office to get some work done, but I don't usually have appointments, and I don't have any today. Of course, I will go be with Ginger, maybe bring her back here if she's willing. As soon as Primrose and I finish chores, we're going to go to the house and have some breakfast. Jasmine is making hot-cakes and sausage and, of course, coffee. There will be plenty. Do you want to join us?"

"It sounds inviting, but I had breakfast with Ginger. I'd better ride on to town and talk to Jim Tolliver and get him started to work on this problem."

"Stop by here when you come back with Jim. He will probably want Ginger to ride with you out to the home-stead. I'll ride with you. Maybe you could see if Brady Yates could bring a wagon from the livery." She could see the exasperation on Grant's face. He was always chiding her about being bossy and taking charge. She went silent.

"I didn't plan to ride out with you. My intent is to put this in the sheriff's hands, and then I am done with it. The last time I got involved with Jim, he got shot and I ended up county sheriff for a spell. Not again."

She planted a seed. "And the experience inspired a book. *The Accidental Sheriff* will be a great one. You told me your publisher loves the early chapters. This could lead to a new novel."

"I've got plenty of novels in my head without getting shot at again."

"Remember, you have a lawyer to support."

"How could I forget? She sends me a nice reminder in her bill the first of each month."

Chapter 5

AFTER GRANT DEPARTED for Lockwood, Hannah rushed through the remaining chores. Primrose, dressed in baggy britches and a buffalo hide coat that dropped to her thighs and virtually swallowed her tiny body, hurried toward Hannah from the opposite end of the stable. She carried a bucket of rich milk she had coaxed from Belle, the Guernsey cow that was producing more milk than they could use since weaning her calf a month earlier.

The calf still got some of the surplus via bucket, and three barn cats helped, but Jasmine and Primrose, who did most of the cooking, were pressed to make use of all the milk. Primrose offered her impish grin with a suggestion when she came up to Hannah. "Can I make ice cream later, Hannah?"

"Well, it doesn't feel like an ice cream day, but go ahead if you want."

"You said that last Saturday, but you ate your share."

"Okay, you've got me. Let's get to the house and eat breakfast."

Jasmine Dupree was busy in the kitchen when Hannah and Primrose arrived at the house. She appeared in the kitchen entryway. "Ten minutes. Get yourselves cleaned up and in here for breakfast."

Hannah shed her wool-lined coat and went into the water closet to wash up. It was a luxury compared to her office in town, where the outhouse behind the building was still in service and a hand pump along the street was the primary water source. Here she enjoyed a modern cast iron, porcelain coated clawfoot tub, a sink and a commode, all of which were piped to a gully more than seventy-five feet from the house. The handpump that emptied into the kitchen sink furnished water for flushing and casual washing, but a warm bath necessitated heating and carrying water from the kitchen stove.

She was surprised at how easily she had adapted to the two girls who had moved into her home some five months earlier following Moon Dupree's death. Now, she could not imagine life without them, and she supposed that would come too soon, probably three or four years at the most. Jasmine had just turned sixteen and was less than a year older than Primrose. Jasmine was a petite girl but three or four inches taller than Primrose who would have to stretch to reach five feet in height. Both were such pretty girls, each with black hair and dark eyes but Jasmine's lightly bronzed skin was noticeably lighter than her friend's. Jasmine was quarter-blood Sioux, while Primrose was full-blood Arapaho.

As she combed her own copper colored hair and redid her ponytail in the bathroom mirror, she studied her face with greenish-blue eyes, searching for intruding wrinkles or other unwelcome invaders on the smooth skin that was losing its summer tan now. She expected crows' feet to show up any day. She certainly qualified as an old maid now, having turned thirty July 4th. She wondered how her twin brother, Thad, was holding up. It had been a good ten years since she had seen her twin, who was a medical school graduate practicing as a veterinary surgeon in the Flint Hills near Manhattan, Kansas. Her father practiced law with one of her three half-brothers in the same community, and she had been estranged from him during that time—her choice, not her father's.

The girls coming into her home, the tragedies she had witnessed the past year, had set her thinking. Perhaps she was not as wise as she had perceived herself. Maybe it was time for a reunion. She surrendered the bathroom to Primrose and went to the kitchen to see if she could help Jasmine with breakfast, knowing that her ward would tell her to sit down and enjoy the coffee that would be steaming in a mug at her place.

While they enjoyed the sausages and hotcakes buttered generously from the surplus they were accumulating and soaked in maple syrup purchased from the Oaks General Store in Lockwood, Jasmine chattered about her plans for the day. Jasmine did not handle silence well, and Hannah's thoughts were often elsewhere when they ate. Primrose was naturally quiet and reserved, much less inclined to involve herself in casual conversation.

Jasmine said, "What is Grant Coolidge up to?"

Hannah had heard only the words "Grant Coolidge." She looked up, "Are you talking to me?"

"I swear, you and Primrose never listen to me."

"I'm sorry. I was just preoccupied."

"Probably about Grant Coolidge. Half the women in Lockwood get their hearts pounding when they see Grant."

"My heart isn't pounding over Grant."

"I saw him ride in here this morning and head for the stable. I figured he would be here for breakfast, but then he rode out. How did you let him get away?"

Jasmine annoyed her sometimes with her matchmaking talk, and it made her uneasy. Grant had been Moon's lover, and Moon likely died in the boarding house fire as a result of evil men striking out at Grant because of his service as sheriff. Jasmine had blamed Grant initially, but the anger had thawed and she saw him as family now. That would please Moon, Hannah was certain, but for her part she worried that any romance with Grant would be disloyal to her deceased friend.

"Aren't you talking to me this morning?" Jasmine said.

"Grant was here because of something terrible that happened last night."

Both girls were listening now. "Are you going to tell us?" Jasmine said, impatience in her voice.

"There was a lynching. Kade McDowell was hanged. Ginger came to Grant's place early this morning. Grant has headed to town to report the killing to the sheriff. I promised to go to his house to look after Ginger. When Grant returns with the sheriff, I plan to ride out to the McDowell place with Jim Tolliver. As county prosecutor, I think I need to be involved right away."

"Why would anyone hang Kade?" Jasmine asked. "He seemed like a nice enough fella."

Hannah did not wish to furnish any information to the girls until her own investigation revealed more facts.

"That's what we want to find out. Why and who. But I want to speak with you about something that would likely inconvenience you for a while."

Jasmine said, "Go ahead."

"I would like to offer to take Ginger in for a spell. Her house has burned down. I doubt if she has any money. She needs help. We would lose some privacy. I can't say what challenges we might have after her going through something like this."

Primrose said, "I remember Ginger. She was with us at the relay place where we were being held when Jazzie and I were taken by those horrible men. She was nice and wanted to help us in the worst way."

Hannah shuddered. She did not like to think of those days when Primrose and Jasmine were held and raped by men who intended to deliver them to Santa Fe. There they would have been sold into slavery to be delivered to bordellos in the Southwest or Mexico.

"Where would she sleep?" Jasmine said.

"We have the extra single mattress stored under your bed. I thought we could pull that out and put it in my study, and she could sleep on that. My guess is that it would be nicer than anything she has been sleeping on since she moved into that soddy."

"Primrose and I can do that and make up the bed, can't we, Prim?" She looked at her friend, who nodded enthusiastically.

Hannah said, "All right, I will leave that chore to you then."

Jasmine said, "If you can bring her back around noontime, I will have a nice lunch prepared."

"And I will have ice cream ready," Primrose said.

Sometimes, Primrose seemed joined to the crank of the ice cream freezer they had found at the general store a month earlier. Before the girls came to live with her, Hannah had eaten sparingly because she had little interest in cooking. Jasmine, however, had cooked many meals at The Tipi, Moon's boarding house, and Primrose was quick to assist. Hannah suspected the Arapaho orphan had endured near starvation on the reservation in the northern part of the territory before her abduction.

"You work on lunch then. I will capture the guest. She has nothing to bring with her but a horse that she rode bareback to Grant's place. That reminds me of something. I will need to take an extra saddle and tack with me." She finished her pancakes and washed them down with her coffee, stood and snatched up her coat and headed for the stable.

Jasmine called to her as she opened the door. "Stop back before you ride out. I'll have some scraps gathered to send over to Sarge."

Chapter 6

GRANT HITCHED BLUE to the rail in front of the sheriff's office. It was shortly after eight o'clock, and he doubted Sheriff Jim Tolliver would be in yet since he had to ride in from the small farm nearby where he lived with his wife, Sarah, who also happened to be Trouble Yates's mother. Chief Deputy Ozzie White should be in unless he was out for breakfast, probably at The Chowdown, the best restaurant in town for simple food served in generous portions if the diner was not put off by dirt-coated windows and a floor that had likely not been mopped for a year or two.

He opened the heavy oak door and entered the brick building. It was a compact structure with two exterior barred windows in the front section that offered some light for an otherwise dusky room. He noticed that the chair behind the sheriff's desk, which had one end abutting a wall near one of the windows, was vacant. The chief deputy, who also happened to be the only deputy, sat at the rolltop desk along the opposite wall and swung around to face the visitor upon the door's opening.

"Grant, good to see you, pard. Been a spell. Hope you ain't bringing problems," Ozzie White said.

"Sorry, Ozzie. You may have a big one on your hands." He walked over and sat down on the captain's chair next to the deputy's desk.

The young deputy ran his fingers through unruly wheat-colored hair and looked at Grant with cobalt blue eyes. He was a handsome kid, a few years short of twenty-five, Grant thought, on the skinny side, average height and totally honest, maybe something of an innocent. He liked Ozzie and had learned the deputy was tougher than he looked. A fool would underestimate him.

Ozzie said, "It's been quiet lately, but Jim's been worried that a stew is brewing and about to boil over the pot. Lots of strangers in and out of town. Too many with guns slung low on the hips. And now some ranchers have been in chewing Jim's ear about cleaning up the rustlers. Hell, Big River County includes almost two thousand square miles of rangelands, mountains and everything in between. Over sixty miles north and south up the valley. A sheriff and one deputy. County board won't come up with tax dollars for no more, and the sheriff's contingency fund won't carry more than one temporary deputy. How we going to chase down rustlers with just the two of us?"

"Well, somebody did some chasing for you."

"What do you mean?"

The office door opened, and Jim Tolliver stepped in. Grant stood up, and Tolliver walked over and took his extended hand in a firm grip. "Grant, good morning, this is a nice surprise."

"You will likely want to take those words back when I give you some bad news."

Tolliver sighed. "I was hoping this was a social call." He waved him toward the sheriff's desk. "Come on over and sit down and tell me about it. Maybe Ozzie would give you a mug of coffee to suck on."

Ozzie's coffee carried a bad reputation, and Grant would have preferred to do without. He took a chair in front of the sheriff's desk. Jim Tolliver was a formidable figure behind the desk. He was a big, muscular man with a short-cropped black beard and coffee brown eyes and a former U.S. Marshal who was a few years older than Grant. Tolliver had been a Confederate cavalryman, fighting at Gettysburg when Grant was a Union infantryman there. His heritage was reflected in a soft, mellow voice with a twinge of southern accent.

Ozzie placed two mugs on the desk and filled Grant's. When he started to pour the thick, black brew in Tolliver's mug, the sheriff waved it away. "No thanks, Ozzie. I just had coffee over at the Chowdown."

Coward. "Well, are you ready for my story, Jim?"

"Guess I can't avoid it. Go ahead. Ozzie, you better listen in."

As if Ozzie required an invitation. Grant said, "There has been a lynching at the McDowell homestead. Kade McDowell's hanging from a big cottonwood out there."

Tolliver's face was impassive but angry eyes betrayed him. "Go on."

Grant related the story Ginger had told him. "She rode bareback to my place. I think she's lucky she's not hanging with Kade. I don't know why she was spared. They might have been reluctant to hang a woman because of possible public uproar. She says she recognized the voice. She couldn't place a name on it but claims she would know the leader if she saw him. Didn't want to tell me more. Hannah Locke's going over to my place and will probably take Ginger back to hers. She will learn more than we would."

"Yeah, you're right about that. Hannah can squeeze water out of a rock."

"I assume you will be going out to the McDowell place."

"Yep. Can't let the buzzards eat the evidence. I need to bring the body back for Doc Weintraub to examine. Got to verify cause of death when I track down the killers and bring them in for trial. I'm sure Hannah would want that."

"Ginger wanted Kade planted in the ground out there. No coffin. She doesn't have money for an undertaker's burying."

"Well, I might want to bring the body in for Doc to look at. He's the official coroner. We can return Kade to the place or the sheriff's contingency fund can cover the burial cost. You collected nearly a herd of horses from dead outlaws when you were acting sheriff. That sale money is in the contingency fund, and I can't use it for a sheriff's bonus."

"Well, I've told you what I know. I'm going to head home." Grant started to get up.

"Whoa, cowboy. You ain't walking out on me, are you? Do you think you can just drop this in my lap?"

"That's what you're paid for. I am just a helpful citizen."

"Well, Mister Helpful Citizen, I can't believe you would just run out on me like that. I'd like you to at least ride out to the place with me, share your thoughts about what you think."

"I can't see any reason you would need me out there."

"I'll even re-deputize you. Pin a badge on your coat. There's a story here for a writer. You wouldn't want to miss that, would you?"

"I learned last spring that the safest stories are in my head. And you don't want to hear where you can put that deputy's badge."

"Then, just for friendship's sake, ride along with me. I need to talk."

The friendship ploy trapped him. "I'll ride out with you. Then I go home, and that is the end of my involvement. I've got a contract with deadlines for books to be submitted. I don't have time to play lawman. You don't have enough bait to get me to bite on this one."

"Understood."

Tolliver was not going to let him off that easy. The sheriff was a wily fox, and Grant knew it was going to be hard to escape his trap. "When do we leave?"

"Allow two hours before we leave here. I'll want to stop and talk with Missus McDowell. Will she be at your place or Hannah's, do you think?"

"More likely Hannah's by then. We can stop there first."

Tolliver turned to Ozzie. "I think you'd better come along on this one, Ozzie. Go over to Fletcher's Livery and rent a team and wagon. Trouble is out at Taylor Brown's sawmill today about some new project, so you will have to deal with old Enos. You can drive the team, and if Missus McDowell comes along, she can ride with you."

"You can bet Hannah will be riding with us, too," Grant said.

"That's fine with me. Takes some of the load off my shoulders when it comes to collecting evidence."

"I'm going to the post office and see if I've got mail today. I haven't been in town since the first of the week."

"You need to come out of your cave more often, Grant, socialize some now and then."

"Humph."

Chapter 7

GRANT COOLIDGE'S CABIN was less than a ten-minute ride down the rutted road from Hannah's Box L ranch. His twenty acres had once been attached to her land, and the cabin had been constructed and occupied by the craftsman who built her house. The man had planned to move his family to the newly completed Box L house when a diphtheria epidemic claimed the lives of four-year-old twin boys. The wife's mental state had forced sale of the property to Hannah more than five years earlier so they could join family back East.

Hannah had sold the cabin property to Grant after Moon Dupree's death. Moon, as well as the twin boys, were buried in the little cemetery plotted out not far from the Box L house. Grant had employed a carpenter to construct bookshelves and adapt the cabin to his needs, and he had installed a coal cookstove that doubled as a vital heating device.

She reined in as she approached the cabin, spying a rider paused on the trail that passed it. His head was turned toward the cabin, and he obviously did not see her. She slipped her Henry rifle from the saddle scabbard and levered a cartridge into the chamber. She knew how to use the weapon and would if the rider threatened. She moved her buckskin gelding ahead at a slow walk. The rider looked in her direction, abruptly turned his horse away and took off at a fast gallop in the opposite direction.

There was no useful way to describe the rider for identification purposes. He rode a sorrel, which might narrow possibilities to a thousand or so horses in the vast valley. He wore a gray Plainsman hat, but his face was obscured by a coat collar pulled up about it. A bulky winter coat revealed little of the man's size and form.

She trotted the gelding up to the cabin and hitched it at the rail there. Carrying her rifle with her, she stepped onto the porch and knocked on the door. There was no response. It occurred to her that Ginger might be reluctant to answer after the horrifying experience she had undergone the previous night. "Ginger," she hollered. "It's Hannah Locke."

She heard the door latch click. The thick door opened a crack, and Ginger peeked out, confirming the identity of the visitor before she pulled the door back and waved Hannah in. Hannah stepped into the room that constituted kitchen, parlor and bedroom for the occupant. The only other room branching off the bedroom area was reserved for Grant's study and workspace.

Hannah started to embrace Ginger before she realized they both carried rifles. She smiled. "We can probably set our rifles aside for now."

Ginger nodded, and they both found wall space to prop their firearms against. "I'm sorry," Hannah said, opening her arms to Ginger, who fell into the proffered embrace and began to sob. Hannah held the younger woman until she was cried out and then stepped away. Ginger's pretty face was hidden behind a veil of bruised and swollen flesh. A closed, puffed-up eye did not enhance her appearance.

"I have coffee," Ginger said, nodding at the stovetop. "Grant made it, and it's quite good."

"I don't recall tasting Grant's coffee, but he is a man of many surprises."

They sat across from each other at the little table, sipping at their coffee mugs. "You were right, it is good coffee," Hannah said. She was unsure what to say to the young woman, and she was rarely at a loss for words.

Ginger saved her. "I hadn't cried until just now. I don't know why. I don't think any of this had seemed real."

"That's not uncommon. There aren't any rules about grief that I know of. You are certainly entitled to shed some tears. Is there anything I can do to help?"

"I have so many questions. I suppose it seems selfish, but I am worried about what becomes of me now. I have nothing. Everything's gone. I don't know if there is money in the bank. Kade was good to me, but he didn't think women should handle money matters."

"He was far from alone on that score, and as a lawyer I can tell you that many men would be better off better off letting their womenfolk manage the money. A few do have the wisdom to do so."

"I am carrying a child," Ginger said.

Hannah tried not to act shocked. "Oh, congratulations. But I can understand that would add to your worries."

"Kade and I were not married."

"I see. I just assumed . . ."

"Kade concocted a story that we went to Cheyenne and got married. He had the notion that if I was a single woman, I could claim a homestead on the quarter section next to us and double the size of our place."

"Well, it has been done, I guess, but claiming to be married complicates the process."

"But my name isn't on the claim. I guess the land goes back to the government. I'm sure I am not a signer on any bank account. I don't know who owns the mule and horses. What about the mavericks Kade branded?"

"Did Kade have a will?"

"He couldn't read much let alone write. He wouldn't have done his own, and he never said anything about seeing a lawyer. He was a smart man about some things and a hard worker, but he was raised on a little ranch far from town, and his folks didn't have much education. At least I got eighth grade schooling. It was after that my life turned sour."

That was something to talk about later if Ginger wanted. "I will be your lawyer to help straighten this all out if you want me to be."

"But I don't have any money to pay you."

"I take many cases where folks can't pay. Some pay me when they can."

"I would like you to be my lawyer."

"I consider myself hired. My first advice is for you tell no one else that you were not married. In fact, you might have been. We will work to establish that you had a common law marriage. I cannot imagine anyone challenging this, and there are many court cases where a marriage has been legally established for a man and woman who have lived as husband and wife without formal vows or registration of the marriage. It is especially common in the West. Some places it's just nearly impossible to find a preacher or judge or an office where folks can record the marriage. They just agree that they are."

"You can help me then?"

"We will get you through this. You are Kade's widow as far as I am concerned—and everybody else, too."

"My baby will not be a bastard then?"

"Absolutely not." Ginger's smile was all the pay she needed.

"So I guess now I need to find a place to stay until we figure out what to do about the land and anything else that I can come up with. I don't think Grant would be very excited about my staying on here."

Hannah was not so certain about that, and she was not about to give him the opportunity. "You are going to stay at my place just down the road. I hauled an extra saddle and tack along on my buckskin. We're going to saddle up your horse and head over there now. My girls will be making lunch and setting up a mattress on the floor of my study. That will be your room until we get your business straightened out, and you decide what you are going to do."

"I only know what I'm not going to do."

"What's that?"

"I'm not going back to whoring. I will not do that to my child. He or she is going to have a respectable mother."

"You and that baby are going to be just fine. Before we leave, I have just one question that you might prefer to discuss with me."

"Yes?"

"You told Grant you would recognize the leader of the vigilantes without his hood. Can you explain?"

"He was my customer at The Doll House three times on three consecutive nights and then he never returned. That was six months back, not long before the business was abandoned by the crooks who ran the place. It was his voice—I don't know how to describe it. So deep and kind of a crackle in it. He was standing when he was at the farm. I would place him at close to six and a half feet."

"How old was this man?"

"A few years on either side of fifty, I would guess. White hair, though. Pale blue eyes, lightest blue I've ever seen in a person's eyes. Scary looking at first, but he was a gentleman during the hour he bought. Didn't get rough, didn't ask for anything special, if you know what I mean?"

Hannah wasn't certain what Ginger meant but elected not to pursue it. "Well, somebody's voice and height probably would not stand up as solid evidence in court, but your ability to describe and identify him could still be helpful in tracking the man, especially if you saw him."

"I don't want to see him unless he is dead."

Chapter 8

SHERIFF JIM TOLLIVER and Grant rode ahead of the mule team-drawn buckboard skinned by Deputy Ozzie White. They had covered half the short distance to Hannah Locke's Box L when Grant heard someone hollering behind them and then the pounding of a horse's hooves as a rider approached.

"It's Bushwa Sparks," Grant said. "Somebody's riding behind him. I think it's Trouble Yates."

Tolliver signaled a halt to Ozzie, and they reined in and waited for Bushwa and Trouble to join them. When they rode up to the group, Grant noticed instantly the grim look on the sixteen-year-old Trouble's face. Bushwa's face was hidden by a shaggy, black beard with white skunk stripes drooping from lip corners and falling with the rest of the scraggly mass over his chin.

Tolliver greeted the arrivals with a nod of his head. "Bushwa. Trouble. I welcome your company but didn't expect it."

Bushwa, a bearlike man only a bit shorter than Grant's six feet but carrying fifty to sixty pounds more, said, "Nobody over at your office, so I went to the livery to ask Enos where you might be, figuring nobody knowed if he didn't. He said he'd heard you was headed out to Hannah's and that there'd been a lynching someplace. Then Trouble rode in. I told him what I wanted to talk to you about, and he offered to ride along. Fletcher bitched about it because he wanted Trouble to clean stalls. I had to remind him that Trouble owned the livery now and could do what he damned well pleased. That didn't set none too good."

Trouble said, "I'll make peace with the old devil later. It can't be easy trading hats from owner to stable hand." He looked at Bushwa. "There wasn't any need to pick a fight with old Enos. He gave you the information you were after. I would have calmed him easy enough if you hadn't jumped in."

"You're getting a mite big for your britches, boy."

Tolliver intervened. "You settle your differences someplace else, you two. You rode out here to tell me something. What is it?"

Bushwa spat a stream of tobacco, just missing his horse's neck, before he spoke. "I was riding down from the mountain this morning and when I hit the foothills, I seen smoke a few miles north—lots of it. I decided to take me a look and headed up that way. When I reached the smoke, I found piles of burnt up lumber smoldering over red hot coals finishing up their work. Looked like a house, barn and something that used to be a workshop. Privy was even burnt down."

"Any people?"

"One. Laid out in front of the smoking house with a tree branch across his chest and a hangman's noose around his neck. I figure somebody hung him and left him there and the limb broke later. It was a scrawny tree."

Tolliver said, "You don't know who he was?"

"Sign on a fencepost near the trail said 'Richards.' I seen him around town before, but he wasn't a friendly sort. His place was off my path, and he gave me no cause to think he wanted visitors."

Trouble said, "That would be Josiah Richards. I rode along because Bushwa said he didn't see a kid at the place. Josiah bought a horse at the livery on a few occasions, and he had a boy with him. I talked to the kid. I think his handle was Gideon. He went by 'Gid.' Last July, he said he was nine going on ten. He didn't go for joshing much, never saw him smile. Acted like he had a cocklebur in his britches. Still, there was something about him that made me wish I could know him better."

Bushwa said, "You probably wanted to make him a slave for one of them businesses of yours."

"I don't have slaves. I pay the people working for me. They get paid good. But, yeah, I suppose he reminded me of when I was a kid."

Bushwa laughed. "You are still a dang kid. Sixteen aint' growed."

"I'm taller than you by three or four inches."

"I'm talking about your brain, boy," Bushwa said, tapping the side of his head with a forefinger.

The sheriff interrupted the fuss between the two newcomers and looked at Grant. "I got to ask you for a favor, Grant. Would you go with Bushwa and Trouble to the Richards place and see what you can figure out? Especially, look for what might have happened to the boy. I'm afraid he might have burned up in the fire."

Grant sighed. He did not like the way he was being sucked into the sheriff's problems. He had been through this and knew that one thing had a way of leading to another. "Yeah, I guess I can do that much, but you'd better not get yourself shot, because I'm not available for sheriff's duty."

"I don't plan on it. Let's meet back at the Box L later. We can talk then, and you will just be down the road to home. I'll see that all three of you get paid deputy's wages from the contingency fund for your work today."

"Suits me," Trouble said, never one to forego a dollar. "I'm losing money every minute I'm out here anyhow."

"I'll take my share," Bushwa said.

"Forget about my wages," Grant said. "I'm a volunteer today. If I take wages, you will say I was hired on for more."

"Come on, Grant. We're friends. I'll take you at your word if you say you are out after today."

Grant did not reply. "Lead the way, Bushwa. Let's get this party over."

"I know a shortcut," Trouble said. "Follow me."

Chapter 9

IT WAS LATE morning when Grant and his partners approached what was left of the Richards farmstead. It was a bleak landscape, Grant thought, one that he might try to capture in one of his novels. The landscape was snow-frosted, and grayish white smoke drifted skyward from the earth. Cast against a background of white streaked mountains and a gray cloudy sky, it presented a ghostly setting.

They dismounted and walked their mounts over to a row of three trees in front of the smoldering rubble of the house. The dead man lay in the embrace of a broken tree branch, back and legs frozen to the earth, head and arms tangled in the fallen tree limbs. The noose was knotted about his neck, the face swollen and contorted. The scene might have sickened some, but Grant, as a Union infantryman, had been wounded at Gettysburg and witnessed hundreds of grotesque deaths and injuries. He was not unaffected by such sights but hardened to them.

"Trouble," he said, "why don't you walk the perimeter of the place and see if you can turn up any sign of the boy. Keep your eye out for some lumber we might salvage to tie the body to. We'll see if we can fashion a sled. I think Jim Tolliver will want to see the man, maybe have Doc Weintraub examine the body."

Trouble led his sorrel gelding away, eyes searching the yard and buildings as he slowly circled the site.

"Damned nuisance if you ask me," Bushwa said. "The man's dead. He ain't talking."

"He might have some messages for Doc that we can't see or hear."

"What the hell are you talking about?"

"Never mind. Do you have a shovel?"

"Of course not."

"Do you want to dig a grave with your hands in this snow?"

"We just leave him. The wolves and buzzards will clean him up."

"We will take him back. Now, let's get that noose off him. We might be able to tie that to our sled to pull him with. Trouble had the good sense to bring a rope. Maybe we can use one to tie him onto the sled."

As they worked to free Josiah Richards from the noose and broken tree branches, Grant estimated that the balding gray-haired man would have been better than sixty-years-old, nearer the age expected for a ten-year-old boy's grandfather than his father. He obviously would have had a younger wife, but where was she? Of course, childbirth and other hazards had a way of shortening female lifespans in the West, so it would not have been unusual for the mother to have been taken by some misfortune. If the boy survived, he would not be the first orphan in this perilous land. In fact, he knew that orphans were countless.

"This ought to work."

Grant turned and saw Trouble dragging a charred, flat, weathered board over the snow crust. He got to his feet and walked out to meet the young man and relieve him of the load. "At least three feet wide and six feet long, I'd say. That should do it."

Trouble said, "it's part of the barn door that broke off and fell to the outside."

"We'll need your rope. We'll anchor the body to the door with the hanging rope and use yours to pull the sled."

"Fine by me. I found sign of the boy—Gid. He got away from the fire, it appears. I found tracks leading from the barn toward the foothills. I don't know what the kid had in mind, but if we get more snow that's the worst place for him to be."

"Well, let's mount up and see if we can follow those tracks." He turned to Bushwa, who was watching them with suspicion.

"Don't say a dang word, Yarnspinner. You don't got to tell me. Old Bushwa's going to be stuck with the corpse. Go ahead. I'll get this feller all fixed up for a sled ride. But don't ask me for any more favors."

Grant unwrapped the wool scarf that had been warming his neck and ears and handed it to Bushwa. "Use this to wrap the man's face. If we come back with the boy, I don't want him looking at his father's face all the way back to the Box L."

Bushwa accepted the scarf without a word, and Grant and Trouble led their horses away. Near the barn's smoldering remains, Trouble pointed to the tracks in the snow that led away from the farmstead. "Look at your footprints and mine. These have got to be the kid's."

"Let's see where they take us."

Still leading the horses, they walked silently until they came to a steep draw. Grant said, "He took to the draw. You can see his footprints. Looks like he's still headed southwest toward the foothills. We don't know how long he's been on the run, but he could have a half day's head start on us. We can't both waste a day chasing the boy. Why don't you go back and help Bushwa get Richards's body back to the Box L? I'll follow the boy's trail till it burns out. It doesn't take an expert tracker to follow him in the snow."

"You sure? I know the country better than you do, but I got work waiting back in town."

It was a writer's lot, Grant thought, that nobody considered writing real work. Revealing your vocation was good only for smiles and condescending head nods. "Yeah. If you leave word with Jasmine or Primrose, you could take the body into Lockwood and leave it with the undertaker. Tell George to just hold the body till he talks to Jim."

"George Caldwell won't do anything till he knows how he's getting paid."

"That's probably true enough." Sort of like Trouble Yates, Grant thought.

Trouble started to lead his horse away and then stopped and turned back toward Grant. "Hey, Grant, want to invest some money?"

"What in and how much?"

"Lumber business. I made a deal with Taylor Brown to buy his sawmill for three thousand dollars. Includes the mill, saws and warehouse."

"The place looks awfully rundown."

"It is, but it can be fixed up. It's the saws I'm after. I want to cut off somebody else from getting ahold of the place. Mark my word, lumbering is going to be big business around here in a few years. With the railroad we can ship it out now. Poor old Taylor can't even supply the local market. Can't find men to work for him because he's so cranky and doesn't come up with the wages on payday."

"How much do you want from me?"

"Fourteen hundred dollars. I'll do sixteen. I'll have Hannah Locke set us up a corporation. I'll have sixteen hundred shares, and you will have fourteen hundred shares."

Grant was not entirely naïve about business matters. He knew that Trouble's majority ownership would give him total control of the operation. "I will think about this and catch you at the livery in a few days."

"You won't be sorry if you do it. I know I can find another investor, Grant, but I know we can get along."

"We'll talk."

Chapter 10

AFTER TROUBLE DEPARTED to join Bushwa, Grant led Blue along the edge of the draw for several hours before the tracks exited and headed across the prairie toward the beginning of the foothills. He rarely rode another horse these days. Enos had informed him that the horse's coloring identified it as a grulla. The gelding was a grayish-blue horse with a dark mane and tail and a dorsal stripe. Hannah had owned the young horse but turned it over to Enos Fletcher to sell. The moment Grant had seen the big, muscular animal, he had to own him. Enos had seen that and struck a hard bargain that made him pay far more than Hannah would have accepted. Grant did not care. He loved the horse.

He mounted Blue, deciding he could track from horseback so long as he rode on the flatlands. The boy would have been forced to rest sometime, Grant figured. He increased the grulla's pace.

His mind turned to the killings. It seemed likely that the Richards lynching would have been carried out by the same men who hanged Kade McDowell on the same sweep. He wondered if there were others. And why? He was not clear about the legal claims to unbranded cattle, but, regardless, the insignificant number of animals Ginger said were on the McDowell property would not justify a hanging, and he doubted any statute provided for such a penalty. Certainly, the imposition of punishment by either vigilantes or law officers without trial constituted murder. He would ask Hannah to sort this out for him.

The sun had emerged from cloud cover just minutes earlier and informed him it was well past high noon now, and he pulled his timepiece from his britches' watch pocket to confirm it was just past two o'clock. The boy's tracks in the snow remained steady and on a straight course as if he had a specific destination in mind. Grant reined in his mount and studied the horizon. He could see the foothills rising against the backdrop of snow-capped mountains, spotted with clusters of pine and aspen. A spinelike ridge of rock crossed one hill about halfway up the slope, positioned like a low fortress wall. During the war, his infantry company had favored such places to defend against approaching enemy soldiers, protection with the upslope advantage. That was where the boy was headed.

He urged Blue on. Ten minutes would bring them to the spot. The big horse did not seem to be tiring, but they had covered at least a dozen miles today, and he calculated it would be ten back to his place and more if he journeyed back to Lockwood.

He quickly confirmed his assumption about the boy's intention. The tracks led up the slope to the natural fortress. The question was whether he moved on from here. He had already travelled six or seven miles from the destroyed farmstead. Good sense should have kept him from heading into the mountains, but what ten-year-old had good sense? It still eluded this forty-year-old more often than he cared to admit.

He dismounted and hitched Blue's reins to the saddle horn, confident that the horse would not stray. Hannah, his former owner, had trained the gelding well. He started walking slowly up the slope, noting flattened snow at several spots where the boy had slipped, lost his footing and ended up on the ground.

The crack of a rifle shot toppled him to the rocky earth, too, not because he was hit by a slug, but the surprise had caused him to instinctively dodge and back away, slide on the snow and end up on his butt. He rolled down the slope a short distance before grasping the trunk of a scrub pine and pulling himself back to his knees. His Winchester was in its saddle scabbard with Blue some thirty feet distant. He reached under his coat and pulled his old Army Colt from its holster. He had served as a Union sniper, and this was not his weapon of choice.

He needed to confirm the identity of the shooter. If it was the boy, he certainly would not fire back. He must negotiate a truce. He hollered, "Gideon Richards. If that is you up there, I'm here to help. I'm working for Sheriff Tolliver."

The response was another rifle shot, the slug chipping a small stone about ten feet distant. "I put that shot where I wanted, mister. Next one's for you if you don't prove yourself."

At least it was a boy's voice, but he did not doubt that the kid could place a shot where he wanted. Most boys and a fair number of girls in this remote country could handle a rifle well enough. This kid obviously had some grit to go with his marksmanship. "How do I prove myself?"

"How about you just walk up this way with your hands raised till I tell you to stop. You do what I say, and I might not kill you."

Might not? He holstered his Colt and stood up with his hands raised high. "Okay, I'm coming up."

Grant took tentative steps toward the stone wall, taking care to plant his feet firmly, so the slick slope would not take him down. When he was within about fifteen feet of the wall, the boy rose and faced him, rifle pressed to his shoulder and ready. "Stop."

The boy was bundled in a tattered coat, and an entire coonskin with tail attached was tied with rawhide strips over his head and under his chin. The pelt covered most of his head and neck, leaving only some unruly strands of orangish, red hair creeping from behind the edges. A pair of near crimson, freckled cheeks were about all that the garments revealed. "I take it you are Gideon Richards."

"Hell, no, I ain't. I'm Gideon Trout."

"You're not Josiah Richards's son?"

"Nope."

"But you lived with him?"

"Yep. But I never called him 'Pa.' He was 'Joe' to me."

This raised a lot of questions in Grant's mind, but this was not the time to explore the boy's history. "Gideon, I want you to come with me. What do I have to do to prove I'm not going to harm you?"

The boy seemed perplexed by the question and had obviously not thought out the proof he was demanding.

"Where we going if I come with you?"

Now Grant was forced to struggle for an answer. "Someplace safe. We'll talk to the sheriff about it."

"Nope. He'll want me to go to one of them orphan homes. Won't do it. If they take me there, I'll be gone in a day," Gideon said.

"Well, we can't stand here all night. Just come with me. We'll figure it out together."

"What's your name?"

"Grant Coolidge."

"Never heard of you. Are you a rancher?"

"No. Not a cow to my name."

"Are you a gunslinger?"

"Hardly. I guess you could say I'm an ink slinger."

The boy lowered his rifle and clambered over the stone ridge that separated them but did not move far away from the barrier. "What's an ink slinger?"

"I write books."

"You get paid for that?"

"I do."

"Ma learned me how to read some before she died, but I ain't seen a book since. That's been two years. Joe didn't have no use for books. He couldn't read or write and didn't want me fooling with such things. I liked making out the words, but he burned all of Ma's books—her Bible even. Think he might have gone to hell for that."

"You know he is dead then?"

"Yeah, I seen the devils string him up. I was sleeping in the barn when the riders showed up. Seen and heard most of it."

"We'll talk about it, but come with me. You can't live in the mountains for long. You must be half frozen from being out last night."

"Just kept walking. It wasn't so bad."

"Come with me. My horse can carry both of us easy enough. We don't want to be out here after sundown. My cabin is warm as a hot biscuit. We will get some food in your belly and a good night's sleep. We can talk more when you are ready."

"How do I know you ain't going to hang me like Joe was?"

"I guess you've just got to decide whether to trust me. I'm ready to go home." He turned and started to inch his way down the slope. "Come or not. It's up to you."

When he reached Blue, he stepped into the stirrup and swung into the saddle. He looked down and saw Gideon Trout, rifle in one hand, looking up at him with wide, cocoa-brown eyes. Grant leaned down with outstretched hand. The boy grabbed it, and Grant pulled him up as he scrambled onto the horse's back and settled in behind the rider.

Chapter 11

HANNAH RODE HER buckskin next to the wagon within talking distance from Ginger, who sat on the buckboard seat beside Ozzie. His repeated glances at his passenger suggested he was quite taken with the new widow. It was hard for Hannah to envision the match, which she figured made it all that more possible.

They should arrive at the McDowell property within twenty minutes, according to Ginger. The young woman had protested at the sheriff's direction that the body be taken to town for examination by the coroner, but she gave in when he promised that the county would see to the cost of burial in the town cemetery since the body was being brought in because of a criminal matter.

Hannah was curious about the other hanging Grant, Bushwa and Trouble were investigating. She feared this was only the beginning. Something serious was brewing in Big River County. She worried that it had something to do with the local ranchers who had contacted her about serving as legal counsel for the Big River Stock Growers Association in the process of formation. The group was to be an affiliate of the statewide Wyoming Stock Growers Association, commonly known as "WSGA." Major objectives of the organization were to end cattle rustling in the valley and put a stop to encroachment of homesteaders on what they considered public grazing land.

Hannah had conferred with her partner, Ethan Ramsey, who was a member of the territorial legislature. They agreed that too many potential conflicts existed with his position, since the legislature constantly dealt with WSGA issues. Furthermore, Hannah, as the part-time prosecutor for the county, had concerns about vigilante activities that had arisen in other counties as a result of ranch groups enforcing their own versions of the law.

Within a month of her turning down the legal business, a young lawyer arrived in town and set up a new firm associated with a Cheyenne partner. The law firm's most prominent client was the Big River County Stock Growers Association. The Ramsey and Locke firm was already bleeding some longtime clients to the upstart lawyer and his absent Cheyenne partner, and Hannah worried about the impact on future firm revenues. Still, neither she nor Ethan had second thoughts about avoiding involvement with the new organization.

When they reached the McDowell homestead, Hannah nudged her mount ahead of the wagon to catch up with the sheriff. As they rode into the yard, they were greeted by a macabre scene that might have come from an Edgar Allan Poe book. Kade McDowell's limp corpse hung from the solitary tree, and a half dozen black buzzards were scattered in the branches above, readying to dine. She could not see that the eerie flock had descended to do their work. The man's pale face revealed no evidence of the shredding that would have been rendered by the huge birds.

Sheriff Tolliver said, "Hannah, could you coax Missus McDowell away from this while Ozzie and I cut the body loose and drop it into the wagon and get the deceased covered with a blanket? She doesn't need to see this."

Hannah said, "She doesn't seem all that disturbed, but I will try."

She wheeled her horse and signaled Ozzie to stop. She dismounted and led her horse to Ginger's side of the wagon. "Why don't you climb down here, and we'll take a stroll and check the buildings to see what might be salvaged."

"I guess we can do that, but it is probably wasted time. When I left everything was already mostly burned out."

Hannah tied her gelding to the rear of the buckboard with a lead rope to allow the horse some distance from the wagon while the sheriff and deputy were carrying out their unpleasant task. First, they walked toward the house ruins where the thick sod walls remained. They paused next to the body of a big gray dog with blood-caked fur that lay in the dust, and Ginger knelt beside the animal and stroked its head and nose. Ginger said, "This is Mazie. She just showed up here one day, and not long after birthed some pups. She tried to save us. I would like to see her buried before we leave. I can't stand the idea of the buzzards eating her."

"There is a shovel in the wagon. The sheriff and Ozzie will probably take care of it. If they don't have time, I will."

"Two of her pups were still alive. I hope they weren't in the barn. They had been weaned a spell, but I don't know if they could survive on their own."

They continued to the house. The thick sod walls appeared virtually untouched by the fire. Coals from the caved-in roof and contents still smoldered inside, but the heat was bearable, so Ginger could stick her head through the doorway.

"My cookstove is still there," Ginger said. "Some of the ironware is scattered about but not much else."

"It will need to cool some yet before you can sift through for jewelry and such."

"No jewelry worth anything. Colored glass beads and things like that. Kade owned some pistols and at least two rifles that would have been in here. The stocks would have burned off the rifles. I don't know what heat might have done to the rest."

"We can ride out again in a few days and see what we can find. Hopefully, scavengers won't hit before then. There is a new gunsmith in town. He could examine what's left of the guns."

They went to where the barn had stood and found it virtually burned to ashes. Hannah started when suddenly wild barking erupted and two pups thrice the size of her biggest barn cat raced out from behind a pile of stones in the nearby cattle lot. They headed straight for Ginger who dropped to her knees to greet them. The gray dogs had wolf-shaped heads and eyes, Hannah thought, and she suspected the sire might have been a gray wolf. There were more than a few roaming the valley and foothills. The pups climbed on Ginger, front paws on her shoulders and tongues lapping at her face. The young woman sur-rendered her first smile and laughed, giving in to the af-fection from her pups.

Ginger looked up at Hannah. "This is Scamp and Lovey. I can't leave them here."

"Of course not. We'll load them in the wagon. When we get the pups back to my place, we can feed them and figure out what to do then. I gather they have been shel-tering in your barn. I have a vacant stall in mine. We can fix a cozy place to put them for now."

"You are so kind. I can't thank you enough. I won't be able to keep them, I'm afraid. I will have to stay in a boarding house as soon as I figure out how to make a living. I wouldn't live out here by myself, ever, especially after what happened last night, but I will find homes for them."

Things were getting out of hand, Hannah thought. She was taking on too many boarders. Grant Coolidge needed a dog in the worst way. He just didn't know it yet. She would work on that as soon as possible.

Chapter 12

BEFORE GRANT PUT Blue up in the stable, he settled young Gideon Trout at the kitchen table near the coal-fired cookstove. He put together a ham sandwich and laid out a big slice of cake from the chocolate creation Jasmine Dupree had dropped off the previous evening. He retrieved a bottle of milk from the new icebox, the contents of which had been replenished by the Box L milk cow. It occurred to him that his comfort in this valley grassland would be greatly reduced without the amenities furnished by Hannah Locke's household. The three women there spoiled him more than he cared to admit.

"I have to put Blue up and see to the sorrel mare I've got in the stable," he told Gideon. "I'll be back in a half hour. Maybe you can get acquainted with Sarge after you eat."

"I don't like cats."

The boy had not talked much during their ride from the burned-out farmstead to the cabin, and Grant's efforts to make conversation had fallen flat. He mostly faulted his own lack of experience with children for that, but his relationship with his nephew and nieces told him that not all youngsters were this hostile.

Regardless, Sarge's feelings toward Gideon appeared mutual. The tabby did not seem especially pleased to welcome a visitor to the house, keeping his distance from his favorite spot on the bearskin rug in front of the fireplace. If cats frowned, that is what Grant saw on his companion's face.

He went outside and unhitched his grulla from the rail and led the horse to the small stable. Dusk was slipping into nightfall now, but the reflection of the moon and stars off the snow offered ample light. Approaching the stable, he noticed boot prints coming from the draw east of the building and stopping at the smaller stable door that was accessed only by human entrants. There was no sign of exit, however.

Someone must be in the stable. He released Blue's reins, slapped the horse's buttock to move him out of the line of gunfire and then slipped the Army Colt from its holster. He walked quietly to the door, knowing that the occupant would be aware of his presence. Two of the westside windows provided a view of the cabin's front.

He opened the door a crack and yelled. "I know you are in there, mister. Throw your gun out and walk out with your hands raised."

"Go to hell." A gunshot echoed from inside the building, and a slug drove into the door.

Grant flung the door open and dropped to his belly, crawling through the open doorway. Another gunshot with the missive passing well above him. Inside now, he lay on the dirt floor waiting for his eyes to adjust to the darkness. Then he saw the gunman's form on the opposite side of the barn half hidden behind a water barrel across the alleyway. A black hood covered his face, and a black cloak covered most of his upper body making the shooter nearly invisible.

Grant was surprised the man had not spotted him and speculated that the hood's loose cloth limited his range of vision. Grant aimed his Colt. He had been an Army sniper but had never enjoyed the killing. Without a warning, however, he liked his odds.

The ambusher, clearly nervous now, yelled. "I didn't come to hurt you, mister. Just want to know where the McDowell woman is. Our man tracked her here. I know she ain't in the house and her horse's gone. Just tell me where she's gone to, and I'll be on my way."

Grant squeezed the trigger and got off two shots before the man dropped his weapon and tumbled to the ground. He scrambled to his feet and walked over to the body that had fallen into the alleyway. He bent over and pulled off the blood-soaked black hood. Head shot above one eye and a neck wound that was bleeding profusely. The would-be killer was a mustachioed man not much past thirty, Grant estimated. So much of potential life unlived now. Fool. What possessed folks to invite death this way?

At least, he was not a big man and could be dragged from the stable easy enough. First, though, he needed to get Blue inside and assure Gideon that everything was fine.

He opened the sliding stock door just enough to allow him to lead the horse in. After placing Blue in his stall without unsaddling, he hurried back to the house to find that the deadbolt on the door was in place. Smart kid. He pounded on the door. "Gideon. It's Grant."

The door opened a crack, and the boy peered out. Grant could see the rifle in his hands. "I heard gunshots."

"It's all right now. A man tried to ambush me in the stable. I have some work to finish. Then I'll be up."

"I can make a sandwich and some coffee, slice a piece of the cake."

The boy caught Grant off guard. "Uh, yeah, that would be nice."

Grant went back to the stable and drug the dead man out, laying the body along the outside stable wall out of view from the house. Then he hiked down the draw and located the hooded man's mount, a bay gelding, and led it back to the stable. After tending to Blue and his mare, as well as the guest gelding, Grant returned to the house, where he found Gideon sitting on the bearskin rug with Sarge in his lap, the cat purring loudly with eyes half closed.

"I thought you didn't like cats."

"Don't care for most, but this one ain't so bad. Coffee's ready in the pot on the stove. Ham sandwich and cake on the stove. I cut myself another piece while I was at it."

Grant decided that maybe the kid wasn't as bad as he first thought. He shed his cap and coat and hung them on the pegs near the door. He was cold and hungry. The stove and coffee cured the first concern, and a bite of the sandwich got him started on the next. He was readying to take on the cake when Gideon claimed the only other chair and sat down across the table. The boy said nothing but seemed to be studying his face.

Grant broke the silence. "I thank you for making the coffee and putting some vittles out. I've got an extra pillow and some blankets. I'll make you a bed on the bear rug near the fireplace."

"That will do fine. Been sleeping in the barn most nights."

"The barn? You didn't sleep in the house?"

"No bed there anyhow. That was Joe's. He wanted me to sleep with him, but I wouldn't do it no more. Liked it better in the barn. Worried about the worst of winter coming on, though."

Grant did not press the boy, but he had a feeling something had been terribly wrong in that house. "Well, from now on you will be sleeping where it's warm."

"Will I be staying here?"

"Just tonight. We will see about other arrangements tomorrow."

"I ain't leaving."

"We can talk about it tomorrow."

"Don't matter. I ain't leaving. You'll have to tie me and haul me over a horse's back or toss me in a wagon. It'll take more than you to do it. And you take me to some orphanage, I'll be out and on the run in a day."

"I'm sure we can find a nice couple in town to take you in and care for you like their own."

"They put bastards in orphanages. That's what Joe always said. And I'm a bastard. He let me know every day."

This poor kid. Grant had no notion of how to respond. And how in blazes was he going to get this boy out of his house? Gideon was a scrawny kid—looked half starved—and Grant had no doubt he could handle the boy physically, but he could never bring himself to hogtie the youngster and haul him off. He needed to talk to Hannah about this, better yet, turn the problem over to her.

"How long has your mother been gone, Gideon?"

"Call me Gid, since I'm going to be here a spell. What do I call you?"

"Uh, I guess Grant would be all right."

"Ma died about two years back. We come here two or three years before that—don't remember for sure. Never knew my pa. We lived in a shack near the railroad tracks in Denver before that, and Ma cleaned houses for the rich folks there. I don't recollect much about them days."

"Was Joe with you then?"

"Nah. Ma met him at one of the houses she cleaned. He was kin to some of the rich folks. Claimed to have a gold mine in Wyoming and talked Ma into coming up here with him. Always said they'd get married, but it never happened. She wouldn't have anyway. He beat on her, whipped my butt and back raw more than once. We tried to leave different times, but he always caught up and drug us back. I'd have killed him by now if Ma was alive, but after she was gone, I knew I'd have to wait till I was old enough to be on my own. He didn't like me, but I was big enough to do some work around the place. He'd say, 'Hey Bastard, do this or Bastard do that.'"

"So, Joe did not have a gold mine. How did he make a living?"

"Rustled cattle. Two or three in a bunch. Some wasn't branded, and he put his own iron to them. Others, he sold to rustling outfits. A few riders showed up once a month to see what he had. Joe bitched all the time they cheated him on price.'"

That explained the lynching. Grant believed that the vigilante mentality could not be tolerated in a free society, but if there was a case to be made for it, Joe Richards would rank high on the list of the deserving. He decided to shift the topic since the boy seemed willing enough to talk. "Do you feel like talking about what happened tonight?"

"Don't make me no difference."

"Why don't you just tell me what you saw."

"Well, I was sleeping in the front barn stall, and the first I knowed anything was happening was when I heard some gunshots. I looked out the window across the alleyway and saw these men with black sacks over their heads dragging Joe out of the house. He was barefooted and wearing just his woolens, screaming, cussing, howling something awful."

"How many men were there?"

"Eight. All of them with the black bags. Black coat-like things tossed over their shoulders, too, now that I think of it."

"Is there anything special you noticed about any of the men?"

"Yep. One man was in charge, and he had this voice that sounded like an echo but was real deep, sort of like a bear growling. He was riding a strange-colored, horse, sort of gray, maybe yellow, depending on the light. Don't want nothing to do with that feller."

"Did you hear anything he said?"

"Heard some of what he was saying to Joe."

"And what was that?"

"He asked Joe if he ever seen a horse like his. Joe was blubbering, but I guess he said 'No' cause this leader says, 'It's a pale horse.' Joe didn't say nothing, and the feller asks, 'Do you know who rides a pale horse?' Joe says 'No,' and this leader says, 'Death rides a pale horse, and Hell follows.' The way he said that almost made me piss my britches. I stayed long enough to see those men put a noose around Joe's neck and put him on top of one the horses and then I grabbed up my rifle and run like a scared jack rabbit."

Grant nodded. The same bunch that hit the McDowell homestead. "I'm going to make up a bed for you on the rug. You ought to be tuckered out after what you went through last night and walking all those miles. The privy is out back, and the path is cleared to it. I can stand watch outside if you want to use it."

"Rather step out and do my water in the snow."

"Okay. Whatever suits you."

Grant tossed a few more logs into the fireplace and checked the coal-fed cookstove. They should be fine till morning, he figured. He doubted he would sleep much that night, worrying about what to do with Gid Trout and a request he was certain would be coming from Sheriff Jim Tolliver. Later, he discovered he was wrong.

Chapter 13

HANNAH WAS SURPRISED that she had not heard from Grant this morning. After their return from the McDowell farmstead, the sheriff and Ozzie had continued to Lockwood with Kade's body. Later, a rider had brought a message informing her that Bushwa and Trouble had arrived in town with another body and that Grant had remained behind to track the deceased's son.

It irritated her that Bushwa and Trouble had apparently abandoned Grant. How did they know that some of the vigilantes had not taken the boy? Perhaps they were watching the place. She worried that she had not had an opportunity to tell Grant about the man she had caught watching his cabin.

They had finished breakfast, and Ginger, surprisingly cheerful, was helping Jasmine with cleanup. Primrose had ridden her favorite horse to town for Sunday services at the Methodist Church. Hannah found it ironic that the household member most likely to be called a heathen by the proper prigs of the community was the seriously devout one.

She had been staring out the window expecting Grant to ride up the trail to the house astride Blue, but her patience escaped her now and she went into the kitchen to speak to Jasmine and Ginger. "I'm going to saddle Dusty and take a quick ride over to Grant's. I haven't heard anything about his coming back. His mare might need some care if he hasn't."

Jasmine said teasingly. "I think the mare is the farthest from your mind. It is okay to be concerned about Grant, you know."

Hannah rolled her eyes and gave Jasmine an exasperated look. "I won't be gone long."

"Spend the day if you like. I would suggest you make him lunch, but he might not survive it."

Jasmine, having cooked in her mother's boarding house, had quickly assumed culinary command in the newly improvised family, and Hannah had surrendered without resistance. She hated cooking. "I'm not that bad," she said.

"I know. Sometimes, I can't help myself. I'm sorry, I wasn't very respectful."

"I expect you to lose a night's sleep over that remark. Now, I will be on my way."

Jasmine called after her. "I'll be doing roast beef and fried potatoes for Sunday dinner, why don't you talk Grant into coming over?"

"That probably won't be hard. His cooking is worse than mine."

Less than a half hour later, Hannah, taking the wagon road that passed by the Box L headquarters and Grant's cabin, approached the Coolidge property. She froze and her heart raced when she saw the body lying in the snow on the near side of the stable. She reined in her mount and studied the scene. The figure wore a black hood and cloak. The body must be that of one of the so-called vigilantes—the Justice Riders, Ginger said they called themselves. That calmed her some, but there had obviously been a gunfight here, and the dead man did not guarantee Grant's safety.

She kneed Dusty ahead and then reined the horse off the road angling toward the stable. She had to be certain. When she reached the stable, Hannah dismounted and stepped over to the prone form, frozen now by the cold. She bent over, grasped the hood and yanked it off. The man was no one she recognized. She dropped the hood over his face and led Dusty toward the cabin.

She hitched the horse to the rail and pulled her Winchester from the saddle holster. She stepped onto the porch softly and eased over to the door. She knocked and backed away raising the rifle to her waist with the thought of shooting from the hip if necessary. The door opened.

"Why don't you come on in, Hannah?" Grant said.

She lowered the rifle. "You knew I was out here?"

"Sarge heard you. His ears perked up, and he looked to the door. I peeked out the window and saw you leading Dusty up to the cabin."

"And you didn't come out to greet me?"

"You looked like you were on the hunt. I didn't want to risk it." He opened the door wider and waved her in. "I've got somebody I want you to meet."

She walked in, her eyes searching the room until she saw the red-headed, freckle-faced boy sitting on the floor in front of the fireplace. He glared up at her, and she instantly felt like an intruder.

"Hannah, this is my, uh, guest, Gid Trout," Grant said.

"Good morning, Gid." She turned to Grant. "He's not the Richards boy then?"

Gid answered before Grant could explain. "I'm the Trout kid. That was my ma's last name. I'm a bastard."

Hannah was left speechless for a moment and then replied, "You are a boy and a mighty handsome one at that. I'm pleased to meet you." His face told her she had not softened his hostility.

Grant said, "Coffee, Hannah? Come in and sit down. I need some advice."

She followed him to the kitchen area which she assumed would escape the boy's hearing if they spoke softly. They sat down at the table and Grant poured two mugs of coffee. "Gid made the coffee. It's better than mine."

"Your coffee isn't so bad. Are you going to tell me about this boy?" Hannah said, her voice just barely above a whisper.

Grant gave her a quick summary of his first encounter with Gid and what the boy had heard and seen when the raiders hanged Joe Richards.

"I saw the body next to your stable."

"He was looking for Ginger."

"I hadn't seen you, or I would have told you a man was studying your place when I came over to talk to Ginger yesterday. She's settled in at my house now until she decides what to do. I will be helping her with some legal matters that must be sorted out."

"Gid says he is not leaving here. What should I do?"

"You could let him stay."

"I wouldn't know what to do with him."

"You would figure it out."

"That's easy for you to say."

"What do you mean by that? I've taken on two girls since spring."

"It's not the same. They're sixteen or seventeen years old. They're old enough to help around the place. I know Primrose works with the horses and milks the cow, and Jasmine has practically taken over running the house."

She could not deny his statement. Life had become easier since the girls moved in, although the addition of Ginger was crowding the house some. "You said the boy made the coffee. It sounds to me like he's accustomed to doing a man's work. I suspect he would make a place for himself."

"Hannah, I cannot let this happen. I am not ready for this kind of responsibility."

"Not ready? Grant, you are forty years old. It's about time you got ready. This will be good training for the children you will have someday."

"I've got two former wives in my past. I don't see another in my future. It is best that I remain childless."

"What are you going to do with him?"

"I thought I just asked you that."

"I am your lawyer. I am not responsible for your domestic concerns."

"I can't just drop him in the sheriff's hands. He would send Gid to an orphanage. I promised Gid that would not happen. I was thinking we might find a couple that would take him in, but I don't know that many folks around here, and I don't know if he would stay if I found somebody."

"It sounds to me like your options are very narrow. Grant Coolidge or Grant Coolidge."

"Your girls would dote on a little brother. I know they would."

Her eyes narrowed, and she stared at him in disbelief, but she found that she was enjoying his struggle with the dilemma. She decided to torture him a bit more. "Ask yourself what Moon would do. Maybe that will help."

"That is not fair. That is totally unfair."

"Jasmine said I should invite you over to Sunday dinner. Of course, that includes Gid."

"I don't think he will come. He will think it is a trick to make him leave."

"I will handle it." She got up and went back to Gid who remained with Sarge on the bearskin in front of the fireplace. He looked up at her, obviously still suspicious of the intruder.

"Gid, you and Grant are invited to my house just down the road a bit for dinner this noon. I promise a meal that will be far better than anything you will get here."

"I ain't going. You're just trying to fool me, get me to go there. Then you'll hogtie me and dump me at an orphanage."

"Lockwood doesn't have an orphanage."

"Then you'll toss me on a train and send me to one or give me to some folks that will take me in. I won't stay nohow, and I ain't going."

"I promise that after dinner, you will come back here with Grant." She looked at Grant who stood just a few steps away. "That's right, isn't it, Grant?"

"Uh, yeah. I promise, Gid. You will come back here with me."

"I don't know," Gid said.

Time for the kill. Hannah said, "Do you like puppies, Gid?"

"Yeah, I had me a dog named Red. Best dog ever. Joe kilt it after my ma died. Red tore into him when he was giving me the belt. Joe shot him dead."

Hannah did all she could do to hold back tears. This poor kid. She would take him in if Grant refused, but he should be with Grant. The Box L bunch would back the novelist. "I have two pups over at my house. They need homes. You can pick one out and bring it back here if you like. It will be your dog—if this is alright with Grant."

The boy looked at Grant. She knew she was not playing fair, putting the man on the spot like this.

"I don't know. I suppose it could sleep in the stable."

"Give it a chance in the house," Gid said. "If it don't work out, I can stay in the stable with it. I done that plenty. But Sarge will love the pup. I know he will."

Grant said, "You can choose a pup. We'll bring it back here after dinner and figure out what to do."

"How soon can we go?"

Grant pulled out his timepiece. "When do you want to eat, Hannah?"

"Let's make it one o'clock. Get there about noon, and he can choose the pup before we eat. I have a hunch I will be taking the other one, so the siblings can see each other now and then."

Grant sighed. "It sounds like this is going to be great fun."

Chapter 14

"OLSON SHOULD HAVE been here by now. Where is he?" Reaper said, raking his thick, white hair back with long, thin fingers, as he stared out the window of the stone house set on a rise near the base of the dead-end canyon wall. Danek, the man Reaper considered the overseer of his Riders, sat in front of the fireplace of the house he shared with Reaper.

"He should have been back a day ago," Danek said. "I sent Joker to town to see if there are rumors floating about. The woman should have been dead by now. If Olson couldn't find her or get her alone, he would have reported back. I told him not to take chances. Joker left first thing this morning. He will be back by suppertime, a few hours from now. I still think we should have left the woman alone."

Danek, a Polish immigrant with light brown hair and a short-cropped beard, spoke with a slight accent, but had mastered the English language before coming to America. Reaper knew his overseer was a man of considerable education, and he claimed to have been an officer in the Polish army during which time he had taken part in a failed military coup of the monarch, forcing him to escape the country.

Reaper did not know if 'Danek' was a first name or surname. The stout man had been with him for five years now, and when they had met in a Fort Worth saloon, he had said "Just Danek will do." Why not? The employer was known by all only as "Reaper." He was saving his birth identity to retire to someday, should he choose to do so before his own neck stretched in a noose.

Reaper turned away from the window and stepped over to the fireplace and claimed the sturdy rocking chair on the opposite side of the hearth, so he could face Danek. "I should have strung the bitch up with her man. I was a fool. A soft heart is my curse. I didn't recognize her as the whore that worked at The Doll House when we first showed up there. I was with her more than once. She was one of the best at her work, beautiful and clean. I can't stand a dirty, stinking woman. I just walk away from that kind."

Danek said, "Don't be so hard on yourself. She was wearing britches and half hidden by that big coat and a hat pulled down over head. I didn't think of it till later. There was something about her around the nose and eyes that seemed familiar. Then I connected that later with her voice, but I was back here and in bed before I made a connection."

"You never said how you knew, but you had her, too, didn't you?" Danek shrugged.

Reaper did not press. Danek was the only man among the Justice Riders who could choose not to answer his questions, the only one among the men who could occasionally intimidate him. He trusted the Pole to a point, but the man's blood ran ice cold. He had witnessed Danek dispensing death calmly and methodically like a butcher carving up a beef carcass. If Danek knew the meaning of fear, his face did not display it.

Reaper said, "Do you think this Ginger woman recognized me?"

Danek shrugged again. "Not from your appearance. You were hooded and cloaked in black. It is unlikely she had ever seen you astride a horse. But your voice . . ."

"What about my voice?"

"Let us say it is distinctive. Like no other. It comes like an echo from your throat, deep like the growl of a grizzly. It is a voice one might remember."

Reaper had told no person about his own night on the hanging tree not quite ten years earlier when the noose had crushed his throat, and the rancher and his foreman had left him for dead. He had freed his hands from the rawhide bonds, pulled himself upward hand over hand over the suspended rope until he grasped the limb, swung his body over it and freed himself. Two days later the rancher and his cohort suffered painful deaths, and Reaper compensated himself with an unbroken pale colt and a black gelding from the stable in the Texas panhandle before taking leave of the area for a spell.

"I have been told before about a certain quality to my voice." ·

"I am sure. That does not mean the woman would remember it or attach it to the men who dispensed justice at their farm."

"Justice. Yes, that's what we do, dispense justice for money." And since that night of his near demise, Reaper had made a nice living rendering justice. He had

rustled his last cow that night, finding that there was a fertile market for those willing to bleed ranchers of their dollars from the other end of the rope.

Three distinct raps at the door snatched his attention, and reflexively he sprung from the chair and reached for his holstered Colt. Danek remained seated, his eyes fixed hypnotically on the fire. "Come on in, Joker," he hollered.

The door opened slowly, and Joker Johnson's craggy face with the handlebar moustache appeared. He stepped in and doffed his low-crowned planter's hat, revealing an unruly nest of salt and pepper hair. He nodded at the other men, "Reaper. Danek."

It annoyed Reaper that Danek presumed to grant admission to the house, but he conceded that a knock at the door tended to make him skittish as a colt. He removed his fingers from the Colt's grip. "You got the couch. Put your ass down and tell us what you learned in town."

Joker was a tall, lanky man but several inches short of Reaper's six and a half feet, and he sank into the stuffed, cowhide-covered sofa, causing his knees to rise to his midsection. He was clearly uncomfortable. That was why Reaper avoided the furniture piece.

"Coffee or whiskey?" Danek said.

"Given a choice, whiskey wins."

Danek got up, disappeared into the kitchen-dining room and returned with a whiskey glass and bottle and set the items on the tea table in front of the sofa. Joker poured himself a glass of the amber liquid, drank it in a single gulp, belched and poured another drink.

Reaper had tolerated enough delay. "No more whiskey till after I get your report."

"What do you want to know first, boss?"

"Ole Olson. Any sign of him?"

"Didn't see him to prove it, but I'm betting he's the feller planted in the new pauper's plot at the town cemetery. Sheriff's deputy brung him in yesterday morning I was told. Cowhand I talked to at the Salty Dog seen the body slung across the back of a bay gelding—likely Olson's. Said some writer fella gunned him down."

Reaper said, "That was Coolidge. I know about him. He was sheriff for a short spell not long after we got to the county last spring. I haven't read a book for some years, but the rumor is that he actually sells the stuff he writes. Where did the killing take place?"

"At Coolidge's place, but I didn't hear how it came to be."

"That's where Skip tracked the woman to," Reaper said. "That's why Ole went there."

"Ain't there no more."

"Well, where the hell is she?"

"Near as I can tell she's moved in with the lady law wrangler. The Locke woman. She's also the county prosecutor."

Reaper flinched at that thought. Ginger living with the prosecutor. "Where does this lawyer live?"

"Couple miles west of town. Less than a mile from Coolidge. I rode past coming back here. No nearby neighbors or nothing. Coolidge is closest."

"Does she have a husband?"

"Nope. She's an old maid. Got two older schoolgirls living with her. No man around to protect them."

Danek finally spoke. "She can use a gun. When all this business with the Indian orphan girls was taking place last spring, the Locke woman jumped into the middle of it. Killed her share of the kidnapping ring. Besides, she's part of the law in these parts. I wouldn't be making any moves against her."

Reaper said, "I would still like to see that Ginger woman dead."

Danek said, "She did not see you that night. I am not a lawyer, but I doubt if recognizing a voice would carry much weight in a courtroom. There's not much chance she will even see you again. It seems to me that the greater risk lies in killing more folks and drawing more attention while you are trying to get to her. If it was up to me, I would just back off and let her be. You can always change your mind if you are forced to make a move. You can't reverse it if you go after her and shouldn't have."

Danek was right, of course, but Reaper could not bring himself to admit it outright. "We will wait for an opportunity. Besides, the Stock Growers Association has a new assignment that demands our attention. Success assures that we will have work here for months, perhaps several years."

Chapter 15

GRANT HAD WON a major battle with young Gideon Trout yesterday when the boy surrendered to his unofficial guardian's demand that he attend school. Gid had refused at first, insisting that he did not need schooling and wanted no part of meeting a bunch of strange kids. He had relented, though, when Jasmine dropped by the cabin with a frosted apple cake and told him that it would be the last food coming to the Coolidge place if Gid did not go to school. She had assured Gid he could ride to school with her and Primrose if Grant would furnish a horse.

The boy already adored Jasmine and evidently did not want to disappoint her. He seemed not to care what the man he lived with thought. Grant felt he was living a chess match with the boy, and so far, he was losing.

Grant had gladly assented to assigning his mare to school duty. He felt a bit of guilt at his relief at avoiding child supervision while the boy attended school. He had not written a word in four days after taking in an often-sullen boy and a rambunctious pup that was obviously destined to be a cabin resident. To Gid's credit, however, he had chosen Lovey, the female pup, a gentle affection-ate soul, and apart from a few accidents seemed to be successfully convincing the young dog that the house was not a dog privy. The boy had explained that before Josiah Richards entered his life, he had trained the dog the man eventually killed. Gid had also taken on the responsibility of collecting scraps for feeding Lovey and saw that the water dish always had fresh water.

Gid was at the Pennock School just outside of Lock-wood now, and Grant, finally free to resume writing, was working at the desk in his office putting pencil to paper to complete a Marshal Buck Tyree dime novel for his pub-lisher, Beadle and Company. He had just finished a chap-ter when Lovey started barking from the front room. He stood and took his Colt from the holster that lay on his desk, a new habit since his interlude as the county's act-ing sheriff.

He walked into the front room, peered out the win-dow and saw Hannah's buckskin gelding, Dusty, tied to the hitching rail in front of the cabin just before the rapping on the door. He placed the pistol on the fireplace mantel and told the pup, "It's all right, Lovey. Friend." He bent down and patted the pup's head. "Good pup."

He opened the door and gestured to Hannah to enter. She wore shirt and riding britches, which he thought was strange on a day she would ordinarily be in her law office. Saddlebags were also slung over her shoulder.

She walked in and headed for the kitchen table. "I came for lunch," she said.

"Uh, is it lunchtime?"

"Twelve-thirty. It is for most folks."

"I forget lunch sometimes when I'm writing. I don't think I've got much to eat here. Some of that apple cake Jasmine brought over."

"That can be dessert. Jasmine cooks so much for your house lately, she forgets to save some back for me."

"I'm sorry. She is not expected to do these things, and she won't take money. It's like you are feeding Gid and me. I'm sure Jazzie's not paying for the food."

"It will be hidden in your bill someplace, Grant. Don't be so serious about this. Friends and neighbors don't keep score out here. I see you've got a coffee pot on the stove. If you will get some mugs, I brought beef sandwiches from The Chowdown." She pulled a paper sack from the saddlebags and placed them on the table. "I've got another bag of meat scraps for Lovey and Sarge for your icebox."

She worked a big sack out of the other pocket and handed it to him. "Compliments of Charlie at The Chowdown."

Hannah handed him the sack, and Grant placed it on top of the icebox. "This will last a spell. Thanks. I have trouble keeping up with animal meals these days. Sarge is too lazy to hunt, and Lovey's too young."

"Thank Charlie. I told him about your growing family, and he offered to send supplies."

"I will." He set mugs on the table along with two plates, forks and the cake pan.

As he poured the coffee, he said, "Gid made the coffee again. He has pretty much taken over that responsibility. Strange, since he doesn't drink the stuff. He prefers the cow's milk you folks send over."

"It appears that the boy had been taking on grownup responsibilities at least since his mother's death."

"Yeah. He can cook some, too. I haven't found much he can't do if you let it be his idea. He doesn't take orders well, so I am having to learn how to deal with him. I was thinking, the boy's not afraid of work. Trouble Yates ought to take him."

"You can't be serious. Trouble won't be seventeen till spring."

"But he's going to get married. They would have a nice start to a family."

"He has Samantha Morris's permission to court. She told me that she will not under any circumstance marry him before they are both eighteen. They are the same age, and their birthdays are only a few months apart, I think. And she says they will not marry if he does not learn to think of something besides making money and getting into her bloomers."

Grant chuckled. "I never thought about the money part the two times I got married."

"You are disgusting. And see how those marriages worked out."

"Okay. I'll take Trouble off my list."

"You have a list?"

"Well, no. Not yet, but I should make one, I suppose."

"You would send that boy away to strangers?"

"He was a stranger to me until less than a week ago."

"Eat."

They ate the sandwiches and drank their coffee in near silence until he took a knife and began to slice the cake. "You will have a slice of cake?"

"Yes, please. A big one."

"Yes, ma'am."

She nodded toward the fireplace where the cat and pup were sleeping. "Sarge is curled up against Lovey. Do they always do that?"

"After the first day. Once Sarge did a little hissing and spitting and made clear who was in charge, they struck up a friendship."

"That's good. I know you were worried about how they might get along. Are you getting some work done now?"

"I got a good start again on a Tyree book this morning. I am ahead of schedule on the dime novels, about where I should be on the book for Percy Garth and Mark Twain. I didn't have a chance to tell you that I mailed sample chapters to Percy a few days ago."

"Your lawyer likes to hear that news. But I meant to ask how school enrollment went this morning?"

"Well, as you know, I rode Blue to school with Gid. He's going to ride Lady. The principal seemed glad to have a new pupil, especially one who will pay the private fees."

"That doesn't surprise me. Ralph Turner must watch the money carefully. The Lame Buffalo Association pays tuition fees for all students who are at least half blood Sioux, as well as for other students who cannot afford the cost. But that is at three-fourths of the usual private rate.

Of course, the county supplements the budget some, but not much."

"Anyway, Gid will ride home with the girls, and they have promised to keep an eye on him. He is taking some tests today to see what grade level he should be placed at. I fear he won't be happy with the result. I don't think he has had much formal education and will likely be forced to start out with much younger kids."

"He can move up quickly. Until high school, the children advance by achievement not age."

Grant cleared his throat. "You did not interrupt your workday and ride out here with lunch for the conversation we are having. Did you even go to work? You are not dressed for it."

Her face flushed. "I wear riding clothes to the office and change there. You should know that by now. I can't wear a dress when I am traveling back and forth. I don't even know how to ride sidesaddle. I grew up on a ranch. And, yes, there is something I want to discuss with you. Two things for that matter."

"I am listening."

"Trouble came to my office this morning and told me about his plans to buy the sawmill and that you had agreed to be an investor. Is that true?"

"Yes. We spoke at the livery early this morning after I left Gid at the school. He said he would be speaking with you. Since he is not of legal age, I understand that you have agreed to act as trustee on his behalf."

"Yes. That means your agreements will be with me. I will hold his shares if I approve of the purchase. I am your lawyer, as well as Brady's lawyer and legal substitute. You must procure other legal counsel to represent you on the transaction."

"No. I will sign any waiver of conflict that you prepare, but I am just an investor. I will not employ another lawyer. What is the other matter?"

Hannah's greenish-blue eyes shot daggers at him, and the firm set of her lips told him that she was struggling to choose her words carefully. "I must think about this," she said. "I may not be able to approve the transaction."

She would, Grant figured. Not even Hannah Locke could outmaneuver Trouble Yates. He would convince her that her veto would stand in the way of his opportunity to make a fortune. "Again, the second matter?"

"Jim Tolliver asked me to invite you to a meeting tonight—a private meeting with some of the citizens of Lockwood and surrounding ranchers."

"Not interested. It's a trap to pull me into something I want no part of. My latest involvement has placed a disagreeable boy and a dog in my home. I don't have any more room in my heart or head."

"Grant, please come and listen. Something terrible is happening to this county. It's beyond vigilante justice. It's more like war, and nobody within the range of opposing armies escapes the consequences. With your war experience, you should know that better than anyone. Jim respects your opinion, and you bring a perspective of one who can view this with more objectivity than some who have been here for years. You don't have to commit to anything beyond tonight's meeting."

"Do you honestly believe that?"

"Grant, you have become a valued client, but more important, a special friend. You owe me nothing, but I would consider it a personal favor if you would attend."

She was wearing him down. Since the death of Moon Dupree, he had come to think of Hannah as his best friend. "I can't leave Gid here alone."

"Bring him to my place. We can ride into town and back together."

"But is your place safe? With Ginger there, I worry about the risk of that vigilante bunch coming for her if they have learned where she is at. The man I killed was looking for her."

"Ozzie White and another deputy will be there to stand watch."

He sighed. "You had this all planned out, didn't you? The trap was set, and old Grant Coolidge just had to step into it."

"Please don't feel that way about it."

If she had not played the friend card, he could have resisted. "What time shall we come by?"

"Thank you, Grant. I do appreciate this." She reached across the table and squeezed his hand. "Come for an early supper at five-thirty. The meeting is at the Methodist Church at seven."

Her mission accomplished, Hannah got up from the table and left. Grant stood at the window and watched her ride down the wagon road back toward the Box L and then on to town. His most profound thought was that there would be dog piss and dung to clean up when they got home. Gid insisted that Lovey would use the newspaper if they laid it out. Well, they would see. Maybe the *Lockwood Journal* was good for something besides the privy.

Chapter 16

GRANT HAD BEEN something of a grump since he stopped at the house to leave Gid with the girls, Hannah thought. Gid was happy enough, though, and he obviously loved having Jazzie and Primrose doting over him. Grant had brightened some when Gid reported that he had been assigned to fifth grade level at school. This was age appropriate and higher than many students his age given that schooling opportunities were sporadic, often non-existent, in many parts of the West. Grant had seemed both proud and surprised at the boy's placement.

Hannah suspected that Gid would soon have plenty of books to choose from, and she intended to visit Oaks General Store tomorrow to find something to contribute to the boy's library. Strangely, she found herself excited by the prospect.

Grant and Hannah rode silently most of the twenty-minute trip to town. As they approached Lockwood, Hannah said, "Are you mad at me for dragging you to this meeting?"

"Mad at myself for not declining the invitation."

"You don't like meetings, do you?"

"Nope."

"I'll bet you don't like dances or church socials either?"

"This is not a church social, but as a matter of fact, I don't."

Darn him. He would not even think to ask her. "Then you're not going to escort me to the barn dance at the town hall Saturday?"

He hesitated. "If it's a barn dance, why is it at the town hall?"

"The town hall has two big fireplaces. Barns are too cold this time of year. To tell the truth, most barn dances are at the town hall anyway. It's an event, not a place."

"I learn something every day, I guess."

"You didn't answer my question."

"Are you asking me to accompany you to a barn dance?"

"Yes. I suppose you can put it that way."

"I haven't danced for a dozen years, and back in those days, I was a drunk. I don't know if I have ever danced sober."

"I'm sure you can if you put your mind to it."

"You're really serious about this, aren't you?"

"I am."

"It feels strange, somehow. My lawyer. There is probably some rule against this."

"Not in Wyoming where men outnumber women at least two to one."

"Moon's best friend, too. But okay, yes, I'll go. But you will have to get one of the girls to watch Gid."

"Not necessary. He will come with us. The girls will want to go, too. Folks often bring the whole family."

"Okay, I guess I can have a go at it."

"More enthusiasm would be nice."

"The answer is 'yes.' I will be looking forward to it."

"Liar. But I will take you at your word."

After they reached the Methodist Church, they left their rifles in the church vestibule in accordance with a sign posted by Reverend Frederick Meyer, and then Hannah and Grant split up. She joined her friends, Skye DePaul Ramsey and She-Bear "Carissa" Oaks, who were conversing on the east side of the sanctuary with what seemed an unlikely pair, Katy Culper, a young teller at the Gaines Bank, and Maggie White, the local moonshiner who also happened to be Ozzie White's mother. Maggie was attired in bib overalls and clodhoppers, but at a few years short of fifty still caught the eye of most of the county's bachelors and more than one man who was not. Skye, like herself, wore denim riding britches and boots, but the other two women still wore their workday dresses.

She greeted the others but after a bit of small talk turned her eyes across the sanctuary where the men were gathering. Strange how men and women seemed to habitually divide into separate tribes at gatherings like this. She noticed Grant speaking to Bushwa Sparks, the good friend with whom he quarreled half the time, never about the war, though, during which Grant wore Union blue and Bushwa dressed in Confederate gray.

Grant and Bushwa were approached by Sheriff Tolliver and her law partner, Ethan Ramsey, now, and handshakes were exchanged. Matt Gaines and Brady Yates entered the sanctuary entrance together; the bank president had been Trouble's mentor years before either learned they were biological father and son. Gaines had been unmarried when Brady was conceived. Brady's mother, Sarah, had been married to a no-good, Alfred Yates.

Some years after Alfred's mysterious disappearance, Ethan Ramsey had assisted Sarah with legal proceedings to have the man declared dead. She later married Jim Tolliver. Hannah figured that Tolliver and Gaines's wife, Martha, were the only others who shared the secret besides Brady, Ethan and herself. Hannah suspected she was missing part of the story. Ethan had on several occasions spoken with certainty of Alfred Yates's death that suggested the exact circumstances of the man's disappearance were known by him.

There was a racket raised by stomping boots in the vestibule outside the sanctuary, and Con Callaway, owner of the Double C Ranch and county board chairman, walked in, followed by his son, Bobby, and five other ranchers, all of whom she recognized as law firm clients. These were evidently the men the others had been waiting for, because Ethan Ramsey now walked to the front of the sanctuary and stood in front of the pulpit, clearly trying to avoid the appearance that the meeting was a church sanctioned gathering.

Chapter 17

GRANT SLIPPED INTO a pew with Bushwa Sparks, his eyes on Senator Ethan Ramsey who stood quietly, waiting for all to be seated. He had met Ramsey once when Hannah introduced them at the law office. He was a relaxed, down-to-earth man and seemed to hold himself above no man. Still, there was a presence about him, a bearing that commanded attention and respect. Grant guessed the man to be about his own age. He was a tall, lean man with dark hair and steel-gray eyes that appeared to be constantly searching.

Ramsey and his wife Skye were legends in the county. Ramsey was a former Army scout called "The Puma" by the Sioux for his stealth and patience in the stalking of an enemy. Skye was half-blood Brule Sioux and had lost her left arm below the elbow during an abduction by outlaws some years earlier. Months later she had been abducted with She-Bear and other young Sioux women from a Sioux village by raiders seeking gold that had allegedly been hidden by her deceased French father. Grant had heard only fragments of the story, but the most intriguing was the supposed vision of Sioux chief Lame Buffalo on the "night of the coyote" when he proclaimed that Ethan and Skye were destined for each other.

There was a powerful story there to be written, Grant thought. Would the Ramseys ever reveal how they came upon the fortune that allowed them to endow the Lame Buffalo Association that had done so much for both Indians and whites in the valley? Intriguing. As a fiction writer, of course Grant could change names and places and solve the mystery in a story.

Ethan Ramsey raised his hand, and the chatter in the room ceased instantly, every eye fixed on the man in front. He spoke with a clear voice that was not thunderous. "I want to thank you all for coming in this evening. We will make this as brief as possible. Sheriff Tolliver asked if I might preside at this meeting. You were all asked to attend because you were identified as folks who might help with a crisis facing Big River County.

"You all have heard about the hangings of Kade McDowell and Josiah Richards. We have reason to believe this is just the beginning. We are about to be in the middle of a range war that can tear our county and town apart. The ranchers here tonight were invited because they have publicly expressed opposition to the county Stock Growers Association. The membership is secret, so we have no way of identifying members with certainty. My best guess is that the ranching community is split about half and half in terms of opposition and support.

"I do have a source of information, however, and I have good reason to believe that the Stock Growers have collected an army of mercenary gunfighters led by a man who calls himself 'Reaper.' The objective is twofold and simple. First, bring what they call justice to all suspected rustlers. Secondly, to eradicate the valley of all homesteaders who are taking up grazing lands. They have hired lawyers to defend their actions and to help with termination of homestead rights on the public record. This is a well-organized effort. More are going to die, many more if this cannot be controlled. Questions, so far?"

Con Callaway stood. "Ethan, I obviously don't like rustling, and I wish the homesteaders would head someplace else. However, I realize the government has made certain land available for homesteading, and those folks have their legal rights. A few have turned into good neighbors that I hire on sometimes. But the rustling needs to be stopped."

Ramsey said, "Of course, it does. But everyone should understand this. Rustlers must be prosecuted under the law. The territory of Wyoming does not provide a death penalty for rustlers, however. If theft amounts to less than five hundred dollars value, it is a misdemeanor and punishable by either sixty days in jail or a five hundred dollar fine plus restitution, or both jail and fine. Theft of greater value will be a felony and could result in a year or two in the territory prison. But no man will hang under the law for rustling."

Callaway said, "But folks are hanging."

"And the perpetrators are murderers and should be brought to justice."

Callaway said, "I wouldn't be against a legal hanging."

"Well, Con, the law doesn't allow for one. And once we disregard the law for one crime and deny a man his day in court, who is to say where it stops? That's why our founding fathers established a constitution."

"Yeah, I do understand that." Callaway sat down.

Ramsey continued, "We gambled that the folks invited here tonight would conclude that this vigilantism cannot be allowed to continue. It's not just in the community's interest that we stop this, it is in your personal interest. In the end nobody escapes the devastation rendered by a mob. Our problem: Big River County extends fifty or more miles north and south in the valley. East and west, you are talking about thirty-five to forty miles and half of that includes mountain country. We have a sheriff, one full-time deputy and one part-timer to cover this. It is impossible. We need to collect an army of law-abiding citizens who will be deputized to help when called upon. With that, I turn the meeting over to Sheriff Jim Tolliver."

Tolliver walked to the front of the sanctuary and took Ramsey's place. He seemed ill at ease in front of the group, but after surveying the room a few moments spoke in a voice devoid of emotion. "I thank you all for coming tonight. I won't waste time. I am trying to put together an army of deputies. I think a war the likes of which the people in this county have not seen is coming soon. I am helpless to cover this county with my two deputies. I am trying to compile a list of folks who will be sworn and deputized as volunteers and come forth to help track and capture any lawbreakers, whether they be rustlers, vigilantes or any other outlaw. I'm afraid if we don't act soon, things are going to get out of control, and this county will be like a battlefield. Some of us have seen that, and I can't imagine anyone wants to see it here."

Con Callaway stood. "I ain't disagreeing with what you say, Jim, but the folks here have businesses and ranches to tend to. We can't just drop everything and leave our work."

Tolliver said, "Not asking for that. I want you to help me find other volunteers, and I want to organize three posses. I will head up one, Ethan Ramsey will lead one. I haven't talked to him yet, but I am hoping Grant Coolidge will take the other."

No. Grant wanted to scream out in protest. Trapped. He said nothing and froze in his seat, looking straight ahead.

The sheriff continued. "I have asked Bushwa Sparks to be second in command of Grant's posse, and he has consented. She Bear will back Ethan, and Ozzie will stay with me. My group will move out first if there is a problem. If I am going to be out more than a day, I will send word to Ethan or Grant to be on stand-by near Lockwood. The other will call on his posse to be prepared to ride out wherever needed. I will meet with the leaders in a few days after posse members are assigned to work out more detailed plans."

Maggie White stood. "I ain't leaving my place for more than a short spell. I don't know why Ozzie even asked me to come here."

"Talk to me after the meeting," Tolliver said. "Jeb Oaks is going to be in charge of getting local merchants prepared to defend the town or come to our aid whenever violence threatens Lockwood. That will be a tough job, because many will be worried about losing customers if they are seen as favoring one group or the other."

Callaway said, "With the general store, Jeb's got more at risk than anybody."

Jeb Oaks stood and looked about the room. A former first sergeant with the buffalo soldiers during the Red River War with the Comanches, Oaks was a lean, sinewy man with flawless, mahogany skin from mixed Negro-Cherokee ancestry. Since his arrival in Lockwood, Grant had learned that few men were more respected than the highly successful merchant who operated the largest general store in the territory and bowed to no one.

Oaks spoke with a soft Southern drawl. "Folks must be convinced that everybody loses if the law of the rope rules. Nobody is safe when the law gets stomped on. We can close our eyes to it for a spell and pretend it don't concern us, but sooner or later the raging mob will find us, and the price will be a dear one. It might be the destruction of our property or the death of loved ones, and if we don't make a stand, it will be the loss of our freedom. I ain't backing away from this, and I damn well intend to do my part to stop it."

Oaks sat down, and Tolliver spoke again. "Ethan and I have got pencils and paper. If you can help, sign up before you leave. Talk to other folks you think you can trust. Sign-up papers will be in my office. We would like to gather at least ten men—or women—for each posse, and it would be nice to have some in reserve."

The shattering of several east sanctuary windows shocked the group. Grant dodged a stone that flew over him, but the smoking object rolling down the aisle grabbed his attention. He yelled as he leaped from his pew. "Hit the floor. Take cover."

"What the hell?" Bushwa said, as he dropped to the floor and rolled under the pew in front of him.

But Grant did not have time to answer. He was already in the aisle, scooping up the hissing dynamite stick. The burning fuse told him that time was up. He launched the cylinder with all the power his arm could muster, praying it would clear the frame of the broken window. It did by an inch. The explosion outside shook the church, shattered any remaining windows and drove him backwards. He tumbled toward the floor, cracking his head against a pew before he went to his knees.

The blow's impact was overcome by his anger and barely fazed him. Grant clambered back to his feet and headed up the aisle to the vestibule and his Winchester.

He burst through the doorway, snatched up the rifle, levered a cartridge into the chamber and charged out the church entrance. The black-cloaked and hooded men were mounted and preparing to ride away. He squeezed off a wild shot. A man grunted and slumped over in his saddle. Several guns fired from the riders before they rode away, leading the slumped rider's horse.

He ran down the stairs to give chase when he realized all the horses had been unhitched and driven off. The explosion had probably scattered them all over town and beyond. He had seen the man Gid had spoken of, though, the tall rider astride the pale horse. He had been set apart from the others, farther from the church, his mount facing the structure. Grant swore he could feel the man's stare and the hate and contempt that came with it.

He started when he felt a hand on his shoulder. He turned and saw Sheriff Tolliver and Ethan Ramsey.

"You saved a lot of lives tonight, Grant," Ramsey said.

"Is anybody hurt badly?"

"A few scratches and bruises, that's all," the sheriff said. "Reverend Meyer won't be happy about the damage to his church, but Ethan says he and Skye will deal with that."

Grant saw Blue walking down the dirt street toward the church with Hannah's buckskin and several others following. "I'll collect those mounts and hitch them. Go on in and get your sign-up sheets out. I'll be in to sign and get a few riders to help round up the missing horses. As soon as that's done, I've got to head home. I'll stop by your office in a few days, Jim, to see what you want me to do."

Chapter 18

WHEN GRANT AND Hannah reached the Box L ranch, they were greeted by Ozzie White and another man who had been standing at the corners of the house. "This here is Zeke Dale," Ozzie said, nodding toward the short, slight young man who walked out of the darkness. "He's working as a part-time deputy right now, but Jim's hoping to convince the county board to bring him on full-time."

Zeke stepped forward and offered Grant a handshake and a polite bow to Hannah. "Howdy. Pleased to meet you."

Grant could make out a broad smile and futile efforts of a moustache in the shadow of a wide-brimmed Plainsman hat. "It's a pleasure to meet you, Zeke. I hope things work out for you." He thought the young man's chances had improved after the chaos at the church tonight.

"All quiet here?" Grant said.

Ozzie said, "Yep. No trouble. Missus McDowell come out with coffee and cookies, talked to us a spell. She is one nice lady. Terrible what happened to her husband. Just awful. Wonder what's going to become of her?"

Grant sensed that Ozzie was more than casually interested in Ginger's future. Ginger and Ozzie? Impossible.

After the deputies rode out, Grant walked with Hannah to the stable to retrieve and saddle Gid's mare while Hannah put her buckskin, Dusty, up for the night. Their ride back to the Box L had been almost as quiet as their destination trip, but suddenly Hannah wanted to talk.

"I've been thinking," she said as she closed Dusty's stall gate.

"That's what I like my lawyer to do."

"Not funny. I wish I hadn't invited you to that meeting."

"More command than invite, as I recall."

"I think you ought to back away from this. You have got new responsibilities with Gid and all."

"Already signed on."

"I'm sorry I got you into this. You could have got yourself killed tonight."

"I suppose I should have stood there and watched that stick of dynamite blow?"

"Well, no. You likely saved us all, and I thank you for that. More to add to Grant Coolidge's local legend. But you were a damned fool when you took off after those raiders on your own."

"Hit one, I'm pretty sure."

"That's not the point. You should have waited for others. You were crazed. Maybe that bump on the side of your forehead had something to do with it. It's still oozing blood. If you will come in the house, I'll clean it up some, put a gauze patch on it."

"It will be fine."

"Tough feller, huh?"

"Did you check your saddle for a bur when you put it away tonight?"

"I'm just worried about you, and I am regretting my part pulling you into this fight."

"Think about it. I was in it the instant Ginger came to my house. I dug in deeper when I took Gid in, and there was no way out when I killed that gunslinger in my stable. And after that attack at the church, I was in by choice. It's my choice now. Understand that."

She nodded.

"And we had better quit fussing with each other, because you're stuck with me taking you to that barn dance."

She looked at him, nodded again and surrendered a faint smile.

Chapter 19

"WHAT DO I do about Tommy Bean," Joker asked.

"Where is he?" Reaper replied.

"I had the boys put him in the extra bed in my cabin. Didn't think you would want him in one of the bunkhouses just yet. Cobb's trying to doctor him some, but Bean took the slug in his lower back. It's still in there. Seems deep. He needs a doc. Cobb's not bad with horses, but he says he can't be cutting on a man. Wouldn't know where he was headed with a blade, and he ain't got nothing but a big penknife."

"And where would we find a doctor?"

"A good one in Lockwood, they say. A Jew, I've heard."

"Would you want a Jew cutting on you?"

"Don't think I'd care much if I was going to die if he didn't. Don't know that I ever seen a Jew. Guess I'm not sure what one is. Some breed of Negro?"

Why did he keep this idiot around? He guessed loyalty and obedience were worth something, but at moments like this, he wondered. "We take Bean to this doctor, and the sheriff will be there in five minutes. And Bean starts talking in ten."

"So what do I do?"

"Not a damn thing. When you leave here, send Cobb back to the Rider bunkhouse."

"That leaves me to look after Bean."

"You are catching on. I don't want you to shoot him. A gunshot might stir up the boys. You're handy with a rope. Work one around Bean's neck and pull till he can't breathe anymore."

"Strangle him?"

"You are catching on. Is he conscious?"

"Not when I left to come over here."

"Your other choice is to just let him die. But we aren't taking him to a doctor. Now, I want to know who the son-of-a-bitch with the rifle was—the one that shot Bean. He came down those church steps like he thought he could whip the bunch of us," Reaper said.

Reaper, Danek and Joker were sitting in the canyon hideaway's parlor in front of a roaring fire. Reaper sipped at the whiskey in his glass, savoring its taste, giving the golden liquid time to do its calming. His companions were well along on their second glasses, and Reaper would grant the two men a few extra tonight. He always restricted himself to a single, refusing to impair his thinking for even a few minutes. "I said I wanted to know who the crazy fool was. Can our man with the enemy tell us?"

"He might not be so inclined to cooperate after tonight. He would have died if that dynamite had exploded inside the church," Danek said.

"Tell him that we didn't know he was there if he says anything. He will want to believe it, because he can't stop sucking at our money tit."

Joker said, "No need to ask. I seen the feller around more than once when I first come up from Texas looking for a place for us to set up a headquarters. That was Coolidge, the feller that kilt Olson, the one we talked about before. He was the substitute sheriff when Tolliver got laid up by a gunshot."

"So that's the famous writer."

"Wouldn't know about that. Don't care much for books."

Reaper figured Joker might be able to read and write his own name but not much beyond. "He's becoming a nuisance. He will likely need to be disposed of before we are finished here, but I think we should back off for a week or two, at least until we get some word from the Stock Growers Association. Last word I had, they want to move careful like. Mostly, they want the rustling cleaned up before spring calving and the homesteaders on the run by that time, too."

Danek said, "Another month, the snow's going to be ass-high in a lot of the valley. We won't be doing much over the winter."

"And folks won't be expecting us. If we're patient, we might be doing a lot. Surprise is a huge edge in war. There are two places at the far west end of the valley I would like to strike before the bad snows move in. We will be a long way from the law, and it will give some satisfaction to our employers. They may be upset about the way tonight went."

Danek shrugged.

Reaper said, "Yeah, I know. You said it was a step too far."

"You don't blow up churches amongst the god-fearing people out west. And an attack on the leaders is inviting big trouble."

"But if it had worked, we would have owned the county and been free to do our job without interference while folks cowered in their homes."

"But it did not work."

Chapter 20

TWO DAYS AFTER the church attack, Grant accompanied Gid to the Pennock School before a visit to the sheriff's office. The boy had not resisted attendance, and Grant thought he might have detected some hidden enthusiasm. Another boy was waiting outside for him, and after leaving Lady the mare at the school stable, Gid had raced away to greet his new friend.

Grant stopped at the principal's office to discuss Gid's grade placement, since he had received his information secondhand. Principal Ralph Turner was a short, sixtyish man with a shiny, bald pate and a big smile and seemed pleased to speak with Grant about the new enrollee.

Grant sat across the desk from the principal, who handed him a sheet of parchment paper setting forth the boy's grade levels based upon examination. The name imprint at the top said "Gideon Coolidge." He scanned the sheet which included the examining teacher's supplemental notes. The evaluation summary left him scratching his head. Third grade for history, sixth grade for arithmetic and seventh grade for reading and writing. Class assignment: fifth grade

Turner said, "I was going to send the report home with Gideon today, but I'm delighted we have an opportunity to chat."

"Well, I am, too, but there is a mistake on the report. I am not Gideon's father. His name is Gideon Trout, and I am looking after him until other arrangements can be made."

The principal frowned. "Perhaps that was the name you gave my assistant, Miss Greenwald, but the boy insists his last name is Coolidge and writes it on all his papers. Does it really matter? We don't want a name fuss to get in the way of his learning."

"I guess not. It just seems strange somehow, and I hate to encourage any illusions he might have about residing with me permanently. I know nothing about being a father."

"Does anyone? Gideon is obviously very bright. We could have set his grade level higher, but he does need some work on history. Also, we try to group by age even though the teacher instructs by achievement levels, a challenge with as many as twenty various grade levels in her classroom. He will be in a class of children ranging from fourth through seventh grade levels, and we try to stay alert to challenging those at the upper levels and focusing on deficiencies."

"If he reads well, it appears I should encourage him to do some historical reading."

"Yes, and thanks to the Lame Buffalo Association, we have an excellent library at our school."

"A boy met him outside the school. It appears he has a friend. I had worried about that."

"That would have been Toby Harms. He's a very shy boy, and their primary teacher, Miss Collyer, was thrilled that the boys seemed to hit it off so quickly. Before Gideon arrived, we had four boys in their age group, and Toby had never been accepted by the other three for some reason, perhaps because he is more of a scholar and a bit of a loner. His father is a superintendent with Valley Coal Company at the mines, and his mother sews at Sarah's Fashions. Good, hardworking folks with five children enrolled at our school and another arriving next term."

Grant said, "I'm glad the boys met up. Maybe they will be a boost to each other."

After meeting with the principal, Grant rode into to town to speak with the sheriff, hoping he could finish his town errands in time to return home and spend a full afternoon at his desk. A Marshal Buck Tyree novel was waiting for P.J. Bowie to finish. Then he planned to spend a month on the longer novel he was doing for Garth and Twain. His income after years of writing had finally risen beyond mere subsistence since his arrival in Lockwood, thanks in no small part to Hannah Locke, who had taken over contract negotiations.

Fortunately, Sheriff Jim Tolliver was at his desk when Grant arrived. Tolliver did not even bother to swing his feet off the desk when Grant sat down across from him.

"Reporting for duty?" Tolliver said.

"Just checking in."

Tolliver reached in his desk drawer and flipped a handwritten sheet of paper across the desk. "Your posse. You should meet and get acquainted soon."

Grant perused the list. He did not recognize some of the names. "Bushwa, of course. Brady Yates."

"Yep. Trouble insisted he ride with you. His ma won't like him riding with anyone, but he lives in the stable loft these days and she's got no say."

"Bobby Callaway and Maggie White."

"Bobby's old man is riding with Ethan, and Bobby didn't want to go with Con. They live in the same house off and on but can't be together five minutes without a quarrel. Kid's good with a gun. Twenty-four or five years old in years, sometimes fifteen years in the brain. His two older brothers have their own homes and families on the Double C. Bobby ain't found his niche yet."

"And Maggie White. She said she couldn't leave her place for serious time."

"I want you or somebody in your group to stay in contact with her. She's going to be our eyes and ears out there. Her still does a big business, especially with the cowhands. She knows what's going on in the county. Send Bushwa out to talk with her regular-like. He's had his eyes on the woman as long as I've been around but won't take a bath or shave to court her."

"If you see Bushwa, tell him I want to talk to him."

"Bushwa and Trouble can tell you about the others on your list if you don't know them. Like I say, you should get word out for a get-acquainted meeting. I'll leave it to you how you want to work out contacting these folks and organizing the bunch. After all, you've been sheriff of this county."

"Don't remind me."

Tolliver tossed a deputy's badge to him. "You're sworn. I don't have enough badges for all the posse members, but the leaders should wear one."

"I swore I would never pin on a badge again."

"Sometimes, things don't work out the way we planned. Be careful about what you swear to."

He was already corralled, so Grant figured it was time to abandon the debate over his service as a lawman, and there was something that had been troubling him. "How did the vigilantes find out about the meeting at the church?"

The sheriff said, "I've been scratching my head about that."

"A lot of folks were told about it considering the size of the group gathered there. I assume there were others who couldn't make the meeting or chose not to get involved."

"That's true enough."

Grant said, "Regardless, it appears that somebody who was identified as a friend is not."

"Appears so."

"If we plan anything ahead of time, I'm thinking we don't share anything till the last possible minute."

"Makes sense."

Grant stood up. "I'm heading home. I've got work to do."

"Is that what you call writing those damn storybooks?"

Grant did not reply and walked out the door, hoping he could catch Trouble Yates at the stable. His sixteen and a half-year-old mind was a virtual encyclopedia when it came to the people and geography of Big River County, and Grant had a few questions.

Chapter 21

HANNAH SAT ON the front of the buckboard with Grant. He handled the mules' reins, as she struggled to keep her mouth shut about his ineptness at driving the team. The critters were hers, as was the wagon, and she would have preferred to be the muleskinner this evening. Men being men, however, she had decided not to start the social evening with an insult. She would be damned, though, if she would ever ride with him on a mountain trail. Of course, Grant was so skittish about heights, he would likely need to ride with a sack over his head.

Jasmine, Primrose and Gid rode in the wagon bed, the girls attired in new gowns by Sarah's Fashions sold through Oaks General Store. Gid had even seemed excited about the new shoes, shirt and britches Grant had let him pick out for the dance. Poor Grant. The kid had come to him with nothing but rags to cover him. Oaks General Store had done well off the writer from the East since his arrival. For that matter, during the week before the dance, Jeb and Carissa Oaks must have hauled a fortune to the Gaines Bank.

Ginger had remained at the house, thinking it was too soon after her husband's death to appear at a social event. Ozzie White had volunteered to stay with her as a precaution in case the vigilantes were still looking for her. Ozzie had volunteered with enthusiasm. He was a fine young man, but Hannah feared he was on his way to a broken heart.

She watched Grant, his eyes intent on the road ahead. He was wearing a western-cut suit tonight mostly hidden by his thick wool coat, but when he shed the garment for a spell at her home, he nearly took her breath away. He had no idea how the ladies were going to drool over him tonight. She should have brought a stick to chase them away with. In Wyoming Territory, the ladies were not shy and demure when it came to showing interest in a man.

She told herself that Grant should have been accompanying her friend, Moon Dupree, to this dance, and she felt sad and a bit guilty about that. She knew Grant was likely suffering twice the guilt. He seemed to carry a sack of guilt from his past upon his shoulders. She smiled when she remembered that a few days before her death in the fire, Moon had teased her that she was grooming Grant for Hannah. Moon said this even though the half-blood Sioux mystic was sharing his bed at the time. It occurred to her now that Moon was not entirely teasing, that she had a sense that her time with Grant would be brief.

Grant reined the team in at the town hall and assisted Hannah and the young ladies off the wagon before moving on to Fletcher's Livery, where he had reserved space for the mules. He had insisted they be out of the bitter wind and had reserved a stall at the livery even though current owner, Trouble Yates, had increased rates for the barn dance.

"Supply and demand," Enos Fletcher, owner emeritus and now livery employee, had informed Grant. "Blame Smith, whoever he is." The writer took the price increase with a sense of humor and had laughed when he told her about his conversation with Fletcher.

Trouble had been introduced to Adam Smith's writings at an early age by his biological father, Matt Gaines, and could quote the writer's works the way some folks quoted the Bible. Hannah knew that Enos Fletcher could not read more than a few words, but the wizened man had lived Smith's economic philosophy for as long as she had known him. He could blame Trouble for the price increase, but if it had been his decision, the price would have risen for the night, also.

Hannah and the two girls waited just inside the entryway for Grant. Gid's friend, Toby, had been waiting at the door, and the boys had already disappeared into a crowd of youngsters gathering at a far corner of the big building, which lacking a false ceiling was more barnlike than some barns, she thought. She looked over the expansive room, picking out the familiar faces in the conversation groups strung out across the floor.

The seven-member band was tuning up on the stage with a diverse collection of instruments: a piano, two violins, a flute, a bass drum, a guitar and a banjo. Thank the Lord for the piano and Winifred Beard, a colored woman about her own age, whose husband, Phil, worked in the coal mine while Winnie gave private piano lessons to children in the area. She also assisted several days weekly with a music class at the Pennock School where her own three children attended classes. The elegant Winnie, an accomplished pianist, would keep the tune moving when the other musicians lost their ways, usually to return for the chorus.

The walls were lined with plank benches. No more than a half dozen ten-person rectangular tables with chairs were scattered at the near end of the building, leaving ample room for the dancers. The Methodist ladies had set up two tables on each side of the hall where cake, cookies, and other culinary delights were served with coffee and punch. A tin for a free will offering sat at the end of each table, and it was rumored the church enjoyed lucrative evenings at the barn dances that were held four or five times annually.

The music began just as Grant walked into the building. "Camptown Races" started shaking the building. Grant shed his coat and dropped it in the men's pile off to one side of the door. Hannah hooked her arm in his and led him to one of the benches, where they sat down. "Where are the kids?" Grant asked.

She could barely hear him above the racket. "They disappeared." Then she saw them and pointed to the dance floor where two parallel lines had formed, boys on one side, girls on the other. Jasmine and Primrose each faced a boy, stepping briskly forward, then backward, forward again, and the boy would take the girl's hand, twirl her around a time or two and the process continued.

"Do you want to try it?" Hannah said.

"Could we wait a bit? I've never done anything like that."

It was going to take some work to get the stuffiness out of the tenderfoot tonight, but she was determined. She sat silently through the next few numbers, waiting for the right song.

Grant said, "I recognize Matt Gaines on one of the fiddles and your associate Hamilton Fish on the bass drum. The guitar player cooks at The Chowdown. That's Katy Culper on the flute. The old fella on the other fiddle is Polecat Smith. He works sometimes at the livery. The banjo player looks familiar, but I can't place him."

Hannah laughed. "Put a long, black beard and shaggy hair on him."

"It can't be."

"It is."

"Bushwa Sparks? His hair sheared down and his cheeks and chin all naked skin? Nice coat and clean Levis, shiny new boots. I'll bet he's even had a bath. What happened?"

"Across the dance floor on the bench nearest the stage."

"Is that Maggie White? Ozzie's mother. The moonshiner?"

"She's a handsome woman when you get her out of bib overalls, isn't she?"

"She and Bushwa? When I asked him to be her contact that's not what I had in mind."

"It might not be a bad cover. If he's courting her, it might make their meetings less suspicious."

"Courting? You are rushing things, I'd say."

She took his hand and coaxed him to his feet. "We're dancing now, and Winnie just said she is going to sing, 'Lorena,' the old song from the Civil War years. I will probably cry."

It was a slow, sad song, and Winnie's soprano voice rose above the soft piano music and echoed through the building, and a few tears did roll down her cheeks.

> *The years creep slowly by, Lorena*
> *The snow is on the grass again*
> *The sun's low down the sky, Lorena*
> *The frost gleams where the flowers have been*

She suddenly realized that she and Grant were gliding across the floor and people were stepping back and watching. She could not believe it. He was a magnificent dancer, instinctively anticipating each step she took. She did not hear the words for a bit, and Winnie paused to allow the violins to play the melancholy tune, sending shivers down her spine. Then Winnie continued.

Ron Schwab

It matters little now, Lorena
The past is in the eternal past
Our heads will soon lie low, Lorena
Life's tide is ebbing out so fast
There is a future, oh thank God
Of life this is so small a part
'Tis dust to dust beneath the sod
But there, up there, 'tis heart to heart

The music ended, and the hall was silent as Hannah's teary eyes fixed on Grant's. Applause broke the silence, and she saw that they were on the floor alone, everyone watching them. Strangely, she found she was not the least embarrassed, but she saw that Grant's face was red as a spring rose. She gave a wave of appreciation and led him off the dance floor.

Immediately, Jasmine appeared and claimed a dance, then Primrose. She accepted the invitation of other men to dance but kept her eyes on Grant, chiding herself for a twinge of jealousy she felt when he was dancing with the other women. She did enjoy watching Bushwa and Maggie dance when he abandoned his station to join her for "My Grandfather's Clock" and the new song "Oh My Darling Clementine," before marching around the room with some of the folks to "Tramp! Tramp! Tramp!"

During a break, Grant strode up to Winnie, the pianist, and spoke to her at length. She got up and lifted the lid of her hinged piano bench. She took out some sheets of music and placed them on the piano. What was he up to now?

After the band gathered on the stage again. Winnie came to the front of the stage. "Folks, I have a request, but I have granted it with the condition that Grant Coolidge will help me out with this one. Obadiah Sparks knows this song, and he will accompany us as the whistler. This song is dedicated to the late Bright Moon Dupree. Ladies and gentlemen, please "Listen to the Mockingbird.""

Hannah looked at Grant in disbelief. He shrugged, "Listen carefully," he said before he got up and headed for the stage. He stood beside Winnie, who sat on the piano bench, her eyes focused on her music sheets. Bushwa stood off to the side. Winnie nodded at Bushwa, and he whistled the tune of the first verse of the chorus. Winnie started singing a solo. Then Bushwa whistled before Grant joined Winnie for a duet for the chorus, singing with a powerful baritone voice that she found mesmerizing.

Listen to the mockingbird
Sing his sweet song.
Listen to the Mockingbird
And know that life goes on.

A solo by Grant. Then Bushwa whistles. A duet for the chorus. A solo by Winnie. Finally, it was Grant's solo again, and his eyes were fixed on Hannah's. She could not make out the detail of those searching hazel eyes, but she knew.

On that morning dressed in black,
I began my journey back.
Through old cobwebs blew.
From my footsteps shadows flew.
Through these eyes of light now
I began to know
All good things in time will come and go.
The whistle and the duet again.
Listen to the mockingbird
Sing his sweet song.
Listen to the mockingbird
And know that life goes on.

Chapter 22

AFTER THE DANCE, Grant helped Jasmine and Primrose out of the wagon. He started to assist Hannah, but she waved him off. "I'll go to the stable with you and help with the mules. You've got horses to saddle, too." She looked at Gid who still sat in the wagon box. "Gid, why don't you go in with the girls. We'll saddle Lady and bring her up to the house."

"You bet." He bounded off the wagon and fell in behind the girls.

Grant did not know what to say to Hannah as they unharnessed and tended to the mules. She had seemed buoyant, almost giddy early in the evening, but as the dance neared the end, she had turned more somber, perhaps retreating into her own mind. He understood that because he lived in his own most of the time, often oblivious to what was happening around him. "Do you want Mabel and Albert to share a stall?" Grant said.

"No, they can take the two stalls occupied by Blue and Lady."

"I'll get them out to make room." He retrieved his horses and hitched them to support posts while he started to saddle the mounts.

After Hannah finished getting the mules settled in, she came up behind him and spoke, "You said you couldn't dance."

He turned to face her. "I said it had been years since I had danced sober or something to that effect."

"You are beyond good as most of the young women in town now know."

He grinned sheepishly. "I give the dance partner I escorted to the dance all the credit."

"You do have a clever way with words, don't you? And I had no idea you could sing. You have a beautiful voice."

"Thanks. I'm not schooled or anything. I enjoy music. I used to sing 'Mockingbird' around the campfires when I was in the Army. Everybody joined in for the chorus. Some would whistle. Soldiers liked the song. I can't remember when I didn't know the words."

"Why did you request it tonight?"

"You will think I am a lunatic. Moon told me."

She looked at him, astonishment in those greenish-blue eyes. "Moon told you. Are you seeing ghosts?"

"Not like that. But it was like she was whispering in my ear, 'Life goes on.' And the words of the song came to me. I finally realized that she would never leave my heart and my memories. I learned so much from her. But life does go on, and I was hoping you would receive that message from me. I am ready to move on and see what life brings my way, and if you are willing, to explore how we are meant to share it. Maybe we are. Perhaps we are not, but I confess that you are more than my lawyer to me now."

For once, she was speechless. He stepped toward her and took her in his arms, kissed her lips lightly, and when she responded, shared a lingering kiss that ignited his desire for this incredible woman. She pulled her head back and said, "And you are more than my client."

They kissed again, this time the embrace pressing them together snugly.

"Uh, sorry folks. I didn't mean to interrupt."

Instantly, Grant and Hannah pulled apart. It was Ozzie. Grant wondered how long he had stood there not more than a dozen feet away.

As if answering Grant's question, Ozzie said, "I just come in the side door. Didn't hear you in here or I'd have backed off. Come to get my horse and head back to town. The girls was jabbering about the dance. Sounded like they had a good time. Miss Ginger and me got along good just talking. She's quite a lady. Oh, and I did take regular walks outside the house to be sure strangers wasn't about. All quiet."

Grant said, "I'd better finish saddling my horses, too. Time to be getting home. At least Gid doesn't have to get up for school tomorrow."

Ozzie took that as his signal to move on, and he seemed relieved to escape the awkwardness of the encounter. Grant worried for Hannah's embarrassment. He looked at her. She just shrugged and smiled mischievously.

He finished saddling the horses, and Hannah took Lady's reins and followed him and Blue out of the barn. "Goodnight, Ozzie," Grant called to the young deputy who seemed to be taking time with the saddling of his mount. "I'll stop by the office later next week."

"Goodnight, Grant."

As they walked toward the house, Hannah said, "You will be over for Sunday dinner tomorrow noon, won't you?"

"If you like."

"It's a tradition now. The girls are already making plans. They would be disappointed if you and Gid didn't come." She hesitated. "I would be, too."

"We will be over about noon, then." Suddenly, he felt tongue-tied, uncertain what to say after their kisses in the stable. He was saved by Gid running from the house to join him. He was not about to attempt a goodnight kiss in front of the boy.

Hannah said, "Thank you for a very special evening, Grant."

She stood no more than four feet distant with the mare's reins in one hand. He felt like they were playing chess, and it was his move. She often spoke with her eyes, and tonight they were teasing him, daring him to take her in her arms again. "Uh, it was nice. I am glad I went. We will see you and the girls tomorrow." He thought later that as an author he could not have written a clumsier ending to the chapter.

Chapter 23

REAPER HAD BEEN assigned the homestead at the northeast end of the valley for this night's mission. It was located some thirty miles from Lockwood. There would be no need to fret about the law learning about their visit too quickly. The place was isolated, an island in the middle of prime grazing land. The area had been opened by the government for homesteading only a year earlier, but the county Stock Growers Association members expected a flood of homesteaders in the spring. They wanted to send a warning.

His association contact had informed him that they wanted no hangings unless there was evidence of rustling. "Just burn them out," he had directed. If possible, the occupants were not to be physically harmed. Reaper had long ago learned there was no homesteader who would simply sit back and watch his home and farm buildings burned down. More than likely, someone would get hurt tonight.

As usual, there were eight Riders including himself to carry out the task. Tommy Bean had taken up residence in hell, and he had sent Joker to Lockwood for a several days' scouting mission, where he would also meet up with their spy for an update. He hoped to learn more details of the law's plans for resistance. And he wanted to know about the man who had shot Bean and fired at his retreating Justice Riders after their attack on the church.

He had a half dozen men in reserve, however, mostly gunslingers who had worked with him for at least three or four years. The men were interchangeable for a mission, and Reaper liked to hold men back, partially to protect their hideout, but also to preserve his resources in case an assault turned sour and serious losses were incurred.

It was a half hour before sundown when the black-hooded men rode into the farmstead's yard. A man dressed in a coonskin cap with earflaps and a bulky coat was crossing the yard, carrying a bucket in each hand. When he saw the riders, he dropped the buckets, spilling the liquid contents, and raced for the little log cabin.

Reaper spoke to Danek, "Looks like the fella was coming back from milking. It appears he turned out the milk cow in the lot. I don't see a calf. Anyway, there's no sign of rustled cattle. I guess that's to the man's credit. Report said he has a wife. Not sure about kids."

Danek said, "It's damn cold out here. I wonder if we shouldn't settle for the barn and chicken house. Leave these people a roof over their heads. Your Association folks should consider public reaction to what they're doing. They seem to be willing to risk public opinion turning against them. Most folks will stay neutral, avoid a fight unless somebody goes too far."

"Sometimes you sound like an old woman, Danek. Leave the house, and they'll have a new barn up by spring. This one's not much of a barn anyhow."

Reaper dismounted from the pale horse, and the other men followed his signal. They hitched their horses to a livestock fence out of gunshot range from the house. Reaper said, "Doggett and Crane, you stay with me and Danek. The rest of you turn out the horses and any other stock in the barn, then fire it up. Same with the chicken house. Turn out the chickens if you like. Makes me no mind. If there is a horse worth taking, and you can catch the critter, it's yours. On second thought, save one horse and tack back for the homesteaders, too. We'll give them a fair chance to get to town."

As half his crew headed for the barn, Reaper and Danek, followed by the other two men, walked slowly toward the house. "No sign of a dog," Reaper said. "That's good. This man's name is John Ridge. Is that right?"

Danek said, "That's what the Association's contact told Roper."

Reaper stopped and hollered at the house, "Hey, John Ridge, come out, so we can talk."

The cabin door opened a crack. "I'm listening," came a male voice.

"You and your missus won't be harmed if you come out peaceable. I give you my word. You stay put, and you will burn with the house. All you got to do is walk away from this place. Go back where you came from or move on. Your choice."

"I'll meet you halfway. You got to holster that rifle, though. I'll leave mine behind."

"And how am I to know your woman won't be shooting at me?"

"She'll watch from the doorway, where your men can see her."

This seemed too easy, but the fool was outnumbered. It didn't seem likely he would take on Reaper's entire crew.

Ridge stepped through the doorway and started walking toward him. Reaper handed his horse's reins to Danek, confirmed that the woman was within his men's view and took a few tentative steps toward Ridge, who was still bundled in the big coat that covered his neck and chin and the coonskin cap that dropped low on his forehead. Ridge stopped when Reaper did. They were still at least thirty feet apart, and Reaper figured that was near enough.

"Now, Mister Ridge," Reaper said, "I'll lay out the rules."

"This is my property. I make the rules here."

"Look around you, Ridge. There's eight of us. I make the rules tonight. And here they are. You and your wife have got fifteen minutes to get a few personal things out of the house. Then we're going to have us a fire. My men are going to hold back a horse for you and your woman to ride to town. If I was you, I'd stay here by the fires tonight and wait till daylight to head out, but that's up to you. No debate about this. Now get your ass moving."

Reaper could not see much of the man's face, but the set of his head as he glared at the farmstead's invader told him to be watchful. This was a man who had not yet surrendered. Ridge wheeled and marched back to the cabin, his wife stepping away and slamming the door be-hind him when he entered.

The light haze of dusk had shifted to darkness now, and he noticed there was no lantern light in the house. He called, "Time's up, Ridge. Grab your things and get the hell out here."

Silence. And then the crack of a rifle and a horse's scream. Reaper turned and saw Lucifer, his pale stallion, rear and pull against the fence where he was hitched. He raced toward his precious mount, consoling himself that the horse had not gone down.

Reaching the horse he grabbed the reins, started speaking softly to the animal, calming him and settling the animal down, at the same time examining him for a wound, relying on his probing fingers in the darkness. In a few moments he felt the sticky blood on the horse's muscled neck and then when the stallion whinnied and pulled back, the entry wound. The bleeding was not pro-fuse, and the location would not affect a vital organ. His momentary panic now turned to rage.

"Return fire," Reaper ordered the Riders. The rifles let loose a barrage of gunfire that shattered the two front windows and splintered the door.

The door opened a crack, and a hand appeared waving a white cloth.

"Hold your fire," Reaper said. "Are you coming out?"

A woman's face appeared. She sobbed as she spoke. "My husband's hurt. He's down. Please, help him. We will do what you say." She backed away from the door, leaving it partially open.

He did not trust her, or any woman for that matter. "Approach the house carefully. Vince, you take the door but be ready to pull back."

Vince Doggett, one of his older Riders, a Confederate Army veteran, ruthless and reliable, stepped ahead of the others.

"Are you coming, Reaper?" Danek asked, when Reaper lagged some distance to the rear.

Reaper did not reply but thought not for the first time that Danek's insolence was wearing thin. He was tiring of the man rendering an opinion so bluntly and challenging his employer's courage on occasion. He paid men to follow orders. Generals rarely led the charge.

When they reached the cabin, Doggett yelled into the darkness behind the open door. "Ma'am, show yourself. Light a lamp, so we can see to your husband."

"I can't find the matches. I'm beside John on the floor. He is wounded terribly. I can't tell if he is breathing. Please. Help."

Doggett stepped cautiously through the doorway, but the shotgun blast nearly cut him in half and knocked him backward onto the snow-crusted ground outside the door. Danek leaped over the body with a grace that belied his stocky frame and disappeared into the house. Reaper tensed, anticipating another shotgun blast.

A lamp went on in the house. "All clear. Come on in," Danek called.

"Let's go," Reaper said to Dirk Crane, the other Rider. "Drag Vince out of the way." Too bad about Vince. He had been a steady, dependable sort. Never asked questions. Less wages to pay, though. Everything had trade-offs.

He stepped into the single room cabin. It would have been cozy enough without the wind whipping through the shattered windows. Danek held the sobbing woman's arm. The shotgun and a Winchester rifle lay on the floor not far from John Ridge's quiet form. It appeared the body had absorbed at least a half dozen slugs, the fool's price for not surrendering or taking cover after firing his challenging shot. Of course, it didn't matter. Wounding the pale stallion carried a death penalty.

Reaper studied the woman. She wore a wool coat over her dress. Blonde and blue-eyed, pretty enough even with red, swollen eyes that stared at him with contempt and hate. "Did you fire the shotgun?" Reaper asked.

"Damn right I did," she said. Totally unrepentant.

Reaper walked over to her. "Let go of her," Reaper instructed Danek.

"If you say so." Danek released her arm and stepped away.

The instant Danek released her, she leaped on Reaper like a mountain lion, screaming at him and pommeling his face, pulling at his black hood. He stepped backward, trying to push her away, but she seemed oblivious to his blows. He stumbled over Ridge's body and went to his knees, but his hood remained clutched in the woman's hand. She looked down at him, seemingly frozen as she studied his face.

He reached beneath his coat and felt for his holstered Colt. Clumsily, he slipped the weapon from its holster and pointed it at the woman. "Back off while I get to my feet."

"Go to hell." She spat on him.

He squeezed the trigger twice before she fell, the echo of the shots resounding like claps of thunder in the small cabin. He struggled to his feet and looked around. His eyes met Danek's. The overseer shook his head from side to side and turned away and walked out the door.

Reaper found his hood on the floor next to the dead woman and picked it up and placed it back over his head.

He saw flickering light outside the cabin window. The barn and chicken house were burning now. He went outside and spoke to Crane who waited alone outside the cabin. "Can you get Vince inside?"

"He ain't that big. Yeah, I can drag him in."

"Do it and fire the place. We need to be on our way."

Chapter 24

TROUBLE YATES SAW Grant ride up outside the Pennock School with Gideon Trout, the boy who had taken up residence at the writer's cabin. Trouble had just finished a conversation with Principal Turner about his graduation status and now was conversing with Samantha Morris, the young woman he was currently courting, just outside the high school entrance. He waved at Grant and raised a hand signaling his friend to wait.

He turned back to Samantha. "I need to talk to Grant Coolidge, Sammy. Can we talk about this some other time? This ain't a good place or time anyhow."

"We had better talk about it, Brady, because I am on the verge of calling off the courting business. There is no shortage of young men in Wyoming Territory. I told you

I was in no hurry to get married, and I said not before we were both eighteen, and that's a year and a half away."

"I ain't in that big of a hurry."

"I know what you are in a hurry for. And it is not going to happen before we are married. And I am not going to marry a man who says 'ain't' all the time."

"I will stop by Sarah's Fashions in the next few days, and we will set up a time to talk. I promise. I love you, Sammy. More than anything. And I ain't going to say ain't anymore."

He could not resist annoying her before he turned away and headed toward Grant, but maybe it was time to send the word off on the wagon. It would likely give Sammy a sense that she was reforming him and bring a little peace to the courtship. He did not want to lose her. He could not imagine they would not be married someday. Besides that, she was the bookkeeper for all his business enterprises. He paid her for the work, but anybody else would charge twice as much. It seemed only reasonable that he would have a free bookkeeper after marriage.

Grant had dismounted while he waited for Trouble to join him. It appeared Gideon was leading his mare away to the Pennock stable. Outside his newly discovered banker father, Matt Gaines, he had no better male friend in Lockwood than Grant. They had hit it off from the day

Grant arrived on a train from the East. "Morning, Grant. Surprised to see you here. I thought the young feller usually rode into school with Primrose and Jasmine."

"They aren't coming till afternoon. They are working on a geography presentation of some kind. They've got maps they've drawn strung out all over the Box L ranch house. Ginger's helping, too. It seems she is quite the artist."

"Matt always says folks have talents hidden even to themselves until they or somebody else discovers them. The terrible thing is for those things to stay buried for the person's lifetime. She ought to keep an eye out for someplace she can use her skills and get paid for it."

"Ginger's an ambitious hard-working woman. She'll find a niche someplace, I'm sure."

"I'd hate to see her go back to whoring."

"That won't happen. You wanted to talk to me?"

"Yep. Did Hannah tell you about the sawmill?"

"She hasn't said a word about it. She's had plenty of chances the past few days."

"Yeah, I saw you and her at the barn dance. Sammy danced with you once, and you sure as hell caused me trouble. Is there anything you can't do?"

"I could write a book on that. I can't cook worth a damn. I couldn't build a doghouse for that big pup we've taken on. You saw my skills at trail riding that time I had to ride the high country blindfolded while you led my horse. I'd starve trying to make a living as a cowhand. But I don't see how my dancing caused you problems with that pretty young lady."

"Well, first, I brought her to the dance but only danced with her twice. I mashed her toes a few times when I did. That's when she started comparing me to you. I think she'd drop me like a rotten fish if you showed her some interest."

"I am old enough to be Samantha Morris's father."

"Lots of women out here are married to older fellers. Some came as mail order brides."

"Well, I am not going to intrude on your romance, I promise that. Anyway, I saw you circulating around the hall during the dance, talking to some of the business folks in town. Maybe you should have dropped business for the night and paid more attention to Samantha."

"You're not much help. That's what Sammy has been chewing my ear about. That and what she calls my deficiencies in the social skills."

Grant said, "I thought this conversation was going to be about the sawmill."

"Yeah. Sammy just got me kind of worked up. About the sawmill, Hannah has signed on. She's agreed to hold my shares in a trust till I'm of age, just like the other businesses. She's going to set up a corporation like we talked about. She will hold the sixteen hundred shares for me, and you will take fourteen hundred. We will call it 'Yates and Coolidge Lumber Company.' I would like to get a bank account set up this afternoon if you can meet me at the bank."

"Wait a minute. I said I'd do this, but I don't want my name publicized on a business."

"Why not?"

"I can't explain it. It just doesn't feel right somehow."

"Hannah said you wouldn't like it. I've got a backup: 'Y and C Lumber Company.' You should know by now that there aren't any secrets in Lockwood. Folks will know you are involved whether your name is on it or not."

Grant sighed. "I'm having second thoughts, but I guess 'Y and C' is alright. As to the banking, I am going back into town from here. Could we go to the bank this morning, and I can authorize a transfer to the sawmill account. I can't wait around till afternoon. I've got work waiting for me at home."

"I guess I can work that out. What kind of work would you have at home?"

"Nine o'clock when the bank opens. I'll meet you there." Grant turned away and mounted Blue, reining the gelding toward Lockwood.

Chapter 25

GRANT WALKED AWAY from his meeting with Matt Gaines and Trouble Yates at the bank feeling much poorer and plagued with second thoughts about his new venture in the world of commerce. The investment had drained his bank account about dry. He would need to keep an eye on his expenses until his next royalty check from Beadle's arrived. With luck, it would show up in a week.

He reminded himself that Trouble Yates, kid or not, appeared to have the Midas touch, a natural shrewdness that turned every venture he touched into gold. And Trouble had mastered and now lived the code of the economic philosopher Adam Smith. He had plans for his enterprises plotted for years in the future. Grant suspected that Trouble's business acumen would soon be unparalleled in the county, someday the territory. No, he would ride this horse with his young friend and see where it took him.

But what would the young man's ambitions do to Trouble's personal life? Would he have one? Alcohol had been Grant's curse, helping him destroy two marriages before he had grasped sobriety ten years earlier. Was business obsession Trouble's alcohol? Perhaps Samantha Morris recognized the dangers that lurked in Trouble's future and was determined that her suitor establish some balance in his life before they took their vows. Was Sammy the custodian of a crystal ball of wisdom for the couple? Grant would watch their story unfold with interest.

He smiled. He had best figure out his own romantic life before he worried about Trouble's and Sammy's. At Sunday dinner, Hannah had seemed distant, and he admitted to himself that he had had been clumsy as a small boy in striking up a conversation. Fortunately, Jasmine and Primrose had been buoyant and chatty. He and Hannah had shared no private moments, and he had not sought any.

After picking up some foodstuffs at the Oaks General Store, Grant tossed the gunny sack he kept in his saddlebags for such purposes over his shoulder and walked briskly down the boardwalk to Fletcher's Livery to retrieve Blue. With luck, he could still get home before noon and capture a full afternoon's writing before Gid returned from school. There would be no avoiding a conversation with Enos Fletcher at the livery, though, and escaping his gossip and stories would be a challenge.

As usual, despite the cold, Enos was sitting on his bench in front of the stable when Grant arrived. Enos kept his watch on the world from there. If Enos was not cleaning stalls or dealing with a customer, he could be found perched on the weather-warped bench. Grant assumed that the old man with ragged hair and beard, would retreat on some of the winter days ahead.

"Howdy, Enos," Grant said. "Don't get up. I'll fetch Blue. Add the charges to my monthly bill." He hoped to avoid a gab session if he kept moving.

"Might want to wait a bit," the liveryman said with his gravelly voice.

"Why?"

"You ain't heard about them killings out north?"

"No."

"Homesteaders. John and Mary Ridge. Knowed them since they come here a year or so back. Seemed like nice young folks. Sold them a mule team."

Grant hoped the couple didn't get skinned like he did when he made a deal for Blue. He treasured the grulla gelding that had been raised by Hannah and sold by Enos acting as her agent. He still could not forget how the old devil had outfoxed him to a higher price. "What happened?"

"Don't know for sure. Do you know Rags Yeager?"

Grant knew it was futile to try to rush the old man, who had to be at least eighty years old and looked older. "I never heard of him."

"He's a young rancher at the northwest end of the county. Married to a Sioux gal. Started a herd of half-breed kids. I heard Morning Flower might be from old Lame Buffalo's line, but I ain't nailed that down yet."

"I'll take your word for it."

"Well, Rags, he smelt smoke last night. His home place sits on high ground, and he looked south and saw the south sky all lit up. So, he mounts up and rides down that way and finds the Ridge place burning, goes back home and tells Morning Flower he's headed to town. Gets two fresh horses and rides all night. Gets to Lockwood and stops at the sheriff's office, comes over here, and we do some horse trading—got the best of him if I say so myself. Anyhow, he's on his way back north. Don't know why the rush. His wife's papa and brother live out there and help work the ranch."

"What's all this got to do with Blue?"

"Sheriff stopped over to see if Blue was here. That would mean you was in town."

"Go on."

"Sheriff wants to talk to you before you leave. Figured you'd want to leave old Blue till you was ready to hit the trail."

So much for an afternoon working on the book.

Chapter 26

"I WOULD LIKE you to ride out to the Ridge homestead with me, Grant. I'd bet those folks are dead. If they had escaped whoever hit the place, they would have been in town by now. Rags Yeager did what he thought was his duty as a citizen in the county, but he's not looking for trouble. He worries that his Indian family might be vulnerable to an attack."

"That's understandable, but it doesn't look like these folks are after Indians."

"We wouldn't get to the place till nightfall if we left today. I would like to ride out first thing in the morning. We'll each take an extra mount, and we could reach the place early afternoon. If we keep the river in sight, there won't be rough ground to travel. It will be a long day, though. We should probably hole up for the night, but my lame leg doesn't handle sleeping on the ground all that well. I'm thinking Rags would put us up in his barn. Bring a bedroll with a few wool blankets."

"If I go, I've got arrangements to make. I'm looking after a boy now, you know."

"I could take Ozzie or Zeke Dale—he's a fulltime deputy now—but I'd like some time for us to talk away from any other ears. I trust Ozzie, but the right person could likely trick him into saying something he shouldn't."

"Like I said, I've got the boy. I would have to work something out for two nights in case we have to camp someplace. It gets complicated."

"You stop over at Hannah's office. She will have it all figured out by now."

"Hannah knows about this?"

"I walked over and talked to her about my problem. She said she would see you were free to ride with me. I figured she would. She's the county prosecutor. She's got a stake in this, too. And the two of you seem to be getting along well enough these days." Sheriff Jim Tolliver offered a sly grin.

Grant wondered how much Ozzie had said about the scene he had witnessed in the Box L stable. He hated to think about how much the tale had grown. By now, Enos Fletcher had likely wrangled every detail from the deputy and had the couple naked in the hay. Grant did not find the image repulsive, however.

"What time tomorrow morning?" Grant said.

"Eight o'clock. The sheriff's office will rent you an extra mount from the livery. You can choose one when you pick up the horse. Tell Trouble or Enos to bill the rent to the county."

When Grant entered the Ramsey and Locke office, he was greeted by Hamilton Fish hammering at a typewriter behind the counter in the waiting area. The young former clerk had recently passed the territory bar examination and was now officially the firm's newest partner. "Are you lost, Ham?" Grant asked.

"They are a day or two from getting my office ready. I don't mind. I've sat here for several years. I kind of hate to give up the spot. Hannah doesn't have a client. Just go on in."

Grant guessed his own status had been elevated since the last visit. He stepped into the hallway beyond the reception area, made a left turn and rapped on the half-closed door. "Hannah, it's Grant."

"Come on in."

He entered and sat down in front of her desk. She appeared to be signing some letters, dipping her pen in an ink well, signing the parchment sheet. blowing on the damp inscription and laying the paper on a small sack.

After she signed the last sheet, she put the pen down and looked up. "You are here about your little journey with the sheriff."

"Yes. Jim said he had spoken with you. I sometimes feel like there are conspirators plotting to keep me from my chosen career."

"I think I have a solution to caring for Gid."

"I figured that."

"You get him up and bring him by my place in the morning when you leave. We will feed him breakfast, and the girls will ride to school with him as usual, and, of course, will bring him back to the house after school."

"I have a cat and dog. I can care for them before I leave. The dog's broke to the house if I'm around to let her out. She won't make a full day, but she will use the papers I put out. Sarge has a sandbox he will use if he must."

"I know that. I am going to stay nights at your house till you return. I'll go home if you get back by the second night. One of the girls can take Gid over to care for the animals after school. They will come back to our house for supper, and then I will take him back to yours for the night. That should work fine. We already have Ginger as a house guest and your pup's littermate. It will be too complicated to move them all in at the Box L."

"You plan to stay at my cabin?"

"Why not?"

"I won't have time to get everything cleaned up. I haven't done dishes for a week. I can do that this afternoon, I guess, if I ever get out of town. Some sweeping to do. Where will you sleep?"

"Think about this, Grant. Is your bed sacred or something?"

"Uh, my sheets haven't been washed for a month, and Gid's using the only extras I had on the floor where he sleeps."

She rolled her eyes and wrinkled her nose, which was her usual sign of disgust. "I'll take extra sheets from my place and change them. I'm surprised at your low sanitation standards. How long do you and Gid wear your underwear?"

"That seems rather personal, but as a matter of fact, we change daily. I have it figured out. I take everything to the Lockwood Laundry every week. I used to pay Moon for laundry services when I lived at The Tipi boarding house. I think Jasmine did a lot of it."

"Have you ever done your own laundry?"

Grant said, "When I was in the Army, usually in a creek. Then, of course, my wives did it when I was married."

"Of course."

He detected a bit of sarcasm in her voice. "After that, I hired it done. I didn't walk around in filthy garments."

"I'm glad to hear that. Don't worry about cleaning up your house. You won't have time. You could do the dishes this afternoon, though. I hate that chore."

"Then I guess it's settled."

"I should think so, as far as Gid's care is concerned."

"Well, I suppose I had better be on my way then."

"Not yet. We have been avoiding any conversation about the other night in the stable."

Grant said, "I don't know what to say. The town likely has us living in sin by now. Indications are that Ozzie did not keep his mouth shut. And I wasn't sure how you felt about it."

She smiled. "I rather enjoyed it."

He grinned back. "I did, too. And I was cold sober. It's not like it was a drunken impulse. I would do it again if I thought I could get by with it."

"You probably could."

"Then it's alright between us?"

"It is alright between us. We just need to go forward very, very slowly."

He nodded in agreement. "Yeah, I do have things to sort out in my head. But I want you to know that you have become very important in my life and not just because you are my law wrangler."

"Then we seem to be at about the same place."

Grant stood to leave, and Hannah sprang from her chair, hurried around the desk and blocked his exit. "Do you want to see if you can get by with it?"

He took her gently in his arms, and their lips touched. Suddenly, there was a single knock on the door that was still partially open, and Ham Fish stepped in. "Hannah, I have that contract you wanted . . . oh, Lord . . . pardon me. I didn't mean to . . ." He turned away and disappeared into the hallway.

Hannah stepped back, shrugged and smiled. "Perhaps another time we can enjoy a private moment."

Chapter 27

THE JOURNEY TO the Ridge homestead took longer than anticipated, and it was approaching midafternoon when Grant and Sheriff Jim Tolliver rode up to the building site where parts of the house and barn still smoldered. They dismounted and staked their horses in the yard before surveying the remnants of the barn.

Tolliver stepped inside the barn's foundation and onto the charred ground, weaving through the piles of smoldering boards, poking here and there with the shovel he had brought with him, kicking aside burnt timbers.

The sheriff said, "No signs of animal carcasses. We can't be certain, but it appears they turned the critters out before setting fire to the place."

As if in confirmation, a mule brayed north of the destroyed barn. Another answered. Two mules, a sorrel horse and a Guernsey milk cow, were moving tentatively in their direction now, pausing intermittently to inspect the visitors before stopping not more than fifty feet distant.

"They want something more than dead, snow-covered grass to eat," Tolliver said. "The barn would have held most of the current feed supply. There are probably some haystacks they could get to about the place, but they're missing their grain treats this morning."

"Two riders headed this way."

"They're not trying to hide their approach, and from their pace I don't think they're a worry."

As the riders drew near, the sheriff waved, and the riders responded in kind. "It's Rags Yeager and his brother-in-law, Tall Tree. I'm not surprised. He said they would keep an eye on the place. Somebody likely saw us coming from way back and rode to the Walking Y to let Rags know."

"Rags is a strange name. Not his baptized tag, I am guessing."

"You've heard of 'rags to riches?'"

"Yep. Poor man becomes wealthy."

"Enos told me once that Rags was poor and hungry as a desert grasshopper when he showed up in Lockwood. He wasn't more than fifteen then. Worked at Fletcher's

Livery a year or two for sleeping space in the loft, meals and a dollar a week. Took to horses and mined Enos's brain for everything the old devil knew about the critters, and nobody knows more about equines than Enos Fletcher. Of course, he wouldn't know what the term 'equine' meant."

The riders rode into the yard, reined in and dismounted. Grant said, "I would like to hear more of the story later."

"We will have plenty of talking time on the way back to Lockwood."

The first thing Grant noticed about the men walking toward them was the stark difference in height. The shorter man was average height, slim and wiry looking even under his bulky coat. The other bronze-skinned man with aquiline features towered above his companion. Grant placed him at a good half foot above his own six feet.

Tolliver stepped out with hand extended to greet the newcomers. "Rags, this is my acting deputy, Grant Coolidge."

Rags offered his hand to Grant, more than matching the writer's firm grip. "Howdy, Grant. This here's my brother-in-law, Tall Tree Lincoln."

"Pleased to meet you both." Grant flinched when Tall Tree's giant paw closed on his. The man nodded but did not speak.

Rags said, "I had Tree not far away watching for you and he came and got me when he seen you coming." He gestured toward the livestock that had backed off some with the appearance of the riders. "I see the beasts are lonesome for human company. What do you plan to do with them?"

"I don't know," Tolliver said.

Rags rubbed the neatly trimmed, brushy moustache above his lips. Ladies would find him handsome, Grant thought. He guessed the man's age would not be more than thirty years. Rags said, "We can herd the animals back to the Walking Y for now and hold them till you tell us what to do with them. Don't like to think of them wandering around out here through the winter, maybe starving or wolves making meals of them. Flower's milk cow is going dry, and we can put the lady here to work. From the looks of her bag, she needs relief yet tonight."

Tolliver said, "Take them. You might end up with the stock if the Ridges don't turn up."

"Have you checked the cabin yet?"

"That was next. Avoiding what I am afraid we'll find."

"Me and Tree stayed away from it. We didn't want to get in the law's way."

"Let's look."

Rags Yeager had brought a short-handled shovel, too, and the group walked over to the cabin ruins. Hot coals were sparse here, but thick smoke hovering over the site obstructed the view. The structure was burned nearly to the ground, but blackened fragments of the walls still reached upward from the base here and there. They were greeted just inside the former door frame by charred skeletal remains and a grinning skull with several missing front teeth.

The sheriff said, "Damn. Must be the husband, John. Guess it's a man."

Rags said, "What do you think, Tree?"

Tall Tree took the shovel from Rags's hands, stepped into the rubble and pushed the smoldering timbers away from the fleshless corpse. He knelt beside the remains, tracing his fingers over the bones, studying the skull. "Man. Not a big man."

Grant doubted that any man looked big to Tall Tree.

"Don't think it's John Ridge," Rags said. "I suppose somebody could have knocked some out, but the last I seen him he had a full-toothed grin."

Tall Tree stood and looked about the cabin. He pointed to fallen half burned timbers that had obviously supported a roof and now were scattered haphazardly across the dirt floor. "Under the timbers." He stepped over to several large support logs that formed a vee that held up other debris, took his shovel and began pushing the timbers aside.

By the time the others joined Tall Tree, he had cleared the timbers away, revealing the remains of two people almost side by side. Some flesh remained on the bones, even patches of clothing that had been seared into the bodies. Tufts of blonde hair remained on one skull.

"That would be Mary Ridge, other has got to be John," Rags said. "Ain't right. These was good folks, just trying to make their ways through life. I tried to help them out some, giving them a beef now and then, hiring on John when I needed an extra hand. I been trying stay clear of all this fussing. I don't belong to the Stock Growers Association. I try to mind my own business. I'm in the fight now, Sheriff. You let me know if I can help put a stop to this."

"I will likely take you up on that, Rags. But now we've got to get these folks buried. I'll bet the top layer of dirt is hard as granite."

Grant said, "Not where the buildings burned down. That would be thawed out."

The sheriff hesitated and seemed to be pondering the suggestion. Finally, he nodded his head. "Why not?"

"We'll clean this out come spring," Rags said, "and put some stones there to mark the graves. If any other fool claims this quarter section someday, he can re-build someplace else. Nobody would want to put their house on top of grave sites."

The sheriff sighed. "We had better get to work. It's going to be dark by the time we head back to Lockwood." Grant suspected Tolliver was fishing for an offer.

Rags said, "I've been figuring on you staying at the Walking Y tonight, Sheriff. Our little bunkhouse ain't got occupants this time of year. Flower is planning on you for supper. Those are puny bedrolls on your mounts. We got plenty of warm blankets. Fix you up a good fire in the bunkhouse."

The sheriff said, "We had considered riding through the night."

"You're apt to be lost and dead if you do."

"What do you mean?"

"There's a mean blizzard could bring snow as high as Tree's ass moving in here tonight."

"I see clouds up north, but they don't look all that threatening."

"Be safe. You ain't got nothing to lose but time. My daddy-in-law, Talks-Too-Much, says snow is coming. Ain't been wrong in all the years I've knowed him."

Tolliver looked at Grant. "What do you say, Grant?"

"We both made it through the war alive. I didn't come all this way to die in a snowstorm. I say we stay the night."

"Even if it turns out to be more than one?"

"Yeah. Trouble will look after your wife, and Hannah will see that Gid has a roof over his head and food in his belly."

"We will stay then, and we thank you for your hospitality."

They decided to bury the Ridges in a common grave inside the parameters of the burned-out house. The other remains, assuming the source was one of the raiders, they buried in one corner of the barn.

Chapter 28

GRANT AND JIM Tolliver sat on cedar log-hewn chairs in the six-bed bunkhouse at the Walking Y. They were both stuffed from a meal of roasted beef with baked potatoes and boiled beans grown in Morning Flower Yeager's garden, topped off with coffee and apple cobbler. Flames crawled over logs in the stone fireplace that was twice the size the small building required for heating.

It was not quite eight o'clock, but Grant was ready to call it a day and slip under the blankets on the bed that had already been made up when they arrived. He and Jim Tolliver had been treated like kings since their arrival. Flower Yeager had been an attentive hostess, a tiny bundle of energy. She had seemed delighted to welcome guests in the expansive, log ranch house, a simple, functional structure.

Ron Schwab

Flower had been assisted by a Sioux girl fifteen or sixteen years old, introduced as her niece, Doe Runs. Grant had not yet sorted out the relationships in this large family that included three boys under eight years of age and a suckling girl baby in a crib only three or four steps from the long dining table. He had noticed that the children were all called by traditional English names—Jonathan, Peter, William and Alice. He was convinced this family, including a few generations back, could be fodder for an epic novel.

Grant said, "Rags is bringing his father-in-law and Tall Tree over to talk about the attacks that are taking place in the county. The old chief didn't do anything at supper but grunt. I don't know where he got the name Talks-Too-Much. Sarcasm, maybe?"

"Could be. Never saw the old man before tonight. Old man. I doubt if he is more than sixty. Age is perspective, they say. I suppose the twenty-year-old cowhands are thinking this forty plus sheriff is a geezer."

"But you were going to tell me about Rags. I heard Flower calling him 'Adam' during supper."

"Yeah, I guess that's his birth name. Anyway, after Rags learned the horse business from Enos Fletcher, he hired on as a hand at Ethan Ramsey's Lazy R and went about learning the cattle business. Ethan says the kid was like a sponge, always wanting to soak up more information. Most hands wanted to know what or how. Rags wanted to know that, but he also wanted to know why."

"But not much more than ten years later, he's running his own ranch," Grant said.

"Yep. Rags was a working fool, never went to town on Saturday, stayed away from booze, gambling and the whorehouses and stashed every nickel away. In the meantime, he met up with Morning Flower. Talks-Too-Much was of the old school and wanted ten horses for his daughter. Rags wasn't about to let go of his saved money to pay that price, and he and Flower ran off and got married and found housing at the Lazy R."

"And then?"

"Folks that had this ranch went busted, and there wasn't a lot of demand for the land because of the long distance from Lockwood and the fact that it was just a ten thousand acre spread—small for hereabouts—boxed in by government lands that had been designated for future homesteading. With the backing of Ramsey and the Gaines Bank, Rags bought the place with five hundred cows, and he's doubled that by now. Turns out, this land is the best in the county for grass, and it's suitable for farming. For now, the government lands nearby offer ample open range, but he may lose some of that to home-steading down the road."

"He's not truly rich then?"

"Look at that family. A wife who obviously loves him. I doubt he carries much debt. Rich in the ways that count, I would say."

Grant pondered Tolliver's pronouncement. "I can't argue with that. And it appears his father-in-law forgave him for not coming up with the horses."

Tolliver chuckled. "Nope. The old chief wouldn't speak to him for three or four years. Then one day, Rags shows up at the chief's farmstead with a string of ten horses, says he is paying his debt and invites him and Tall Tree to come live at the Walking Y in the foreman's house. That's the smaller place east of the ranch house."

"The chief didn't answer then, but he and Tall Tree showed up a week later with a wagon load of belongings and their horse herd. Been here ever since. The chief can still put in a good day's work, so Rags got two hands with the deal, and they've got family connections to recruit temporaries in a matter of a few days when they're needed."

The door opened and Rags Yeager, Tall Tree and Talks-Too-Much stepped in, brushing white grains of sleet off their coats. Rags said, "She's starting, fellers. The chief says the worst won't hit for three or four hours. Make yourselves at home. You might be our guests for a spell."

Grant hoped the remark was made in jest. He had work to do at home and a boy to care for. "How long will the snow last?"

"At least a day or two," Rags said. "That ain't the problem. It's the digging out and finding a trail out. Chief and Tree can help you with the last. If it's as bad as Chief says, you don't want to hurry yourselves none."

When the men had all pulled up chairs in front of the fireplace, Rags led off the conversation. "Like I told you before, we thought we would just keep our distance from the fighting hereabouts, but we lost good neighbors two nights ago, folks that weren't hurting nobody. They didn't rustle cattle. They was just trying to squeeze some food and a few dollars from the dirt. No man's safe when folks like that go down for no cause. We're in now. As soon as he can ride out of here, Tree is heading for the Brule settlement farmsteads to gather up four or five warriors to help out here and be on hand in case somebody comes looking for trouble."

The sheriff said, "But how do we track the men who are doing this? I don't look for many more attacks this winter, but spring will bring more raids, and people will die."

Rags said, " What do you know about these killers?"

Grant spoke. "They wear black hoods and cloaks, so there are no physical descriptions from the survivors. I have seen for myself that the leader rides a white or light-colored stallion. He calls the animal 'a pale horse.' If we find the pale horse, we are on our way to corralling the bunch. Of course, replacements could show up."

Tolliver said, "I don't think working ranch hands are involved in the raids. It would be too risky for the ranchers to be identified with this. Besides that, secrets in a ranch operation are not very well kept. These men are hired guns. I saw a lot of this in Texas when I served as a U. S. Marshal."

Grant said, "But some ranchers are involved, most likely the county Stock Growers Association. The association is the head of the snake, the source of the funds to hire these men. I wonder if we could do something to cut off the head of the snake."

Tolliver said, "You may be right. As a lawman, I tend to focus on the direct perpetrators of the crime. Maybe you could talk to your lady friend about how we might legally go about beheading a snake."

"I will do that. There is something else I should tell you. All I can say now is that there is someone who would possibly recognize the voice of the leader, the man who rides the pale horse."

"You hadn't told me that."

The sheriff was obviously miffed. "I apologize," Grant said. "I felt I was protecting somebody. These are dangerous people."

"I dream of pale horse."

Everyone turned their heads toward Talks-Too-Much. This was the first time Grant had heard the chief speak more than a word. The chief stared at the fire as if focused on a drama unfolding there, his black plainsman hat pulled low on his forehead and arms folded across his chest.

"What did you dream, Father?" Tall Tree asked.

"See pale horse and rider with war paint. Black paint almost cover face. Rider white man. Fire comes from eyes. Medicine man headdress but horns not buffalo. More like mountain goat. Evil man."

Tall Tree said, "When did you have this dream, Father?"

"Night that neighbors die."

"Where was this horse? Could you tell?"

"River valley. Side where sun go down."

"West," Rags said.

Grant thought that was not much to go on when a man had a forty or fifty mile stretch to cover. The chief had a fifty-fifty chance of being right without any insight. The dream was nearly worthless to his notion.

"Father," Tall Tree asked, "can you recall what was behind the horse and rider?"

"Canyon walls. He come through mouth."

"Mouth."

"Canyon have mouth. Get in when mouth open."

They talked for another half hour, and Rags promised to send a few warriors along the west side of the valley to search for a hideout that might secret a pale horse after help arrived at the ranch. He told them it could be a week or more.

Tall Tree finally said, "Hard day's work tomorrow. Father and I will go to bed now. Rags, you can tell us at breakfast what you want us to do first."

"The snow will decide that but be ready to dig your way to the house."

While Tall Tree and the chief worked their arms into their coat sleeves, Tall Tree turned back to Grant. "I like P. J. Bowie and Marshal Tyree best. I hope you will have another book soon."

Grant was taken aback. "Uh, thank you. There should be a new book out in January." If he was ever granted time to complete the damn thing.

After the two Sioux departed, Rags said, "Grant, I noticed your surprise when Tree mentioned reading your book."

"Well, yeah, I admit I was."

"He's got books all over his place. I never came close to his book learning. Many of the Sioux around here went to the Pennock School back when the Quakers ran the place. Flower went, too. She and her brother trade all the books they get hold of. Flower keeps a diary and writes about everything that goes on here. Don't know where she gets the time. Funny, the chief didn't want them to go to a white man's school, but old Lame Buffalo said they should go, and he didn't cross the senior chief. Betwixt you and me, Talks-Too-Much ain't a real chief. He is Lame Buffalo's little brother, and he claimed to inherit the job when Lame Buffalo died. Nobody much cared by then. Peace had been made, and Sioux in this valley pretty much took up the white man's ways."

The sheriff asked, "What about his dream or vision?"

Rags shrugged, "I don't know. He's right almost always when it comes to guessing what the weather's going to do, and he seems to expect a lot of things before they happen. I do pay attention. Lame Buffalo had visions and made a lot of good decisions based on them. They share blood. Flower's almost spooky sometimes, the things she dreams about and guesses what they mean. I told her I only want to hear about the happy dreams, but she's saved my neck more than once. I didn't know about the chief's vision. I intend to ask Flower about it."

Rags got up, grabbed his coat and headed for the door. He peered outside. "Shovels are in that closet at the other end of the bunkhouse. We won't do breakfast till about eight o'clock given the weather, but you will need to get around early enough to work your way through the snow."

Chapter 29

HANNAH HAD BEEN snowed in at Grant's house with Gideon, Sarge the cat, and Lovey the growing pup for two days and three nights now. The experience had done nothing to stoke her maternal instincts. She wanted out. Gid was an exceptionally bright child she had concluded, but she did not know how to keep him busy.

Finally, she had dug into a cupboard at her house and come across a chessboard and pieces, a gift from her father. She still harbored what she was beginning to suspect was an irrational grudge against her father for surrendering her and her twin brother to her aunt and uncle after her mother's childbirth death.

Still, there had been regular visits at her father's house in Manhattan, Kansas not all that distant from the foster parents' Flint Hills ranch, and he had taught her and twin brother Thad to play chess. He had even given them each beautiful walnut chessboards with square insets of alternating walnut and white oak. The chessmen had been hand carved by a local craftsman. She had brought the set to Wyoming with her and stored it in her ranch house office. Obviously, she had been unable to discard the link to her father. She took the set to Grant's cabin.

Gid had quickly mastered the game and could hardly wait to challenge Grant. For that matter, he talked about Grant incessantly, and she started to fret about future separation, which was still the writer's professed goal. She suspected Grant was clueless about the boy's attachment and affection for him.

Hannah did not mind an occasional chess match, but she was not up to marathon sessions. Finally, she was rescued by Grant's novels. Gid had devoured multiple times the few books in the cabin she thought suitable to his age, but the previous morning she had an inspiration. She called Gid into Grant's office and pointed to the books on the floor to ceiling shelves that took up most of the wall space.

"Do you see all those skinny books written by P. J. Bowie and Jake West?"

"Yep. Lots of them, for sure. Grant says I wouldn't want to read them."

"Do you know who writes those books?"

"P. J. Bowie and Jake West. That's a silly question."

"You are wrong. Grant Coolidge writes those books. Those are called pseudonyms or pennames. They are used when the publisher or writer does not wish to disclose the author's real name."

"Like Mark Twain and Samuel Clemmons?"

"Exactly."

"You're not joshing me?"

"No, he writes those books. That's what he is doing here in the office."

"Can I read one?"

"I don't see why not. I like the Bowie books best. Why don't you try one of those."

That had solved her problems with entertaining Gideon. He was now entranced by the novels, and she guessed he had read a half dozen by now. What a strange boy. Whatever previous formal education he had experienced would have been in bits and pieces, but somehow he had overcome his limited opportunities.

She pulled back the front window curtain and peered outside. The countryside was calm now, the land covered by a seemingly endless blanket of white. There were few drifts about the cabin, the driving winds having swept much of the snow to another obstacle. She had scooped a path to the privy a second time earlier this morning, and it was still clear, something to be grateful for since it was bitter cold outside. She wanted to check at her ranch house down the road a short distance, but she hated to take a presently contented Gideon out into the cold for such a journey.

She was encouraged that the sky had cleared and that a radiant morning sun was working its way over the mountaintops, but it reminded her she should be at her office in Lockwood battling the myriad of projects waiting on her desk. Patience was not her virtue, and occasionally Grant annoyed her with his forbearing persistence when it came to completing a task. She smiled. Last week, he had chided her for 'going after work like she was killing snakes.'

By midmorning she decided she could tolerate the incarceration no longer. The horses could handle two feet of snow for the short distance to her house. Gid had not complained, but she could tell he did not like her cooking, and she had burned out as Hannah Homemaker. She would tell Gid to get ready to ride and she would go to the stable and get Dusty and Gid's mare saddled. Jasmine and Primrose were going to have guests for lunch.

She stepped over to the window again, and her eyes caught sight of a team of huge draft horses moving in her direction along the wagon trail with a curtain of snow spewing skyward behind it. She watched as the horses approached and saw a man standing in a small square wagon box with hands clutched to the horses' reins and trailed by something that looked like a huge wedge carving a wagon's width path through the snow. When the horses reached the cabin, she recognized Trouble Yates's near-scarlet face buried within the bulky layers of clothing. Of course. Who else?

Hannah stepped outside, flinching at the cold's bite. "Come in," she called.

Trouble waved and climbed down from his perch, braking the wagon before he plodded through the snow up to the door. She opened the door and backed into the house, signaling that Trouble should follow. She took him by the arm and led him over to the kitchen stove. "I'll pour you a cup of coffee, but be forewarned that I have yet to receive a compliment for the stuff."

"Anything hot will suit me fine." He pulled off his gloves and untied the floppy-eared rabbit-fur hat. "Can't stay but long enough to drink the coffee. I'll run the plow to your stable and clear a path out from there and be on my way."

"Did you stop at my place?"

"Yep. Did the same there. Talked with Jazzie. She says to get yourselves over for lunch."

"I didn't know you were in the snow plowing business."

"Something I added to the livery operation. I had the team we rented out to farmers during planting and harvest and such. Found some winter work for them. Forgot to mention it, I guess."

She did not recall seeing the expense on the financial reports, but with Trouble you never knew what non-cash deals he was making. She certainly was not about to grumble after he came to her rescue. "You are keeping busy with the plow then?"

"Yep. Got me a contract with the town that will guarantee income all winter. I had to do Lockwood first, or I would have been out here yesterday. I got folks waiting at nearby farms and ranches, but it isn't feasible to go more than five miles out. I haven't contacted the Pennock School yet. I'm betting I need another team and plow by next winter."

"You can't do all this work yourself."

"No, between the sawmill and the livery, I figure by next summer I can use five more men. Sammy thinks I'm crazy. She's already chewing on me about watching payroll. I try to tell her that's how Adam Smith says it works.

We pursue our businesses to make a profit and then we make jobs for folks who can feed their families. They spend their money and help other businesses."

He had Hannah's head spinning, and she could not argue with Sammy's view. This kid wasn't old enough to have all this figured out. She addressed her main concern. "What do you think about Jim and Grant? Should somebody head out to find them?"

"Waste of time. Too many miles up that way. They weren't that far from the Walking Y up near Ridges' place. Hopefully, they had the good sense to hole up there. Rags would see they were looked after. If they were fools enough to head back in this storm, we won't find them till spring."

He must have seen the fear in her eyes. "Hannah, I'm sorry about talking like that. Sammy says I ain't—am not—sensitive enough sometimes. I wouldn't be talking like that if thought there was any chance of something bad happening. I wouldn't make light of it. Grant's my best friend. Him and Matt Gaines, and you know about my connection to Matt. I guarantee Grant and Jim will be fine. But all reports are that there was more snow as a person moves north. Just be patient."

Patience rearing its ugly head again.

Chapter 30

HANNAH TENSED WHEN she heard the horses whinnying from the stable. Lovey whined and lifted her head, signaling she had heard the sound, too. She swung her legs out of bed and grabbed the double-barreled shotgun that leaned against the wall. It was loaded and ready to fire. At least the stove and the coals in the fireplace kept the cabin warm, and she felt no chill through her flannel nightgown. She stepped out to the window and looked in the direction of the stable.

A man stepped out and started walking briskly toward the cabin. Her heart raced. Grant? She could not be certain, wrapped as he was in bulky clothing. He carried a rifle in one hand but did not appear ready to use it. She stepped over to the door and waited.

A soft knock. She spoke softly, hoping she would not wake Gideon. "Who is it?"

"Grant. I forgot the password."

She leaned the shotgun against the wall, lifted the iron bar that held the door fast against possible intruders and opened the door. He stepped in, and she closed the door behind him, positioning the bar in place. He removed his cap and turned to face her. The normally fastidious Grant had slipped away. His hair was a tangled nest and his drawn, windburned face was darkly stubbled with a six-day growth of whiskers. He was the handsomest man she had ever seen, and she went to him and fell into his arms, which enfolded her with the rifle butt bouncing off her hip.

They did not speak for some moments before she said, "Thank God, you are back. We have been worried sick."

He lowered his head and their lips met for a quick kiss. "I was worried a time or two myself, but we were well taken care of at the Walking Y. It's been a day from hell getting back here, though. We left at sunrise, and I feared we wouldn't get back tonight. It was tough on horses and riders. The critters were glad to get put up in the stable, and this toasty cabin is heaven. I just want to drop and sleep."

"Oh, no, and I've taken your bed. I can get dressed and ride back home."

"Not necessary. I can collapse with a few blankets on the floor. I just want to be warm."

"We can share the bed, if you don't mind. For sleeping," she added quickly. "Do you want coffee to warm you up?"

"No, I just want to sleep. I almost fell off my horse riding back, I was so darned tired. Alright with you if I strip down to my long skivvies?"

"Whatever suits you." She thought of qualifying her statement, but he seemed not to notice the open-endedness.

Grant seemed not to be aware of her presence as he shed his clothes. Within five minutes, he was in bed. Another five minutes and he was dead asleep. She crawled in beside him, trying to leave a respectable distance between them. Sleep did not arrive so quickly for her. She could not erase the thought of this man in bed beside her. She pondered how she would have reacted if he had made a move for more. She decided she could not say for certain, but finally convinced herself that her behavior would have been chaste. She smiled. Well, now she could tell herself she had slept with Grant Coolidge.

Chapter 31

HANNAH AWAKENED WHEN only a faint hint of sunrise appeared in the east. She glanced at the man who shared her bed and for an instant worried that he was dead. She reached over and softly touched his back, feeling the faint rise and fall that confirmed his breathing. She crawled out of bed quietly and went into Grant's office. She picked up her clothes, which had been laid out on the desk, and slipped into her undergarments, denim britches and flannel shirt. She decided to forego her boots till she made a visit to the privy which would be calling soon.

On her way to the kitchen area, she put a few more logs on the dying fire ember without disturbing Gideon, Lovey or Sarge and then moved to the cookstove to replenish the coal, which seemed to have near perpetual life.

After she started brewing a pot of coffee, she pondered breakfast. The burnt cornbread crust on the pan in the sink warned her to choose carefully. Bacon would be safe, biscuits not so much so. She decided to go with flapjacks. Gid loved them doused with maple syrup, and she had made them without total mutilation before. She would master flapjacks and then move on to something else to expand her culinary talents. She could do this. Maybe.

She got her ingredients and the frying pan out, so she would be ready when she had morning diners, poured herself a cup of coffee and sat down at the kitchen table. She was grateful that the school had been closed until word got around that the buildings could be accessed again. This would not be the last closing before spring. The kids loved it, but it complicated her life. Thankfully, the girls could look after Gideon while she went to work. She remembered then that with Grant's return, the boy now had a caretaker.

Lovey's whining yanked her from her thoughts. The dog was at the door signaling she wanted out to do her morning chores. She could be thankful for that. Sunrays sifted through the curtains now, and the room was beginning to lighten. She anticipated that Grant and Gid would awaken soon. The boy was not a late sleeper unless school was in session.

She let the pup out, retrieved her boots and stepped out into the chill to make her way to the privy. She hated nothing more about winter than these trips to the outhouse. In Cheyenne folks were increasingly installing the indoor water closets, and she enjoyed the luxury of one of the few in the county because she could drain wastewater to a gully. Most folks in Lockwood did not have an outlet without sending the waste to their neighbors, which would quickly trigger a dispute.

Lovey was scratching on the door and barking to get into the cabin after they had both finished their business. When they went into the cabin, she saw that Gid was sitting up on his floor mattress not far from the fireplace staring at the sleeping Grant. He looked up at her and grinned. She pressed a finger to her lips.

Hannah whispered, "Don't wake him. Go do your water while I fix breakfast. And at least keep it off the path." She knew that Gid rarely made the trip all the way to the outhouse to perform the duty. The yellow spots in the snow were not all contributed by Lovey. Males had an unfair advantage on that score.

The bacon and flapjacks turned out fine, and she concluded she now had the touch. She sat down at the table with Gideon and forked two hotcakes and a bacon slice onto her own plate. They spoke in soft voices as they talked.

"Why didn't you wake me up when Grant got back?" Gid asked.

"It was very late, and he just wanted to drop in bed."

"I was worried but don't tell him."

"We were both worried."

"Where did you sleep last night?"

"I shared the bed."

"Makes sense."

Thankfully, Gid was ten and not fourteen. "After breakfast, you need to clean Sarge's sand box. There is plenty of sand, so you don't have to dig any from the sandpile out back."

"Okay."

It was after nine o'clock when Grant rolled out of bed. He grabbed his britches from the pile of clothes on the floor and pulled on his boots. "Good morning, Hannah—Gid."

Gid offered him a subdued "hello." He sat on the mattress in front of the fireplace, seemingly engrossed in a P. J. Bowie dime novel.

"Good morning," Hannah said. "Flapjacks and bacon for breakfast?"

"Sounds good. I'll be back." He snatched up his coat and headed outside.

She hoped that he was not so uncouth as to relieve himself in the snow, but she did not want to know. The image of him aiming his pizzle out in the open like that was disgusting. He returned too soon to reassure her. After discarding his coat, he went directly to the sink, grabbed a bar of lye soap and washed his hands in the pan there. He emptied the pan and pumped fresh water into it for the next user. She felt better. He was not a total pig.

He sat down, and she soon placed a plate of hotcakes and several slices of bacon in front of him. "I'll get coffee if you won't make a face when you drink it."

"Your coffee's fine."

"Tell me what you have been up to," Hannah said.

He took several bites of the syrupy hotcakes, and then between bites told her about their visit to the Ridge home and the bodies found and buried there and the offer by Rags Yeager to provide refuge from the snowstorm. "The folks at the Walking Y treated us like honored guests—until after the storm. After that we joined the work crew, rounding up cattle and driving them to haystacks scattered about, searching for critters that might be trapped in the snow, that sort of thing. Most had taken shelter in the wooded areas or behind the windbreaks the ranch hands had constructed over the summer. We kept busy for a few days, and I learned a lot about what ranchers deal with during the winter. It's not an easy life, and they could lose everything they've got to snow, drought or other acts of nature."

"More education for the easterner?"

"Definitely."

"It must have been a tough trip back."

"Rugged but not especially dangerous. Tall Tree, the brother-in-law I mentioned, sketched out a route along the southeast side of the river that provided a natural windbreak of trees and brush that left a trail along the edge. Some places we had to break through drifts, but not often. The best part was that the river kept us oriented. We just had to follow it home. In a snowfall like that the land starts to look all the same, and it wouldn't be hard to get lost."

Hannah said, "But we still don't know who we are looking for besides a pale horse."

"True. The old chief's vision I mentioned told him the horse and rider were on the west side of the valley near a rock wall with a mouth. I am going to ask Trouble if he has any ideas. He has somehow covered almost every inch of the county in his brief life. I have a question, though.

I think some pressure needs to be put on the head of the snake."

"What do you mean?" Hannah said.

"The Big River County Stock Growers. They have got to be behind this, or at least the leaders. Can you investigate them?"

"I can't just direct the sheriff to go in their offices and search or acquire banking records without a judge's order and warrant. I would have to justify applying for such an order by showing some evidence that I had cause for requesting it."

"Could you just interview the president, for instance, to make him worry a bit?"

Hannah said, "The organization has attorneys. I would need to go through their lawyers, who would insist on being present. They would not be forced to consent, but I might be able to make them curious enough to agree to an interview. I will think about it."

"Do that."

She got up from the table. "I'm going home. Gideon is your responsibility again. I am going to take a bath. I will see if the girls can prepare a late noon lunch for about two o'clock if you and Gideon wish to ride over."

"You can count on us."

"I trust you will bathe and shave."

"It's that bad?"

"I slept with you last night, you know."

"Was it memorable?"

"You certainly would not know. Once, I thought you were dead."

"I was thinking of growing a beard."

"You look like an old saddle tramp. A beard suits some men. A beard would not flatter you, and that would likely end our kissing days."

Grant stood. "A kiss before you leave?"

"You heard what I said." She turned away, picking up the carpet bag she had packed with her personals this morning, admitting to herself that she would have relented to Grant's suggestion if Gideon had not been in the room. She was not ready to have the boy witness such affection and then pass the information on to Primrose and Jasmine.

Chapter 32

GRANT WELCOMED A break from the snow, and unseasonable warmth had melted most of the snow from the roads, turning much of the underfooting to mush. Snow patches still covered much of the landscape, and healthy drifts remained against some building walls or along tree lines that shaded them from the sun's reach. A week had passed since his return from the Walking Y, and the Pennock school was open, freeing him from staying home with Gideon.

He and the boy had worked out an agreement of sorts while school was not in session that Gid had surprisingly respected. Hannah had left her fancy chess set and board at the cabin, so mornings they played chess or left the cabin and hiked or rode their horses, sometimes running errands in town. Afternoons, Grant worked on his current manuscript, finding that the words came quickly and flowed easily onto the paper. One day, they had eaten at The Chowdown, and Grant had been surprised to learn Gid had never eaten at a restaurant. He had devoured a heaping plate of roasted beef, fried potatoes and beans and topped it off with a piece of cherry pie. When they departed the restaurant, the boy had asked when they might come again. It had warmed Grant to see the boy so thrilled by the experience.

Now, he was headed to Fletcher's Livery to drop off Blue before he kept a promise to stop at the sheriff's office and discuss the current status of the range war cases. He also planned to inform his lawyer that he should be ready to submit his latest Marshal Buck Tyree novel in a week's time. She handled all correspondence with the publisher, a task he was glad to delegate. He had little interest in handling the business details.

He also had not seen Hannah for five days, and he would admit he was looking for an excuse to see her. She had seemed a bit distant when he and Gideon went to the Box L for lunch the day after his return, almost like something had changed since their visit at the cabin. But he would be among the least competent to judge a female's moods. His former wives would attest to that. Of course, he had been drunk more hours than sober during both marriages.

Enos Fletcher was apparently alone at the livery this morning, which was no surprise. Trouble Yates was usually out of his hayloft bed and on the road to supervise one of his other enterprises at sunrise.

Grant led Blue through the livery entryway and stepped over to Enos, who was leaning on a pitchfork handle in front of an empty stall. "Good morning, Enos. Boss is gone?"

"Yep. He's always gone. Don't know why I sold the kid this place. I still got to run things and do most of the work."

Grant suspected the wizened man would not take orders kindly under any other arrangement. "Trouble just knows he can count on your judgment and experience to do things right."

"Ain't swallowing that. He's got it figured he's going to make money off me so long as I can hang on. I could die any day, you know."

"So could any of us."

He spat a wad of tobacco, some of it dribbling onto his scraggly beard. "True enough, I guess." He nodded toward Blue. "Are you leaving the critter for a spell?"

"All morning. I'll be back after some lunch."

"Don't need to turn him out then. You can put him in this stall. You get the animal unsaddled, and I'll see to his water and hay, maybe a tad of grain."

Grant led the gelding into the stall, and while he unsaddled Blue, Enos kept on jabbering. "I hear you and the sheriff spent some days out at Rags Yeager's place."

"That's right."

"And you found the bodies of John and Mary Ridge and some other jasper?"

Grant hauled the saddle and tack out of the stall and laid it on the ground next to the gate. The geezer seemed to have the story down, so why was he asking the questions? He reminded himself that Enos got to the point of a conversation in his own time. The man was an encyclopedia of both fact and gossip in Big River County, and during his own brief stint as county sheriff, the man had provided vital information.

"You ain't figured out who done it yet?"

"No, I'm afraid not. Jim's working on it."

"He ain't asked me about it."

Enos sounded like he had been offended by the sheriff's failure to seek out the old liveryman's opinion. "He's been overwhelmed by all this. I'm sure he plans to talk to you. Do you know something about it?"

"A few things maybe. Nothing for sure. Can't say who done it or nothing." He hesitated. "Some say the leader rides a pale horse. Is that true?"

"I don't know it for fact, but yes, there has been talk of a pale horse."

"I might of seen that horse some months back. At least twice, such a horse was stabled here overnight. Strange looking critter. Stallion. I couldn't quite call him white. More yellowish-like but not one of them palominos with a white mane or nothing. Some might say he was a clay-bank. All one color except the dark mane and tail. Big devil. Bigger than your Blue even."

"Do you know the owner's name?"

"Asked, but he didn't answer. He visited The Doll House when it was still in business as a whorehouse."

"Do you remember anything about the man?"

"Tall. Not six and a half feet but maybe reaching for it. White hair, longish. Lightest blue eyes I ever seen. Spooky looking. Tried to palaver with the feller, but he made it plain he wasn't the chatting kind. Had a voice and manner like a mad grizzly bear that set me to thinking I didn't want to talk with him neither."

"Tell me more about his voice."

"Don't know how to say it. More growl than anything else. Deep and hollow sounding. It sort of echoed off his throat, like he was hollering in a blind canyon."

Grant decided this had to be the same man who had shared Ginger's bed a few nights during her previous career. "Any idea of whether he is still around these parts?"

"Ain't seen hide nor hair of the feller since then, but . . ."

"But what?"

"You know I ain't charged you a plugged nickel for this information."

"We're talking people's lives. I can't imagine you would be so greedy as to want money for something that could mean somebody's life or death." Grant hoped the old fart had a bit of conscience buried somewhere in his head. "Besides, you stung me enough when you sold me Blue to entitle me to a lot of information paid for in advance."

"I saw him talking to a feller outside The Doll House one day. They talked for a good long spell. I seen this feller around off and on since then. Don't know his name or nothing else about him. So skinny he looked like he'd been weaned on a pickle."

Grant shrugged. "Next time you see him in town, let the sheriff know."

"There's something else."

"Yeah?"

"Twice, I seen the skinny feller talking to Bobby Callaway. Once, they was on horseback like they just run into each other going opposite ways. Feller rode himself one of them Appaloosas. Never left it here, though. Either never in town long enough to need the livery or dropped the critter off at Gaston's Stable, where I wouldn't leave a hump-backed donkey."

"You said there was a second time."

"Yep. Other time was at Milt's Barbering across the street and down a ways. Month or so back. One of them Injun summer days when I was sitting on the bench out front. Bobby just come out of the barber shop when this guy comes along. Talked a little longer then. I never gave it no thought till you started asking questions. You think it might be important?"

"Not likely, I'd say. But I appreciate the information." Gut and brain told him, however, that Enos's observations could be very important.

Chapter 33

"WHAT DO YOU think, Jim?" Grant said after telling the sheriff about his conversation with Enos.

"I don't know what to make of it, but we obviously must follow up on this. I'm not sure how without showing too many cards. I really need to ponder. This is touchy business. Technically, Con Callaway is my boss between elections. He's the county board chairman. Bobby was at the church that night you were playing with the dynamite. It doesn't make sense."

"They wouldn't have told him about their plans, and they would not have necessarily known he would be there or cared all that much."

The sheriff shook his head doubtfully. "I don't know. I want to be slow on the trigger with this. I'm guessing you will be seeing the county prosecutor. Tell her about it and get her thoughts. We'll keep it between us three for now and get together in a few days."

"No argument there, but I think Bobby would have to be our starting place. And we absolutely must keep Enos out of this. He is an easy target at the stable if the wrong people get wind of this."

"Agreed. You just tell Hannah the story."

When Grant walked into the law office, he was surprised to be greeted by a pert, blonde woman with a welcoming smile. "Ginger," he said. "What are you doing here?"

"I'm the new law firm secretary, for a few weeks anyhow. It's a trial. Ham Fish has a private office now, and Mister Ramsey and Hannah agreed to give me a chance. I got eighth grade schooling, and I learned to type on my own when I worked in a Kansas City law office for six months before my life took a bad turn. There aren't many typists in Lockwood, and when I told Hannah that I could, she considered me for the job. I am moving into town in a few days. I think she wanted to get me out of the house."

"Well, congratulations on the new job. I hope it works out for you. Is Hannah available?"

"She is with a client now, but she should be finished in five or ten minutes if you would like to wait."

"Thanks, I will do that." He took a chair, and Ginger returned to her typing. He listened to the clackety-click as her nimble fingers raced across the keys. She was obviously a good typist. He compared it to his frustrating hunt and peck on a barely used typewriter that usually sent him back to writing in longhand. He decided that he would find a way to master the contraption, but he also wondered if Ginger might be interested in typing manuscripts for extra income.

Grant guessed Ginger to be no more than twenty years old. She was educated and well spoken, and she had moved from a secretary to whore to rancher's wife and expectant mother to widow in the blink of an eye. Do not judge quickly, he thought. People are often not what the first encounter suggests.

Fresh starts. That was one thing he was coming to love about the West. There would be a few gossips bringing up Ginger's past in the bordello, but most cared only about what you could do now and were too engaged with their survival to dwell upon such things. Blighted pasts could be put aside by a man or woman. As with many folks, he figured, Ginger's life was a novel if her story were revealed.

He heard Hannah's office door open and booted footsteps in the hallway. The client who stepped into the waiting area was a grim-faced man he had come to know and respect: Con Callaway, owner of the Double C and Bobby's father, as well as county board chairman.

Callaway nodded without changing the solemn expression on his face. "Good morning, Grant."

"Good morning." The man kept moving, so Grant was spared awkward small talk.

"I will tell Hannah you are here, Grant," Ginger said. She got up from her chair and disappeared around the corner into the hallway. Moments later, she returned. "You can go in now."

When he entered Hannah's office, she was staring out her window, which gave her a view of the brick wall of a building that had been recently constructed, leaving an alleyway between the two. "Sit down," she said, without turning.

Her words seemed a bit brusque. No kisses today it appeared. Finally, she claimed her chair on the opposite side of the desk. When she looked at him it was with eyes that seemed distant as if she were somewhere else.

"I can come back another time," he said.

She shook her head. "No, this is fine. What did you wish to see me about?"

"First, I wanted to inform you that the Buck Tyree book should be ready in a week's time."

"Good. We don't want the publisher discounting your royalty payments over a deadline issue. The contract has provisions for that, you know. Leave the manuscript here when you have it completed. I am going to have Ginger type it. Beadle has requested a typed manuscript. You have a new Remington. You should learn to use it. I am certain Jeb Oaks at the general store could order you an instruction book."

"I will ask him about it. Do you type?"

"No, and learning is very low on my list of projects."

He was not going to let her get by with her shortness. "You've got the grumps this morning."

She sighed. "I am given to moods from time to time. The day is not going well. First, I received a letter from my twin brother, Thad, this morning. He wants to bring my father out from Manhattan, Kansas for a visit. I may have mentioned that I haven't seen my father for more than ten years."

"I know you are estranged. It had to do with him turning you and your brother over to an aunt to raise when your mother died. I understand he remained a part of your life, though, and I never grasped why that caused your hostility toward him."

"I confess that as I have gotten older, I have come to realize my attitude may have been a bit irrational. But I am not ready for a grand reunion."

"You are going to wait for his funeral?"

"That wasn't nice."

"I'm not going to argue with you about it. I will keep my mouth shut unless you solicit my opinion. I do have another matter that Jim asked me to speak with you about. Considering the client who just walked out of your office, this is especially uncomfortable."

"Con Callaway is involved?"

"It is about his son, Bobby."

She grimaced. "Tell me about it."

Grant told her about his conversations with Enos Fletcher and the sheriff. "We can't be sure Bobby is connected to the outlaws, but he is the first potential link we have come up with."

Hannah was obviously shaken by the disclosure. "This presents some serious concerns for me. I will have to sort this out. You said Jim wants to get together in a few days. We can use my office. It is more private than the sheriff's. I will need that time to evaluate some things. Also, I am meeting Blaine Garfield this afternoon. He is one of the lawyers for the Stock Growers Association. Maybe I will have something to report after that session."

"Garfield? I saw the name on an office door down the street, but I've never met the man."

"He is about my age, an insufferable snob and cannot be trusted. I dread even dealing with him. He is a Harvard graduate, you know, and will be certain you are aware of it. He refers to himself as an attorney. Lawyer is too lower class. God forbid, someone call him a law wrangler as many folks in these parts do. And he does not consider we unschooled lawyers who clerked our way to the bar examination worthy of the profession."

She seemed to be waiting for a response, but Grant was uncertain how to reply to her little rant without adding fuel to the fire. "I'm confident you will handle him just fine."

"And, of course, I must meet with him at his office. When Ginger delivered the meeting request, his response made any discussion conditional upon taking place there."

"I don't know what else to say."

"I didn't ask you to say anything," she snapped. "You just had the misfortune to catch me in one of my moods." She gave a heavy sigh. "I apologize. This has nothing to do with you."

"Perhaps I could take you to lunch."

She hesitated. "No, I think not. I have work to do. I will ask Ginger to bring me something when she goes out."

"She seems very enthused about her new job."

"She learns quickly and meets folks easily. I think she can make a place here. She found a room at Sally's Bed and Board, which accepts only women now. She will likely have to make other arrangements next spring when the baby arrives, but she has time to prepare. This is a big first step since her husband's killing."

Grant rose from his chair. "Well, I had better let you get back to work."

She stood but made no move around the desk. "This is Tuesday. Tell Jim we will meet here Thursday morning at ten o'clock."

"I will stop at the sheriff's office before I leave town." He turned and walked out of the room, uncertain where things stood between him and this volatile woman.

Chapter 34

AFTER GRANT LEFT her office, Hannah sat back down at her desk. Grant must have been glad to escape the witch from hell, she thought. It had been his misfortune to arrive during one of her black moods. He was likely mystified by her sudden abruptness, yet grateful that he had seen this side of her before their relationship went further. She could have accepted his lunch invitation. It might even have lifted her spirits, probably would have, but sometimes it was like she drove herself to misery.

The letter from Thad had triggered it all, stoked her guilt about her treatment of her father. She was thirty now. Time to grow up. The visit. It wasn't feasible this time of year with the weather risk. Heavy snows could quickly interfere with plans, or they might get snowed in after arriving in Lockwood. Sometimes trains would not get through for days or even weeks.

She knew she was making feeble excuses to herself, but she could not handle spending half the winter with them, and they were both busy men, Thad with his veterinary practice and Myles Locke with his law firm. She would invite them to visit in May and write a letter to her father apologizing for her behavior. Before May, she might even surprise them with a visit to Kansas.

She picked up the notes she had made at her meeting with Con Callaway. The changes Con wanted to make to his will told her the rancher would not be entirely shocked to hear Bobby was up to no good. The present will provided for the ranching properties upon Con's death to go to the three sons, James, Thomas and Robert equally. The changes would exclude Robert, or Bobby, from the division and, instead, grant him payment of an annual stipend from the ranch.

The amount was generous and would be a significant obligation for the other sons to take on but would eliminate the risk of Bobby forcing a sale of the real estate and livestock. Territorial law and the laws of most states granted the right of an owner of a fractional interest in property to force its sale and liquidation. Con feared that Bobby would exercise that right given he had no particular interest in the ranch, showing up to work only when he felt like it. Con should be informed, and she could not participate in any effort to entrap Bobby without Con's knowledge.

Callaway had expressed an urgency about completion of the will, and he would be back in the office to sign in the morning. The changes were simple enough. She would give Ginger instructions for typing a new will. If he wanted further changes pending the outcome of the investigation, they would take care of it while he waited. She prided herself in brevity, and revisions could be made quickly. She found a pencil and began writing the changes to the existing will with the thought of having the documents on Ginger's desk by noon. Then she would try to intercept Grant and negotiate a peace, however fragile it might be.

Later, she sat in the exquisitely furnished office of Blaine Garfield, attorney and apparent junior partner in the firm of Foster and Garfield. She had never met Foster and not even Enos Fletcher could boast of seeing the man. She figured he was either a creature of fiction or resided elsewhere, likely the latter. It might be something to investigate just to satisfy her curiosity if for no useful purpose. The shingle near the entrance wall identified the man as "Alexander P. Foster."

She was beginning to get impatient with Garland who had kept her waiting fifteen minutes now. She would admit to being obsessive about punctuality, but she considered it rude to keep a fellow member of the bar waiting. The door opened, and Garfield strutted in wearing a blue pinstriped suit and gray tie. He was a doughy, pale man with thinning, blond hair and a heavy moustache that curved upward like the horns of a longhorn steer. He stood several inches taller than her own five and a half feet.

He walked directly to her with hand extended, a big smile on his face, "Miss Locke, I apologize for being a bit tardy. I was meeting with new clients in the conference room."

She accepted his hand, which was like holding a limp rag, and gave him the strongest grip she could muster. It pleased her when he flinched and drew his paw back.

He moved behind his desk and sat down, gesturing with his hand that she should do the same. "Your note was rather mysterious, Miss Locke. Something about the Big River County Stock Growers Association. I do represent that fine organization. How may I help you?"

"Mister Garfield, I am not making this visit as a part of my private practice. I am in your office as the county prosecutor, and you should understand that from the beginning."

"Please call me Blaine. I do not understand why the county prosecutor would wish to talk to me."

She was not going to call him by his first name or take the bait to invite him to address her by her own. "I am here about the killings that have occurred on the small farms and ranches in the county. The sheriff's investigation is turning up evidence that the Stock Growers Association may be involved. I would like to discuss this with the organization's president, Cletus Tate."

"Then why did you not do so?"

"He would not have spoken without consulting with you, and you would have advised him not to answer any questions."

"Yes, that likely would have been my advice, although I assure you my client is innocent of any wrongdoing."

"I just wanted to give him the opportunity to be helpful, and to convince me why I should not file murder charges against him and other members of the Stock Growers board."

"What are you talking about, Madam? You know these ranchers did not kill those people."

"They probably did not pull the triggers or put the noose about anyone's neck, but if they ordered the killings and paid for them, they are as guilty as those who did. In that case, I will not hesitate to prosecute. We are convinced that the men committing these murders are hired guns, and I have directed the sheriff to focus on the hiring employers. Shut off the pay pipeline, and we stop the killings immediately."

"Miss Locke, I graduated from the Harvard College law school, and I will not be bluffed like this."

"Very well, Mister Garfield. You will receive no further notice from me before any charges are filed."

"Now, let us not end our conversation on a hostile note. I will discuss the possibility of a meeting with Mister Tate. He is a fair-minded man. I know you are well acquainted with him. He was your firm's client, I recall, before he transferred his business to our firm."

She supposed it would be unprofessional to tell Garfield that Tate was a hot-headed, loud-mouthed fool. "Just send word to my office if he is willing to meet—in your presence, of course."

She stood and walked out of the room.

Chapter 35

BRADY YATES STOOD outside the ramshackle structure that housed the nearly worn-out equipment acquired by Y and C Lumber Company from the previous business owner. He was speaking to his newly hired manager, Birch Reagan, about his plans for the enterprise. He had hired Reagan a few days earlier. At age twenty, the young man was three years older than the not quite seventeen-years-old boss.

Reagan came from a coal-mining family but had no interest in that pursuit. He was a tall fair-complexioned young man with blue eyes and shaggy, straw-colored hair, clean shaven save for a futile attempt at a patchwork moustache. Thick shouldered and muscular, Birch Reagan was the strongest man Trouble knew. Once, he had seen Birch grasp a big yearling steer by the horns and toss it to the earth like laying down a goose-feather pillow. He had worked for Trouble on several occasions, and it was not the physical strength that had pointed him to the man. Birch was a quick learner, could think for himself and could direct other men when called upon, a capable leader, something Matt Gaines said folks were generally born to. Some were leaders. Other good men preferred to follow.

Trouble said, "I won't hire more fulltime men this winter. We'll take on three or four more in the spring. First job is to tear down this building. It's the best site for the new one I want to build. We will need to put up a canvas shelter someplace, so we can keep the saws cutting on days that weather allows. We won't turn out much but just enough to keep customers happy. I'm working on plans for a new mill and stable for the mule teams and wagon storage. I'll go over those with you in a week or so and see what you think."

"These saws won't last long," Birch said.

"I got three big steam circular saws and two smaller ones on order. They're promised by March if weather allows. I got wagon parts and wheels on the way. We got local carpenters that can't find enough work in the winters. They'll build the wagons. We need some extra-long, heavy-duty wagons, maybe a flatbed or two with timber anchors. We'll see how it works. Might even get into the wagon building business."

"You must be planning on cutting a lot of lumber."

"Yep. After we take care of the locals, we'll ship the surplus out by rail. I got Sammy working on that. She's learned a little about that sort of thing with the sewing business she got into. They started with women's dresses. Now her buyers are asking for men's suits and stuff."

"My head's spinning. Where do we get all this lumber? I know there's plenty along the valley's edges, but you don't own it."

"We pay lease fees, cash or share, whatever we got to do. Acres and acres of government land coming up for lease this spring. Cattlemen don't have use for the wooded ground. We'll bid on the leases."

"Looks like you got everything figured out."

"Not everything, but I'm working on it. Stick with me, and I'll make it worth your while. You won't be leaving for more money."

Birch shook his head in disbelief. "You're hitting me with a lot at one time here. I think I'll just start on what comes first. That would be tearing the building down. I could do that with one good man, I think. What do we do with the scrap lumber?"

Ron Schwab

"Sort it out. If it can be reused, stack it someplace. We can sell it or use it ourselves, especially for the stable. The rest we'll offer free to folks who need firewood. Next year, we'll be selling waste hardwoods for burning. We're just two miles from town. Folks can make that trip easy enough."

"Somebody coming this way. Wagon and mule team and at least two riders," Birch said, pointing toward the wagon road that led from town.

They both turned and watched the wagon's approach. As it drew nearer, Trouble could make out three riders accompanying an over-loaded buckboard behind a mule team. The wagon was moving at a brisk pace which told Trouble it had a good distance to travel before sundown. He expected the muleskinner to pull the wagon over for a brief neighborly chat. However, he did not.

Trouble and Birch waved and stepped toward the road. The waves were not returned, and the wagon and riders did not even slow their pace, moving on past and heading for one of the few bridges spanning the North Laramie River that would take them to the valley's west side.

"Friendly folks," Birch said. "Did you recognize any-body?"

"Nope. Ain't ever seen them. I'd like to buy that Appaloosa horse the skinny feller was riding, though."

"What's wrong with your sorrel gelding?"

"Ain't nothing wrong with Tag. Couldn't part with him. But you sounded like you was going to make me a man who could afford two horses."

"Well, it doesn't look like you will get a chance to bargain for the Appaloosa."

"Wouldn't try. That was a sour-looking bunch."

Chapter 36

❝I AM MEETING with Cletus Tate and his lawyer tomorrow morning at Blaine Garfield's office. I don't expect much. Nobody is going to confess to a crime. It is not likely I will learn much—not in the way of facts anyhow. But it might be useful to observe Tate's reaction to my questions. You never know what kind of nonsense this man might blurt out."

Grant sat in the Locke and Ramsey conference room with Sheriff Tolliver and Hannah. They had gathered as agreed to discuss the status of the Justice Riders cases, and she had opened the session with a report on her meeting with Garfield, detailing her conversation with the lawyer. Her distaste for the man was obvious.

"They are meeting with me out of curiosity," Hannah said.

Grant said, "You are acquainted with Tate, I gather?"

"Oh, yes. I have known him for a spell."

Grant suspected Tate was a former client who had jumped ship. Regardless, he was glad to find Hannah calm and more in control today. The letter about a possible visit from her father and brother must have pushed her off balance. He still did not know where he stood with her. She had been businesslike when he entered the office, but the anger and outright hostility had seemingly passed—for the moment anyway.

The sheriff said, "Grant thought we should go for the head of the snake. Could that be Tate?"

Hannah said, "The snake might have multiple heads, but he is a start."

Grant said, "We need to find out if Bobby Callaway is a part of this. If he is, we must figure out how to trap him and convince him to turn on his masters."

"If it makes sense to the two of you, I will speak with his father. Frankly, if I do not, I will be forced to recuse myself from further involvement in the case. I have conflicts I cannot discuss. Besides, Con Callaway is county board chairman. I am not comfortable with law enforcement going behind his back."

Sheriff Tolliver said, "Con is a good man. He had the guts and good sense to stay away from the Stock Growers outfit. I trust him. He's in a tough position. You handle it however you see fit."

"I don't have a vote," Grant said. "The sheriff speaks for his office, but for what it is worth, I agree."

"Very well. I intend to ride out to the Double C and speak with Con this afternoon. I want to do this before I talk with Cletus Tate tomorrow. Be thinking about how Bobby should be approached if Con gives the go ahead. Now, if you are up to an early lunch, you are both invited to be my guests at The Chowdown."

Tolliver looked at Grant and then back at Hannah. "I have an appointment at my office, but thank you. Grant, you can represent the sheriff's office at lunch." He got up and left the room, leaving Grant and Hannah alone, facing each other across the conference table.

Hannah said, "Are you going to join me?"

He squinted one eye and revealed just a trace of a smile. "Why not? I am curious about which Hannah Locke I will be dining with today."

Hannah grimaced and rolled her eyes.

Later, he was pleased to learn that his friend Hannah had appeared at The Chowdown. After they had made their selection between roasted beef and roasted beef on the entryway chalkboard menu, Hannah said, "I apologize for being such a bitch in my office the other day. I'm surprised you would have lunch with me."

"You were having a bad day. I probably was not sensitive to it. According to my former wives, who had the misfortune to be married to me in my drinking years, I had a bad day every day and made their lives constant hell. I am in no position to judge. Besides, you seemed madder at yourself than me."

"Yes. The letter from my brother triggered everything."

"I suspected as much. I understand."

"Truly? Am I forgiven?"

"You are forgiven."

When their meals were served with the obligatory apple pie, they continued talking amiably about the kids and his novel progress. The world seemed right again. He was accustomed to several days or nearly a week between contacts, but the past few days had been different. He had missed her and found himself puzzled by the difference. "I missed you," he said. "I know that is a strange thing to say."

"I don't think so. I know exactly what you mean. And I missed you."

When they finished, Hannah paid for the meals, which felt strange to him. Ladies just did not do such things. He looked about the restaurant, hoping no one noticed. He saw a lady looking their way with uplifted eyebrows and a pitying look on her face. He hoped something else was the cause of her apparent disapproval. He was not about to draw more attention with a fuss about paying the bill.

As they parted in front of the law office, Grant said, "I'm going to pick up Blue at the livery and get back home and get a few chapters written. Good luck with your meeting and thank you for lunch."

"You are very welcome. I will ride over after I have talked to both Con Callaway and Cletus Tate if I don't see you before." She turned to him, clasped the back of his head and pulled it down and kissed him on the cheek. She stepped back and smiled. "And you and Gideon will be over for Sunday dinner as usual this weekend?"

"Of course."

When she disappeared through the office door, he saw an elderly couple crossing the street toward him. Kissing in public was considered inappropriate by many. Sometimes Hannah seemed insensitive to the eyes of others. And the woman was as unpredictable as an unbroken filly. He turned and headed down the boardwalk toward the livery.

Chapter 37

HANNAH, ATTIRED IN her boots and riding britches, reined her buckskin gelding into the Double C headquarters site which included a sprawling log residence and a cluster of nearby ranch buildings. Callaway had resided alone in the house since his wife's death some five years earlier. When he was in her office, he had mentioned the possibility of trading houses with his eldest son Thomas, whose family, including a pregnant wife and three small children, occupied a smaller house about fifty paces to the west. Son James had just recently married and lived at the far end of the ranch.

She dismounted and started leading her horse toward the house, hoping she would find Callaway home.

"Hannah." She recognized Callaway's voice and turned around. The trim rancher, his trademark black Stetson covering most of his white hair, was coming from the direction of the stable. He moved with rapid strides for a man a few years past sixty and a bit gimpy after two broken legs.

She pulled her Plainsman hat lower on her forehead to block the sun from her eyes as he caught up with her. "Good afternoon, Con. I gambled I might catch you at home."

"I paid my bill when I left your office yesterday, so you can't be here to collect. And I ain't dead yet, so you are wasting time if you thought it was time to probate the will. I'm told you've got that writer courting you these days, so it doesn't stand to reason you would be making a social call on this old geezer."

She surrendered a wry smile. "We must talk."

"Sounds serious. Come on up to the house. Young Phoebe always has coffee brewing. I must drink a gallon a day. You've got to be cold. Old Mister Sun is lying about the weather. There's a serious, dang chill in the air."

She followed him to the house, hitching the gelding on the rail out front. He introduced her to Phoebe McIntosh, his foreman's wife, who with the help of her teen-aged daughter, tended to his meals and housekeeping chores. Phoebe, a fortyish, matronly woman said, "My daughter Malinda is at school in town. I wish she could meet you. She thinks she wants to be a lawyer."

"I will talk to my girls and see if we can arrange for Phoebe to come to my office. I can show her around and take her to the courthouse, such as it is." Plans were underway for a new courthouse, but presently the courtroom and offices functioned in a dilapidated, storefront building along Main Street.

Hannah and Callaway poured their own coffee at the kitchen table not far from the wood cookstove, the warmest place in the house. Callaway pressed the hot mug to his lips, testing the brew, and deciding it was too hot, set it back on the table. "Tell me what we must talk about."

"Bobby."

"That cannot be good."

"I don't know. Everything is speculation. Enos Fletcher may have had the pale horse and its owner in his stable. Grant spoke with him and thinks it is very likely the man was there some months back."

"Okay. What has this got to do with Bobby?"

"On one occasion, Enos saw the pale horse owner speaking at length with another man. He thought they seemed well acquainted. Later the other man and Bobby met on several occasions. That is all we know."

"Doesn't sound like much. Are you insinuating Bobby is involved in the killings? He could have died with the rest of us in the church that night, and he certainly was not with the attackers. Pardon me, counselor, but this seems more than a mite farfetched."

"I won't argue that, but he is the nearest thing to a connection we have. At the least, he seems to know a man who may be acquainted with the rider of the so-called pale horse. We need to identify that man. Bobby can apparently do that. Somebody should talk to him, and it should not be you. I should not either. My representation of you presents some ethical problems. You are the county board chairman as well. The sheriff, Grant Coolidge and I met to discuss this. We agreed you should be informed, but the interview is going to take place regardless of your position. I cannot and will not interfere."

Callaway gulped down some coffee from his mug and sat silently for what seemed to Hannah an eternity. He shook his head from side to side. "Oh, Bobby, what now? Yeah, Hannah, do what you've got to do. Can you just keep me informed on what you find out? And I would like to ask that Grant talk to Bobby. Jim's a good man, but he's got a bullying side. Grant has a softer manner. He will probably learn more from a temperamental kid like Bob-

Beware a Pale Horse

by and might be able to convince him not to panic and do something stupid."

She was certain Grant would not be thrilled about being pulled deeper into the case. It would take some gentle persuasion on her part. And there was a possibility that Jim Tolliver would take offense at being cut out of the interview. It was not the prosecutor's job to deal with such things. She had not aspired to a criminal practice, and this was why. She preferred handling matters she could control—wills, real estate, the paperwork side of law. It occurred to her that she would likely be a terrible wife. Her inclination to control and take charge would not be tolerated by any man with a backbone. And she would not want to be married to a man who would put up with it.

"Can you do that? Get Grant to talk to Bobby."

"I'm sorry. I was thinking about it. Yes, I'm sure I can."

"And keep me informed?"

"Yes, of course I will."

Chapter 38

HANNAH SAT IN front of Blaine Garfield's office desk, facing the lawyer sitting behind it and his client, Cletus Tate, seated off to one side. Tate, a balding, jowly man who had always reminded her of a plump toad, glared at her from heavy-lidded eyes, making no pretense at being the affable, cheerful man that was his public face. She was not surprised. This was the side she had usually seen in her office, and she had never missed this client who had abandoned the Ramsey and Locke firm.

Garfield spoke first. "Miss Locke, I understand you are acquainted with my client, Cletus Tate."

"Certainly. Good morning, Clete."

Tate nodded.

Garfield said, "You wanted to ask Mister Tate some questions. He intends to cooperate fully with your office and the sheriff regarding any inquiries. He has nothing to hide, but I may advise him not to respond to questions I consider too invasive of his privacy and that of the Big River County Stock Growers Association."

"I can't force him to answer any questions, but I suggest that if your client and the Association, which is also your client as I understand it, are not involved in criminal activities, it would be in their interest to be forthcoming."

Tate blurted, "What in the hell are you talking about, woman? We ain't done no crimes. It's them damn rustlers that are stealing our cattle and the homesteaders claiming land that's always been open range. Thieves and trespassers. That's what we're dealing with."

"Homesteaders have been granted the right by congress and the president to settle the lands. Those folks, like it or not, are entitled to file a claim and move in to occupy the land and prove up on it by living there and farming it for five years. Whether someone is a rustler or not must be determined by a court of law, and regardless, rustling is not a capital offense in the territory, and no man will hang for it."

"The law ain't always right."

Hannah said, "That could be, but that is not for you to decide. I might not always agree with certain laws, but the jobs of the sheriff and me are to enforce them."

Hannah was grateful when Garfield interrupted. "Now let's calm down folks. Why don't you just ask your questions, Miss Locke."

"Gladly. Clete, you are president of the Stock Growers Association. There are riders who have been raiding homes in this county, hanging and shooting innocent people during the dead of night. Has your association hired gunmen to carry out these acts?"

"First, lady, them folks are not innocents. They're either stealing cattle or trespassing."

"They are innocent unless proven guilty in a court of law. The killers are guilty of murder. You didn't answer my question."

Tate's face turned beet red, and daggers shot from his porcine eyes. "Hell, no. What are you getting at, woman?"

"These men did not show up here on their own. The sheriff is satisfied that the killers are not local ranchers or their cowhands. The motive must be money, so the question is who is paying them. We are searching for the money source. Stop the money. Stop the killings. The sheriff intends to track down the killers, but higher priority is to bring this to an end and to arrest whoever is paying them. You don't have to pull the trigger or put the rope about somebody's neck in order to be guilty of murder."

"Them killers ain't working for the Association or me or anybody else connected with the Association."

"I hope you are telling the truth. I would hate to see you hanging from the gallows outside the Main Steet courthouse." The image did not disturb her in the least at this moment.

"Is that a threat, bitch?"

A nervous Garfield said, "Please, Cletus. Your language . . ."

"I don't give a good shit. I ain't taking this from her."

Hannah said, "I am not threatening, Clete. I am just telling you that anyone who hired these men are as guilty as they are, and I will see they are prosecuted when—not if—they are apprehended. Now, do you have any information that might help us?"

"I don't know nothing, and I ain't saying more."

"Then I guess my business here is finished." She stood and turned to Garfield. "Thank you, Mister Garfield. This has been more helpful than you know."

As she left the Garfield office and headed back to her own, she felt satisfied with the meeting. She had not expected to procure an admission from Cletus Tate. The purpose was to apply pressure to the snake's head and motivate Tate and the Grower's Association officers to pause the attacks, if not bring them to a halt. Her instincts told her that Tate and possibly some of the organization's other members were directly involved in the violence. Hannah's lawyer side reminded her that she lacked evidence.

Chapter 39

"I KNOW YOU don't want to do this, but Jim agrees that we should comply with Con Callaway's request and have you talk to Bobby. As I told you, I spoke with Cletus Tate at Garfield's office this morning. It gave me a sense of urgency about this. We need to keep pressing."

They were sitting at Grant's kitchen table again. Hannah had shown up after supper, bringing a bowl of what she called "Brown Betty" for their desserts. There appeared to be sliced apples in a pudding, and Grant loved anything with apples in it. Gid was eating a huge portion of it as he sat cross-legged in front of the fireplace with the growing pup on one side and Sargent on the other. Grant hoped the animals would not share the pudding, pushing Gid to beg for seconds and leaving Grant with nothing but scrapings in the bowl. Hannah had told him several times that he must learn to say "No" to the boy, although he had not noticed her declining his requests either. She was stricter with the girls.

"Where do I find Bobby?" he asked.

"He is rarely at the Double C. Somebody would put him to work. I'll tell Jim to keep an eye out for him, maybe have Ozzie and Zeke check out the taverns. If you don't come in till late morning, they'll know his whereabouts."

"It appears that first I need to establish that Bobby is a link between the association and the raiders. If so, does he report directly to your friend Tate?"

"That's about it."

"And short of torture, how do I get Bobby to admit this?"

"You are the writer with imagination. You write the script."

Gid called to him. "Grant, you said we'd play chess to-night."

"Get the board set up on the table."

Hannah said, "My cue to leave."

"You created the chess monster. You should give him a match."

"Checkers, yes. Chess could take all night. No, thank you."

They got up from the table, and Hannah, with Grant's help, wormed into her bulky, wool coat. Before she went out the door, she turned and faced him. "You are a good man, Grant Coolidge." She tilted her head upward with an obvious invitation, which he accepted. It was a lingering kiss, one that begged for more.

Then the voice behind him reminded him of his duty. "Grant, the board's set up. I'm taking white tonight."

Grant stepped back and gave a wry grin. "I wonder what it would be like to kiss you without interruption."

"We should try it behind locked doors sometime. Goodnight, Grant."

"Goodnight, Hannah. I don't like you riding back to your place alone at night, but I shouldn't leave Gid."

"I am a big girl, Grant. My house isn't much over five minutes down the road. It would take two or three times as long for you to saddle up as for me to get home. Besides, I love the quiet of riding in the dark and the peace of stars twinkling overhead."

He watched though the window as she nudged her buckskin onto the road, the shadowy horse and rider seeming almost ghostlike in the moonlight as they trotted down the road, leaving him only the memory of the gentle touching of their lips. He realized at that moment how much this woman had taken over his life. He felt a twinge of guilt. He would always love Moon Dupree, but Hannah was inching his lost love into a poignant memory.

He walked over to the game table he had recently purchased with two straight back chairs. He was running out of space in the cabin, and he could not have Gideon sleeping on the floor indefinitely. He had evolved to the realization that young Gideon Trout would not be moving on. Perhaps he should talk to Trouble Yates about building an addition to the cabin in the spring, two bedrooms, so he could get his bed to a private space and ease the crowding. Trouble would not do the work himself, but for a commission he would hire the craftsmen and oversee the project. Grant hated dealing with such details.

He took the chair on the side where the black chessmen were placed. Gideon was already studying the board. The kid had mastered the game and was whipping Grant more than a third of the time now. Grant never cut the boy any slack, figuring there were no life lessons to be learned if he did. Besides, he had difficulty losing graciously even if his opponent happened to be a ten-year-old.

"I won last time; you move first," Grant said.

"Where we going to live when you and Miss Hannah get married?" Gideon said.

Taken aback, Grant said, "Where on earth did you get that notion?"

"I saw you kissing. And Jazzie told me. She said her mama told her that you and Miss Hannah will be getting married."

Moon Dupree, now deceased, was Jasmine's mother. Grant decided not to pursue the subject. "We don't have any plans to get married," he said. "Now move."

Chapter 40

REAPER PACED THE parlor floor early afternoon while Danek relaxed in front of the fireplace as usual. It annoyed him that Danek could handle idleness so calmly. Reaper preferred to be on the move, confronting and punishing transgressors. He thrived on the plotting and execution of his missions.

He paused when he glanced out the window and saw the mere speck of a rider some distance out moving in their direction on the winding trail that snaked through the narrow entry into the dead-end canyon where Reaper's little army quartered. "Somebody coming this way," Reaper said.

"Who is it?" Danek said, not interested enough to get up and see for himself. "We don't have anybody out that I know of."

"I can't tell yet. Half blinded by the sun. Wait . . . I think it's Cletus Tate."

"Tate. Isn't he the man who hired you? The one you report to?"

"That's him. He ain't been out here since he showed me the place. We're on government land you know. Years ago, some fella squatted on the land. That was when Lockwood was nothing but a trading post back before the War of the Rebellion even. Tate said he had some sort of a bargain with the Sioux, raised beef and gave the chief a good share for sort of a rent in trade for them not burning him out. It didn't hold when the Sioux wars broke out. He and his people disappeared, either were captured and killed or abandoned the buildings before. Nobody knows for sure."

"How does Tate know this?" Danek asked.

"His pappy was a mountain man back in the day, one of the first settlers in the valley. He heard the story from the Indians, who warned him off the canyon if he wanted to keep his scalp. His pappy brought Tate over to explore when he was a kid. Since Tate's family was settled in the valley first, he seems to think he should own all the land between the mountains. Everybody else is a trespasser to his notion."

"Sounds like a crazy man. Indians were here first. Under his way of reasoning, it seems like they should own the valley."

Reaper shrugged. "Maybe lots of us are a little crazy."

Danek did not comment.

Reaper said, "Tate's almost here. Go out and wave him in. Have one of the men see to his horse and hightail it back here."

Danek sighed and lifted himself from his cozy spot in front of the fireplace. He donned his coat and headed out the door. Reaper watched Tate walk up the path to the house and climb the steps onto the veranda. Then he opened the door and waved the rotund rancher into the house. "Mister Tate. This is a surprise. Come in and get yourself in front of the fire."

Tate was breathing heavily, huffing like he had just run a mile. He was not an old man. Reaper judged him to be in his mid-fifties, but no one would suggest he was a fit man.

Tate said, "I about froze my balls off out there. Sun may be shining, but the wind is a witch's kiss." He shed his coat, dropped it on the floor and headed directly for the fire.

Reaper joined him and sat down in one of the stuffed chairs. "Sit down. What brings you here?"

"Give me a minute." He turned around and backed up to the fireplace. "I got to thaw my ass some. I swear my blood has turned to ice. It's near ten miles from my ranch to here. I ain't made a ride like this in a few years. You're going to have to put me up for the night. I can't risk being on the trail after sunset."

"You're welcome to stay," he lied. He wanted the obnoxious man out of the house, but he could not ignore the source of the money that funded his latest venture.

Finally, just as Danek returned and claimed a chair, Tate began explaining the reason for his visit. "We got a problem, and you've got to get rid of it."

"What is the problem?"

"A lawyer. A woman named Hannah Locke. She's Ethan Ramsey's partner. He's a senator in the territory's upper house council. She is also the county prosecutor. Ain't been enough lawbreaking around here to hire a full-time law wrangler, she steps in when they need one."

"I've heard of Ramsey."

"Yeah, Wyoming's close to statehood. Got to have sixty thousand people and best guess is it's been reached. Talk is that Ramsey's got his eye on booting Francis Warren out for Governor when statehood comes in a few years. I used his law firm for some years until they wouldn't take on the Stock Growers Association for clients. Ramsey's a cattleman, too, but he's been hostile to the Wyoming Stock Growers Association in the legislature for some reason. Wants an audit of the records, that sort of thing, before he'll vote to release any public funds to the Association."

"So what has this got to do with your problem with Hannah Locke?"

"Just telling you I knew the woman from my dealings with the law firm. Damn smart for a woman. She can be dangerous, and she asked to meet with me and the Association's lawyer, Blaine Garfield. My lawyer said I should be there just to find out what she was up to, so I went." Tate then went on to relate the story of his meeting with Hannah Locke at Garfield's office.

When he had finished, Reaper said, "Watch out for that woman. She's trying to trick you into making a move she can latch on to for evidence."

"Could be. Or trying to warn off the Association from making future efforts for justice. That's what this is about: justice for the ranchers. She's telling us to end our crusade against rustlers and trespassers. She is after my scalp. The bitch is looking to see me hanging from the gallows. I want her to hang first."

"You want us to string her up? A woman and a prosecutor? That might not set so good with folks in your county."

"That will send a message to any troublemakers. They'll think twice about getting in our way. There is a big cottonwood tree in the middle of one of the intersections with Main Street. You couldn't have missed it when you were in town."

"I know the place."

"Two Indian kids was strung up there some years back. That's where I want her to be found, hanging from one of the branches of that old cottonwood."

"This is risky enough business. We can't be carrying out a hanging in the middle of town."

"Do the real hanging someplace else and then just haul the corpse into town, toss the rope over the branch, pull her up and tie it. Won't take ten minutes. Nobody's on the street late nights this time of year."

"I don't like it. We are taking big chances with such a thing. We could make it all worse. The county could pull in another prosecutor from the territory attorney's office, for instance, and they got investigators working for that office."

"I don't give a damn. I want the snoopy bitch dead. And she will be a warning to folks that might try to cross us—maybe even send some of the homesteaders packing and rustlers thinking better of what they're doing."

Reaper turned to Danek, who had remained silent. "What do think, Danek?"

"I think we would be damn fools to get anywhere near this woman. This would be a direct challenge to the law and could bring an army of lawmen to the county."

"Bullshit," a red-faced Tate said. "Reaper, I want this done."

"Have you talked to your directors?"

"Hell, no. The fewer people in on this, the better. They don't want to know the details so they can claim ignorance if the law comes looking. Now, there's a two-thousand-dollar bonus if you get this done, Reaper. Are you in or out?"

"You just sold me. I'm in, but I need a week or so to plot this out."

"You got a week. After you've got her—and I will know—send Joker in for final instructions. Usual contact."

Chapter 41

"BOBBY'S AT THE Salty Dog this morning," Ozzie said, "having beer for breakfast and playing poker at one of the tables near the back. Zeke's over there now, taking a long time to eat his own breakfast. If Bobby leaves, Zeke will follow him. My guess is that Bobby's settled in for most of the day."

Grant remembered his days of breakfast beer, although for him it was more often whiskey. He could not help but feel a bit of empathy for the young man. He wondered how much that demon triggered Bobby's irresponsible behavior. "I guess I'll mosey over there and see if I can figure out how to get him to talk to me. Do they offer a decent breakfast?"

"They do. Just as good as The Chowdown. It's just that they got a rougher crowd since they got booze and The

Chowdown don't, and they got two tables set aside for the local gamblers."

"I guess I'll order some breakfast and figure it out from there. When he comes in, tell Jim I will check back here whether I have any luck with my fishing trip or not."

"He never told me what this is all about."

"I'm not sure any of us know." Grant went out the door and strolled across the street to the boardwalk that led to The Salty Dog a block distant. When he stepped into the tavern, he was greeted by suffocating smoke clouds that delivered memories of his wasted tavern days nursing a bottle of one brew or another. The source of the smoke appeared to be coming from one end of the cramped room where the card players were busy, most with smoldering cigarettes dangling from their lips.

He caught sight of Deputy Sheriff Zeke Dale at a table not far from the door off to his left and decided to join him. By now it was no secret that Grant worked with the sheriff's office. When he claimed a chair at Zeke's table, the deputy's cherubic face brightened and offered a broad smile.

"Boy, I'm glad you're here Grant. Old Porky—Porky Ganz, the owner, was going to run me off. Said I couldn't just hang around the place if I wasn't a paying customer. I think he just don't want the law in his place. Anyhow, I ordered me a second breakfast. I ate it all but I don't think I could have done another, not all of it anyhow."

From Zeke's apple-shaped torso, Grant would not have bet against it. "Well, you can go now. I guess I'll need to order breakfast, too. Any recommendations?"

"Hotcake platter. Comes with three big hotcakes, sausage and a couple of eggs. With maple syrup, it's darn good. Coffee ain't bad neither. I ain't a drinking man, but I've heard the liquor here ain't the best. Porky has all kinds of fancy brew bottles, but he pays kids by the bottle to collect them from trash barrels and puts homebrewed stuff in them. Lots comes from Maggie White's stills, they say. That's Ozzie White's ma, you know."

"Yeah, so I've heard. Any idea how I might get Bobby Callaway to talk to me without getting everybody at the game tables too curious."

"Give Porky a dollar to whisper a message in his ear. I don't think Bobby would want you coming over."

"Maybe I will do that."

"Here comes Porky now. I'm on my way. See you around."

Grant turned his head in the direction of the bar and saw a huge man waddling his way. He supposed describing the man as being as wide as he was tall would be an exaggeration but not much of one. Porky was not more than average height and at least 350 pounds, Grant guessed.

The man came up to the table and spoke with a hoarse-sounding voice. "Never seen you here before, Coolidge."

"First visit. I don't drink."

"Got good grub. You'd better be eating if you're not drinking."

"The hotcake platter and coffee." He plucked a dollar bill from his wallet. "I have a message for Bobby Callaway's ears only."

Porky plucked the bill from his fingers. "What's the message?"

"I want to talk to him at this table the first break he's got. I'll buy his choice of drinks."

"I'll get your order to Gertie in the kitchen and then I'll give him the word."

Grant watched as Porky disappeared behind a curtained doorway next to the bar. Soon he came out and lumbered his way to the gambling tables where eight or nine men were split between the two tables. He bent over and whispered in Bobby's ear. The rancher's son faced Grant's table at the opposite end of the room, and he lifted his eyes from the cards and stared at Grant a spell before shifting his attention back to his poker hand. Grant could not make out the expression on the young man's face, so he was not certain of the reaction to the message.

Soon, a skinny, almost emaciated-looking, woman with gray-streaked hair arrived with a tray so full he was surprised she could carry it. She placed the tray on the table. "Everything you ordered, including the syrup should be there. Just leave everything on the tray when you're finished, and either me or Pork will pick it up. I'm Gertie, by the way. That's a dollar. Includes the tip."

Grant gave her the dollar bill. "Thank you, ma'am."

"My husband says Bobby should have a break in less than a half hour. Should give you time to eat."

"Porky's your husband?"

"More than twenty years in now. For better or for worse, they say. Mostly worse, I found out." She gave him a weak smile and shrugged before she turned and went back to her kitchen.

Grant was ordinarily a plate cleaner when he dined, but he could only eat half the hotcakes, which he figured were at least a foot in diameter. The eggs were not a problem, but he settled for one of the big sausage links. The other he wrapped in a small sheet of paper that he gathered was supposed to be a napkin and stuffed it in his coat pocket, figuring Sergeant and Lovey could share it. He sipped at his coffee while he waited for Bobby.

Fortunately, the wait was not long. Soon young Callaway appeared at his table. Grant stood and extended his hand, receiving a limp response to his own firm handshake. Bobby was smaller than he remembered, almost gaunt, probably drinking instead of eating. "I would like to talk to you a bit, Bobby. Sit down. Can I buy you a drink?"

Bobby turned and hollered at Porky, who was now at the bar taking care of the breaking card players. "Whiskey, Porky. A bottle." Porky waved acknowledgment of the order and turned back to serving his other customers.

Bobby looked at Grant, who noted the young man was tapping his fingers nervously on the table and biting his lower lip. His thin moustache strangely twitching. He was likely accustomed to being in trouble over something and just wondering what he had done this time.

"Bobby, we met that night at the church when all hell broke loose. Do you remember that?"

"Yessir, I do."

"And you are on my posse team."

"Yeah. We getting ready to ride or something?"

Porky appeared with a bottle and a glass. "Just brought one glass. You said you're not a drinking man, right. That's two dollars for the bottle. Should last the kid the day."

Grant tossed two silver dollars on the table. He had drunk enough whiskey to know that Porky was hitting him with a tidy surcharge. The visit to this place was getting expensive. A bottle was not what he had in mind when he offered to buy Bobby a drink. He hoped it would be a good investment.

Porky said, "I like that better than the paper you've been handing out."

After Porky left, Grant said, "I want to speak with you about the killings, but it has nothing to do with the posse."

"It don't?"

"No. Some information has come to me that worries me a great deal, and I wanted to talk to you about it."

Bobby poured himself a drink and gulped it down, then poured another before he replied. "Well, I got me a poker game waiting. What's this information?"

"This information suggests you might be involved with the killers. If it's true, you are flirting with a noose."

The color left Bobby's face, leaving it beyond pallid. He reached for his whiskey glass and started to take a drink, but his fingers trembled so fiercely he could not raise it to his lips without spilling the contents, and he put it down. "I don't know what you are talking about."

"I think you do."

"No. No. I really don't."

"There is a witness who says you have been seen speaking to a man identified as one of the gang of raiders on several occasions. The man rides an Appaloosa horse. Sound familiar? This man was also seen speaking at length with the suspected leader of the gang—a tall man who rides a pale horse. These men are murderers. If you are assisting them, you are an accomplice according to the prosecutor. If you escape hanging, you can look ahead to many, many years in prison."

He was telling Bobby half truths about the evidence, but he seemed to be swallowing them whole. Tears streamed down his face. Grant worried that the young man was on the verge of collapse. "Bobby, don't dig yourself any deeper into this mess. If you have information that would help stop the killings, the truth is the only thing that can save you. If you cooperate and tell us what you know, I am confident the prosecutor will take that into consideration. I cannot promise there would be no charges filed against you, but I'm sure they would be lesser."

"They will kill me if I turn on them. That's what he said."

"Who said that?"

"I just can't say. I've got to think. I need a drink." His shaky fingers worked the lid off the whiskey bottle, and he clutched it and raised it to his lips, taking a healthy swig. He lowered the bottle to the table but did not release his hold on it. Why would he? This was his life preserver on a stormy sea. Grant knew. He had been there. He had been that sniveling, frightened soul once.

"The last thing you need is that drink now, but I know it is a wasted effort to say that. Tell me this much. What has been your role in this?"

Bobby hesitated. "I was a messenger. A go-between. I delivered messages to this feller on the Appaloosa. His handle was Joker. I don't know if that was his real name, but that's what he went by."

"And what were these messages about?"

"I don't know what they said. I swear. Them messages was notes in an envelope sealed with wax. I guess the wax was so they would know if I opened them. I didn't understand what they was doing then, but within a week after I would meet up with Joker, one of the homesteads would be hit. I wanted out then, but I knew they would kill me. Fret about that anyhow. I likely know too much."

"Did you tell Joker about the meeting at the church?"

"Sort of. I told the top dog first. I got paid extra for any extra information I passed on when I thought they'd just want to know. I didn't think they'd do nothing. Figured I could make a dollar or two by going there and learning what I could."

"Bobby, you've got a chance to save your hide. It seems to me that you might not be in as much trouble as I thought you could be. If you are telling me the truth, you probably have not committed a serious crime yet. In fact, if you help the sheriff's office, you could come out of this looking pretty good."

"What do you mean?"

"Carry on as a messenger. The next time you get one, however, deliver it to the sheriff's office."

"They'll kill me when they find out."

"Not if we can put the killers out of business. In the meantime, the sheriff would protect you, maybe lodge you in a cell, so your employer will think you have been arrested. As I see it, you are a long way from hanging or even going to prison. That changes if you tell your boss about this conversation or keep carrying the messages."

"I can sort of see that."

"One more thing, though. You have got to tell me who you are carrying the messages for."

"Cletus Tate, head of the county Stock Growers. I got to know him a year or so back, after Pop and me had a fuss over my drinking, and I moved out. Didn't have no place to go, so I went over to the T Bar T and got me a cow punching job. Clete seemed glad to take me in, and I worked hard for him for three months, even stayed clear of the bottle. I don't like cows much, but I love horses. I helped break and train some critters and learned I can do that pretty good. Anyhow, me and Clete got friendly, and I started doing personal errands for him, carrying messages around the county to the other Stock Growers members and the like."

"But you returned home."

"Yeah. Clete wanted me to. He said Pop was pushing other ranchers to stay away from the Stock Growers and that the Growers was important to the future of the valley. He's been paying me above cowhand rates to let him know what Pop was up to. I guess I was a spy of sorts."

"It was Tate you told about the church meeting, wasn't it?"

"Yeah, I did. And he had me deliver a message to Joker right after that. I went to the meeting with Pop to see what information I might pick up. But after I about got blowed up in the church, I figured out that I must have had something to do with it. That's when I really wanted out but was scared to make a move."

Grant said, "One thing I don't understand is how Joker knew when you would have a message."

"Oh, he comes to town twice a week—Mondays and Thursdays. Tate is in the Growers office those days, too, and I'd check with him to see if there was anything to go. I'd be somewhere outside on the street till Joker showed up, usually before three. Never knowed for sure. Sometimes he came in the night before and stayed someplace. Most times I didn't have nothing, and Joker would grump about spending five hours going to town and back for nothing. Never understood why Clete paid me to do this, but he said he didn't want Joker anywhere near him or the Association office and didn't want direct contact with him, like he had the smallpox or something."

Grant assumed that Tate wanted to position himself to deny knowledge of the crimes if he should be dragged into any accusations. Bobby provided a flimsy layer of protection, he thought, and young Callaway's life would be dispensable if the scheme collapsed.

Grant cast his eyes about the room. "Is there anybody here that might tell Tate about my talking to you here?"

Bobby looked over his shoulder briefly. "Nah. These are mostly summer hands who won't have steady work till spring round-up. They get called in for some day work through the winter and grab a few odd jobs about town, but I don't see none with a T Bar T connection."

"How can they afford to gamble?"

"Aw, we do this with pennies. Nobody's got any money to spare—except for beer and whiskey. Winner sometimes buys drinks, but that's a losing proposition."

"Will you do what I ask, Bobby—take the next message to the sheriff? If you sense you are in danger before, forget about it and go directly to Jim Tolliver. I will talk to him when I leave here, and he will be ready to protect you."

"Yeah. I'm in. Now, I'm going to take this here bottle and get back to the poker business."

Chapter 42

HANNAH HAD NOT seen Grant in the past three days. That day he had stopped at her office to report on his conversation with Bobby Callaway. This was Saturday, and she was looking forward to Grant and Gid visiting tomorrow in response to their standing invitation to Sunday dinner. She increasingly wondered how her relationship with Grant was going to end up. Perhaps, it just stopped with friendship.

She sensed, though, that there was something more between them. Several times a fire had started and died out. Often there had been sparks, but other occasions had brought withdrawal and awkward silence. Was Moon, her lost friend and Grant's former lover, standing between them? Buried some fifty yards distant from the stable, where Hannah now saddled her buckskin mare, Moon Dupree was still a presence in both their lives, but the half-blood Sioux mystic was Grant's ghost more than her own. And, of course, Moon's daughter, Jasmine, residing in Hannah's home was a constant reminder.

Hannah just wanted a trail map for hers and Grant's future, she admitted. She did not live in limbo well. Her mind was fixed on goals and achieving them. With Grant, she was not even certain what she was looking for.

She mounted the buckskin, rode out of the ranch yard and reined the gelding toward Lockwood, where she planned to work at the office for a few hours as was her custom Saturday mornings. The girls understood that she sometimes became absorbed in a project and might work well into the afternoon.

She rode the horse at a leisurely pace, in no hurry this morning, taking in the breathtaking view of the sun just now creeping over the mountaintops to the east. On days like this, she could tolerate the winter cold. Quiet and calm without the wind. Before the day was out the residue of snow cover should thaw and disappear. She had lived in the valley long enough now to know that the respite would be brief.

Ahead of her, she saw two riders coming up the road toward her. They seemed to be in no hurry, and she was uncertain they even saw her. It was unusual that riders would be leaving town this early on a winter morning, but she supposed that they would find it strange that a lone woman would be on the road at sunrise. They did not concern her till they split, one moving to the left side of the road, the other remaining on the right. She would be forced to pass between them.

She reached down and stroked her Winchester's stock for reassurance. She thought of wheeling the mount and racing back to the house only a mile behind her. The riders probably intended no harm, but they would not dare chase her into the yard. Jasmine and Primrose would have rifles within easy reach, and if she fired off a few shots, they would be ready.

She tossed a glance over her shoulder, and her heart raced. Two riders behind her, closing in. This was not coincidental. She reined her horse off the side of the road and angled westerly, readying to race across the rangelands, thinking she would ride toward Grant's cabin. And then another rider appeared in front of her seeming to have dropped from the pale, blue sky like an apparition.

"Stop," he yelled. "You are surrounded."

She reined the buckskin in and yanked her rifle from its scabbard, levering a cartridge into the chamber. Suddenly, she felt her arms yanked abruptly to her sides and the rifle slipping from her grasp. She realized then that a rope was pulling at her torso. She was lifted from the saddle and bounced off the horse's hip, landing with an impact on the frozen ground that sent shockwaves of pain through her entire body. She saw the buckskin lunging away and heading across the range before somebody chased it down and grabbed the reins.

She lay on her back and rolled over, struggling to get to her knees and failing, flinching at the stabbing pain that ripped across her back and down her right leg. Instinctively her fingers clawed at the rope that held her fast. Dazed, she tried to look at her captors and saw that their faces were now covered with black hoods that told her she had been taken down by the Justice Riders, only today they had ventured forth in broad daylight.

She opened her mouth to speak just as a rag whipped across her mouth and sealed her lips. The man kneeling behind her tied the cloth ends and knotted them tightly. Then she was blinded in the same fashion. She could no longer see what was happening, but she felt the rope being loosened and the loop being pulled off her.

"Get up," the man said. She struggled to her feet, her back and leg pain excruciating now. "Now, I'm going to help you back on your buckskin. For now, I will leave your hands free to hold onto the saddle horn, so long as you don't tamper with the gag and blindfold. If you don't do like I tell you, I'll be hogtieing you and tossing you over the horse's back like a deer carcass. We got a two or three-hour ride ahead, and I doubt if you would like that much. Nod, if you understand."

She nodded. The man grasped her arm roughly and guided her to the horse, lifting her hand to the saddle horn. He helped her foot find the stirrup, and she could feel his hand kneading her buttocks as she swung into the saddle with his unnecessary boost. She settled into the saddle, grasping the saddle horn, feeling powerless without control of the buckskin's reins, yet comforted by the familiar feel of the critter beneath her.

The man spoke to the others. "We can't risk being seen. We'll head into the foothills and take the deer trail through the trees. It will slow us some, but I ain't chancing running in to somebody that might cause trouble. We'd have to kill them, and I don't want to leave a blood trail."

When they moved out, she learned quickly that she was embarking on a painful journey. Every step sent sharp needle jabs to her back, but eventually she became almost oblivious to it. The fear and apprehension of what lay ahead turned the pain to mere annoyance.

The riders were for the most part silent as they rode along the trail. Tree branches whipped her face early on, but she quickly learned to ride with her head nearer to her horse's neck. They stopped once at a stream to allow the horses to drink. Her gag was removed then to allow her to drink from a canteen that left a tobacco taste and sticky substance on her lips. Somebody's chew, she supposed, but she no longer cared.

Without being able to see the location of the sun in the sky, she had no idea how much time had elapsed since her capture. It felt like she had been in the saddle for hours, the faceless man had said it would take two or three hours to reach their destination. She wondered how her abductors knew where they might intercept her. Of course, the Saturday morning trip to her office had been her habit for some years, weather permitting, so any inquiries about her routine would have quickly yielded that information.

Of course, Cletus Tate would have been aware of her Saturday trips to town, and she had no doubt that his orders had triggered her seizure. She had threatened him, and he was simply removing the threat. She did not know why these men bothered with the hoods. She could not imagine that there was any intention to release her, but these riders likely were unaware of her fate. Otherwise, why did they bother to capture her like running down some wild animal? Why not just shoot her and be done with it? That gave her hope that she might be held for ransom or as a hostage for some purpose, but it seemed unlikely.

How long before she was discovered missing? It could be late afternoon before the girls became concerned. Jasmine might ride to town and check at the livery and her office. She would eventually go to Grant's cabin. After that he would take charge, and a search would start. The thought of his quiet intelligence and unflagging persistence brought a bit of reassurance. Her task was to stay alive. Every minute she could buy would increase her chances of survival. Grant would find her dead or alive. She would try to make it the latter.

The horses slowed and she heard the bawling of cattle and nickering of other horses nearby. "I'll take it from here, boys. Let me get this woman off the buckskin. Then you get the horses to the stable and put them up. I've got to introduce the boss to his guest."

The man's fingers lingered again where she did not want them when he assisted her off her mount. He grabbed her roughly and pulled her along up a gentle slope. He stopped abruptly. "Steps," he said, nearly dragging her up three steps and onto a wooden platform, obviously a porch. He knocked, and the door opened instantly, offering a burst of welcome heat.

"I saw you coming, Carl. Bring the young lady in." Reaper. It had to be with that growly, distinctive voice Ginger had told her about, a voice once heard that would not be forgotten. She was pushed through the doorway, stumbling on a rug just inside.

Reaper said, "Remove the gag and blindfold. They probably served no purpose." The thought of removal of the impediments brightened her some until it occurred to her that once she saw Reaper's face the prospect for her voluntary release diminished.

First, the gag came off and then the blindfold. When the light struck her eyes, she blinked repeatedly before she brought the room's occupants into focus. A towering white-haired, visage with what some called a Van Dyke beard and moustache stood in front of her appearing like the stereotypical devil some artists drew, a wicked grin seemingly pasted on his face.

Next to her was the hooded man, Carl, her escort to hell. Across the room near the fireplace stood a stout clean-shaven man with an impassive face, who seemed more an observer than participant in this meeting. She had not a clue what was on the agenda here and thought it best she did not know.

Reaper said, "Carl, you may go now. Tell Marty at the cook's shack to send up an extra plate with lunch."

"Will do, boss."

"And Marty?"

"Yeah, boss."

"You probably do not require a hood at this place."

"Yes, boss. I guess I'm just getting used to it." He turned toward the door, removing the hood on his way out, so all she caught sight of was the back of his head.

Reaper said, "Now, Miss Locke, why don't you remove your coat and be seated in front of the fireplace. I suspect you would enjoy the warmth after a long ride in the cold." He nodded toward the sturdy man. "And that's Danek. He doesn't talk much, but you will not find him unpleasant as we get acquainted over the next several days. Danek, do you suppose you could fetch a mug of hot coffee for the lady?"

Danek nodded and left the room. This was bizarre. She was being treated like an honored house guest. Reaper had mentioned "several days." Perhaps her demise was not yet imminent.

Chapter 43

IT WAS NEARLY four o'clock. It was not like Hannah to be in town this late on Saturday. More commonly she was home by one o'clock, rarely later than three. Jasmine turned to Primrose who was reading next to the fireplace. "Rose. Something's wrong, Hannah's never this late Saturdays. I am going to ride into town and check at the office and livery. Would you mind starting chores?"

Primrose put the book down and got up. "Of course. I've been worried, too. I just didn't want to seem silly."

"It's not silly. Something's wrong. I can feel it."

"Now you are scaring me. You are almost always right when you get this way."

"My mother in me, I guess. I am probably wrong. She will probably be riding down the road toward home, and I will meet up with her. If so, I won't be gone long."

"Do you think you should tell Grant?"

"Not yet. I don't want to worry him, too, if it turns out to be nothing. I just wish I had headed for town an hour ago."

When she arrived in Lockwood, she went directly to the Ramsey and Locke office, hitching the buckskin mare she had drafted to service at the hitching post out front. She had snatched up Hannah's extra key from the key rack next to the house entryway and let herself into the building. It was dusky, but window light was adequate, and she rushed to Hannah's office. The door was open, and she stepped in. As expected, no Hannah. There was a chill in the building suggesting the coal stove had not been fed today. Hannah was not inclined to suffering when it came to tolerating cold.

She exited and locked the office, mounted the gelding, and rode down the street to Fletcher's Livery. Both Enos and Trouble were standing just inside. She dismounted and led her mount inside.

"Why, Missy Jasmine, what you doing here this time of day?" Enos asked.

"Has Hannah been here today?"

"Nope. Kind of unusual. I keep her usual stall ready for the buckskin on Saturdays, but she didn't show up this morning. Figured she had things to do at the Box L— or took a day off, God forbid."

Trouble must have seen the tears starting to roll down her cheeks. He stepped closer. "Jazzie, what is it?"

"Something's happened to her, something awful. I know it has. She left for town at sunrise like she always does. I waited too long for her to come home. I should have ridden in earlier. It will be dark soon."

Trouble wrapped his arms consolingly about her, not the Trouble Yates she had always known, but she drew comfort from his embrace. "Now, just calm down. She's probably fine. I'm going to saddle up Tag and ride back to the Box L with you, so I can check for sign while there is still some daylight. She might be home now, but if not, it seems something changed her destination on the way in this morning. Maybe she's at Grant's."

He eased away from her. "Enos, I think Ozzie's handling the sheriff's office today. Would you hobble over and alert him about our concerns and ask him to stay close by till he hears from me? I don't think we need to call Jim in on this yet."

"Hobble? You're talking like I'm a stove-up old man."

"Walk, run, whatever suits you. Just get word to Ozzie."

"Humph."

"Now, Jazzie, just give me five minutes to get saddled up, and we'll take us a ride."

Trouble and Jasmine rode their mounts at a walk on the two-mile trip to the Box L. Trouble's eyes were fixed on the rutted dirt road and about halfway to the ranch he signaled a halt and dismounted and handed her Tag's reins. Jasmine thought he looked like a birddog walking back and forth across the road and then out onto the adjacent grassland bending over and studying something on the ground.

"Stay here," he said and began to run southwesterly for several minutes before he stopped suddenly and dropped to his knees. She could see him studying the ground and raising his head up from time to time and casting his eyes over the landscape. He got up and raced back to Jasmine.

"Tell me what you are doing. What are you finding?" she asked.

"I think Hannah met up with some riders, and they took her."

"Took her. I don't understand. Why?"

"Don't know. I can read some sign, but I'm not the best. It looks like some riders chased her down. Somebody was laying in the dry grass, and there were some boot tracks at that spot, so a rider got off his horse. Ground's frozen, so the tracks aren't deep, but the soft ground helps us some. I'm guessing she made a run, and they caught up with her there. After that, the horses all headed on northwest."

"My God. I don't believe this. What do we do?"

"You go tell Grant. Ask him to meet me at the sheriff's office. I will talk to Ozzie, and one of us will ride out to Jim's and Ma's place and tell Jim. The sheriff has got to know about this. No sense in him coming in before daylight, though."

Chapter 44

GRANT AND GIDEON were absorbed with a chess match when Lovey started whining, bounced off her sleeping rug and went to the door. He assumed she wanted outside to relieve herself. The big pup had become reliable about tending to her chores the past several weeks, and he was glad to interrupt the match and let her out for a few minutes. Then he noticed that Sarge had awakened from his snooze and was staring at the door with ears erect.

Grant got up and retrieved his Colt revolver from the gun belt suspended on the peg near the door. There was a rider approaching the house from the direction of the wagon trail. At first, he could not identify the visitor in the dusk that was beginning to settle over the valley, but as the rider neared, he recognized Jasmine and stepped out onto the porch to welcome her. When the door opened, Lovey ran out to greet the visitor, barking now but not threateningly.

"Jasmine," he said, as she reached the hitching rail, "what in blazes are you doing out this late in the day? Come in and get warmed up."

She dismounted and hitched her horse. "I've got awful news, Grant," Jasmine said as she stepped onto the porch. "I'm scared. Almost as much as when those kidnappers took me."

He put his arm about her shoulder and guided her into the house. "We'll go inside, and you can tell me about it." Lovey raced through the doorway before he shut the door.

"Hi, Jasmine," Gid said, still seated at the chess table but looking at the newcomer. "What's the matter?"

Gid must have observed the tears that streamed down her cheeks, Grant figured. He helped her off with her coat, "Now, tell me what this is all about."

"Hannah's gone. She didn't come home. I went to her office, and she wasn't there, and Trouble thinks someone has taken her."

She spoke so rapidly he could hardly understand her. "Whoa, start from the beginning, slowly. And let's sit down by the fireplace."

Seated, Jasmine told her story, and Grant asked questions as she proceeded, speaking with a calm he did not feel. "So I am to meet Trouble at the sheriff's office. Is that correct?"

"Yes. He didn't think a search could start before sunrise, but he wanted to talk with you tonight."

"I wouldn't have it any other way. Trouble Yates is a sixteen-year-old with a thirty-year-old head most of the time. We will find Hannah and bring her back. That's a promise. Now, I've got to figure out what to do with the creatures here."

"They can all come over to the Box L and stay as long as need be."

"We will put a few things together for the night, and I will help you make the move to the house. I'm afraid Lovey must go with you, too."

"That's fine. She and Scamp can enjoy a family reunion. What about Sarge?"

"He will be happier if he stays behind. I have meat scraps in the icebox and a dish and water bowl next to the icebox. If you can add some coal to the cookstove in the morning, that will keep him warm enough. Don't believe him if he tells you otherwise. The sandbox will need cleaning. Bring Gid with you. He knows about the cat's care. That's one of his responsibilities."

He turned to Gid. "Get your things together, Gid. You and Lovey will be staying overnight with Jasmine. If I will be gone longer, she will bring you back to get anything else you need."

The worry showed on the young man's face. "How long will you be?"

"As long as it takes. You will be fine with the girls. I am leaving to bring Hannah home."

Chapter 45

GRANT HAD HELPED himself to the chair behind the sheriff's desk. He had spent some days there as an accidental sheriff, and he felt comfortable in the spot at thinking time. Trouble Yates sat across from him, waiting for Grant to speak.

"This has got to be related to a conversation Hannah had with Cletus Tate the other day. I will explain later. It's the gang that's been in the lynching business lately. That's what has me worried. They seem to thrive on killing, and women are not exempt. We've got to get after them at daylight. Will you ride with me?"

"Yep, count on it, but we will need more than the two of us."

"I was thinking Bushwa for one."

"Makes sense. He will bitch about it, but he'd be pissed if we left him out."

"What's your chances of tracking these riders?"

"Hard to say. I know a few things, but not as much as some. I'd say get Ethan Ramsey."

"Hannah's law partner?"

"Yeah, he needs to know anyhow. He used to be chief of scouts at Fort Laramie before he took up lawyering. He can track a field mouse over granite rock. I've heard that Sioux called him 'the Puma' because he could get into the middle of a war party's camp without anybody having a clue."

"How do I contact him?"

"As soon as we're done talking, I'll head out to the Lazy R. I can get there, tell Ethan about Hannah and get back in less than two hours."

Grant said, "I would like Jeb Oaks to ride with us, too. She Bear would be welcome, but she's got the little tykes to look after, and somebody's got to be in charge at the general store."

"They might fuss some about who gets to come, but they live just outside of town. I'll stop there on the way out to Ethan's."

"I will head into the foothills and recruit Bushwa. Do you think he will be home or will he be at Maggie White's?"

"Enos says they're not keeping company right now. Bushwa and Maggie had words a few weeks back, and she kicked him out and told him to not come back. You know Enos. He's trying to find out what it's all about, but Bushwa ain't talking. I saw him a few days back. Whiskers are coming back, but it will be a spell before bugs can nest on his chin."

Trouble got up to leave. "I thought about something yesterday that I was going to mention to Jim, but I ought to tell you."

"What's that?" Grant asked.

"Well, Enos was telling me about your interest in a rider of an Appaloosa. Ain't—aren't many around these parts, and I saw one out by the sawmill the other day when I was talking to Birch Reagan about our plans."

"I don't recall hearing about our plans."

"Sorry. I will bring you up to date when we get Hannah back. Anyhow, a loaded buckboard and three riders came past the sawmill headed west across the North Laramie. Unfriendly bunch. Didn't even wave. One of the men rode a handsome Appaloosa gelding. It seems likely they were part of the hired guns outfit. Either Birch or I would have recognized any locals."

Grant said, "And you told me the riders that took Hannah headed northwest, so that makes sense. Something else to think about. I have information that the Appaloosa rider said that it takes him about five hours to make a trip to town and back. Be thinking about where that might put us. Are you acquainted with a Sioux chief that goes by the name of Talks-Too-Much?"

"Yep. Everybody knows Talks-Too-Much."

"He had a dream that the man with the pale horse lived on the west side of the valley in a canyon that opened its mouth to let him in. Sounded farfetched to me, but he appears to be right about the side of the valley."

"Only one other choice."

"Yeah, that's what I figured. Let's get on with our work."

Chapter 46

GRANT CAUGHT A few hours' sleep in one of the jail cells and was pleased to find that Ozzie had a bag of sweet rolls in the office and hot coffee brewing when he walked out of the cell block shortly before sunup. A kerosene lamp lit up the cold room, and Ozzie was scooping coal from the coal box into the new potbelly stove. "I slept in the cell next to yours for a spell and didn't tend to the stove," the deputy said.

"I had trouble falling asleep, but when I did, I was dead for a few hours."

"Snatched up the first rolls out of The Chowdown oven this morning. Got plenty in case some of the others ain't ate yet."

The sheriff arrived as Grant was finishing his coffee and roll. When he walked in the door, he said, "When do we pull out?"

Grant knew Tolliver was going to resist his suggestion, but he hoped the sheriff would see the sense of it. "Jim, Trouble and I have recruited a posse. I think you and your deputies should stay in Lockwood."

Tolliver bristled, and his eyes narrowed. "Hey, mister. You ain't sheriff here anymore. I decide who goes on this posse."

"I'm not challenging your authority. But hear me out."

Tolliver poured himself a mug of coffee, plucked a roll from the bag and went to his chair behind the desk. "At least you didn't take my chair from me. I'm listening."

Fortunately, Grant had claimed the visitor's chair when he got up. "You need to be here, Jim. God knows how long we'll be out. What if Bobby comes in with an important message? Maybe something that needs attention right away. What if that gang takes a notion to hit someplace in town like they did the church? There is too much we don't know about all this. Somebody should keep an eye on Cletus Tate when he is in town. And the guy on the Appaloosa if he shows up. I've got a personal reason for going after this bunch. You've got a wider responsibility to the whole community."

"Damned if you shouldn't have been a law wrangler. I don't like it much, but I guess I'll have to sit this out."

By sunrise, Trouble Yates had arrived with Blue and his own sorrel gelding, Tag. "All you need are your saddle-bags and bedroll," he said. "Jeb will be along with a pack mule and supplies to keep us fed if we're out longer than we expect."

Grant said, "I talked to Bushwa. He was ready to feed me some buckshot when I rode into his place last night, but once I convinced him that I was a friend, he listened to my story and promised to be here. He never even lit a lamp, so we talked in darkness. Or I should say I talked. After he threatened to shoot me, he didn't say more than a few words."

Trouble said, "I hear heavy steps on the boardwalk right now. Betting that's Bushwa."

Bushwa Sparks walked in looking nothing like the cleaned-up version Grant saw the night of the barn dance. Sometimes, Grant thought the big man worked at being ugly. His scraggly skunk-striped beard had not returned yet, but it had a good start with several weeks' whiskery growth. When he saw the sweet rolls, he grinned, displaying the gap left by a missing front tooth.

"Danged if this morning ain't looking better. I'll take two of them things for a start, if you got enough."

Ozzie said, "There is plenty, Bushwa. I made allowances for you showing up."

Evidently, Ozzie was not disturbed by his mother's break-up with Bushwa. The door opened again, and Jeb Oaks, the former buffalo soldier, stepped in, followed by Ethan Ramsey.

The men scattered about the room, standing as they finished up the sweet rolls and emptied their coffee mugs.

"We'll be riding out in a few minutes," Grant said. "Trouble will lead us to where we think the raiders caught up to Hannah. He thinks we should be able to pick up a trail easy enough unless they head into the foothills where the footing tends to turn to rock. We are hoping Ethan can help us if that happens."

"Sometimes, you just can't pick up tracks," Ramsey said. "But there is other sign if you know what to look for. I want Hannah back at her office desk as soon as possible, and we're going to find her. There is one concern I have, though."

"What's that?" Grant asked.

"Word from the Sioux farmsteads is that the holy men are seeing a snowstorm coming, not just a dusting either. Lots of the white stuff and a mean wind, too, maybe a full-fledged blizzard. Sun is coming up now but look to the northwest. There are clouds drifting this way. It may not amount to what the Sioux are saying, but there will be something by late morning."

"I got three canvas tarps on the pack mule, Ethan," Jeb Oaks said.

"We just can't be slowed down," Grant said. "I don't know what these men expected to accomplish by taking Hannah, but once she knows their identity, they can't turn her loose." And once he knew their identity, they could choose to die by the gun or to wait for the rope.

Chapter 47

HANNAH WAS SURPRISED to find that the sun was rising when she awakened. Exhaustion had overtaken her by the time she was shown to the little boxlike room with the single window and a mattress with folded blankets atop stretched out on the floor. She had tossed her coat down, pulled off her boots and collapsed on the lumpy, straw-filled mattress, pulled the blankets over her and dropped instantly to sleep.

She sat up. There was a chill in the room even though the door had been left open, allowing heat from the parlor fireplace to drift in. The situation was bizarre and baffling. She had been treated like a house guest since her arrival. She knew, of course, that any attempt to escape would be thwarted so she played the role of house guest for now. Where would she go if she tried to run? She had been blindfolded the entire journey and did not even know where she was at. She was not foolish enough to believe that she would be released for ransom as a part of some grand bargain. She could just try to buy time.

She did not intend to die. She would think of something. In the meantime, she would keep her eyes and ears open and learn. She pulled on her boots and stood up, brushing her hair back and retying the ribbon that held her ponytail in place. There was no mirror, and that was fine. She must look a fright and did not care.

She stepped out of the room and saw Danek, the quiet man, sitting in front of the fireplace. She wondered if he lived in that cushioned cowhide chair near the open fire. Reaper was not in the room. Perhaps he still slept. She hoped he would sleep the day away. She got chills just looking at the man. Danek, for some unexplainable reason, was a calming presence.

Danek hoisted himself from the chair. "Good morning, ma'am. I will head out to the chuck house and pick up breakfast plates. Coffee pot on the stove. Reaper's out talking to some of the men. Move about as you like but stay close by." He disappeared out the door.

She walked slowly through the house, the first time she had been left alone, taking inventory of possible exits. She found that the front entryway was the only door. Her own window was a possibility, but where would she go? She had visited the privy out back several times the previous day, but still dazed from the tumble off her mount, had not been very observant.

Danek had said she could move freely if she stayed nearby, and it was time for a visit to the privy. She went out the door, and this time she studied her prison setting, moving toward her destination at a leisurely pace. They seemed to be in a box canyon without an entrance or exit. Obviously, that would not be the case. Her eyes caught sight of the wagon trail that approached the building site from east. The distance was such, however, that it disappeared before it reached the canyon wall, but when it faded from her sight, it had appeared headed to a dead-end wall. Possibly the canyon made a sharp turn at that end that gave an illusion of solid wall from her perspective. Regardless, it would be the only route out wherever it led.

She identified the stable, where she presumed she would find her buckskin and tack. If not, she had no doubt she could handle any mount. But how to escape to the exit? Once out with any head start, they would not catch her—not alive anyway. It appeared there were two bunkhouses with a chuck house in between and a few other smaller buildings with unclear purposes.

She noticed a fringe of cedar trees and undergrowth along one canyon wall that would provide some cover if she tried to escape afoot. Perhaps she could make it to a ranch not far distant or encounter a search party that she knew would be out by now. This would be impossible to plan for because she had no notion of where she was at.

She saw Danek departing the chuck house with a covered platter in each hand, so she hurried on to complete her mission. By the time he reached the house, she was at the kitchen sink dipping water from a bucket to pour into the handwash pan, grateful for the bar of lye soap on the strip of counter framing the sink, annoyed at the lack of a towel that forced her to use her britches to dry her hands.

Danek set her tin plate on the small kitchen table and carried his own to his favorite chair near the fireplace. Apparently, he was not interested in socializing. Well, neither was she. She poured a mug of coffee, sat down and lifted the cloth cover from the plate. Two biscuits and a healthy serving of beans, not what she would consider a gourmet breakfast. No butter or honey either. She shrugged, snatched up her fork and started eating. The biscuits she found tasty. Strange how the peril she was in had not subdued her appetite.

When she was finished, she boiled some water, went into the parlor and retrieved Danek's plate and fork and washed their plates and utensils. He had looked at her questioningly when she took the plate and she had enjoyed his confusion. The man seemed lost in thought most of the time, and her gesture obviously caught him off balance.

After setting the clean plates aside for return to the bunkhouse, she joined Danek near the fireplace, and they sat silently for an hour or more before Reaper came through the door. "Good morning, Miss Locke," he said, shucking his coat and hanging it on the peg rack near the door. "I trust you and Danek have been having a stimulating conversation." He laughed, or she thought he did. It was hard to tell with that growly voice.

Reaper claimed his own chair and spoke to Danek, seemingly oblivious to her presence. "I was concerned about clouds to the northwest bringing snow in, so I sent Joker to town with a message. I told him to go the long way. In the unlikely event that he would be spotted by searchers, I did not want him detained anywhere near this place. If he is stopped and questioned, he is just a cowhand passing through looking for a job."

"Seems a strange way to pass through going south considering there's no place to come from north of here."

"Nobody but you would think about such things."

Danek shrugged.

Reaper continued. "He's taking the message to Tate that we've done what he asked. Joker will stay the night in town because he might not be able to find our contact right away when he hits town, and Tate likely won't be in his office till tomorrow. Joker will wait for a reply to bring back. We won't wait beyond Tuesday. Whatever he says or doesn't say, he can forget about that little public show he wants."

Reaper was not making any effort to hide the fact that Tate was the snake's head. That did not bode well for her. It was also apparent that, at best, Tuesday would be the last day of her life if she did not make a move. If Grant found her later today or tomorrow, she had a chance, and she tried to convince herself that he would. But unfettered optimism was not a part of her character.

Reaper turned to Hannah. "Now, young lady, why don't you tell me about your family?"

This man was a lunatic, but she was willing to play his little games. During this pretend dialogue, she might learn something useful, and it would beat staring silently at the fire. Besides, it was unnerving to sit silently in a room with a man who planned to kill you.

"I am unmarried, as you likely know. I am guardian for two teenaged girls. I was born and raised in Kansas, where my father and two of my brothers still reside . . ."

Chapter 48

AS ANTICIPATED, THE so-called Justice Riders had been easy enough for Ethan Ramsey and Trouble to track until they reached the rockier foothills. Grant signaled for a halt until they picked up the trail again. "What do you think, Ethan?" he asked.

The former Army scout, dressed in faded denims, a hip-length buffalo-hide coat and a beaver-skin cap with a flap that fell over his neck and ears, looked nothing like the vested and suited lawyer Grant was accustomed to seeing. Ramsey spoke softly but clearly, "Ten minutes, and I will tell you where they went. They wouldn't be climbing higher if they are bringing a wagon in and out of their hideaway. Ground's rough for horseback and tree growth is getting heavy. They would be wanting to stay out of sight from anybody in the lower valley lands."

Ramsey and Trouble broke away from the others to search out the trail. Grant was confident the two would pick up sign quickly. Ramsey did not seem to miss anything, his eyes constantly sweeping over the terrain in front of him much like a man might read a book.

Bushwa interrupted his thoughts. "You said you had reason to think the hideout was maybe two and a half or three hours out from town."

"Yeah. I hope it's not more than that."

"But that's for a lone rider on horseback. We ain't moving at a third that gait. Even if we don't got to look for sign no more, if we got to stay in the higher country we'll be moving like damned turtles in comparison."

Grant said, "They would have reached their hideout last night anyway. Main thing is that we find the place."

"It's gonna snow, you know."

"I don't know what I'd do without your optimism."

"Optimism? You're using them damn writer's words again."

Grant had not needed Bushwa's remarks to fan the flames of worry. He was aware that the sun had disappeared and that clouds were roiling in the sky to the northwest. It was likely already snowing on the higher slopes. His memories of the struggle with the snow during investigation of the Ridge killings were still fresh, and this time there was no prospect of retreat to a warm bunkhouse and a belly-stuffing feast.

Jeb Oaks, who had been quiet most of their ride, said, "We'd best keep our eyes open for a place to hole up. I'm guessing we ain't got more than two hours before we're done moving for a spell."

Grant could not argue the point. The truth would arrive too soon, he feared. How much precious time would be lost to the fickleness of winter in this high country?

Ramsey and Trouble returned shortly to report picking up the trail. "They entered the trees that cover the slopes along the edge of the valley," Ramsey said. "Plenty of broken branches to show the path they took. They picked a deer trail into the trees. Generously, they left a few piles of horse dung to mark their entry. My five-year-old son could have picked up this trail. I'm guessing they will be following this for as long as it doesn't veer away from their destination. We will need to ride single file for a spell. I'll take the lead and keep my eye out for any change in direction. I would like to have Trouble stay just behind me."

"How long can we ride if the snow comes in?"

"Hard to say. The trees will provide a windbreak that should ward off drifts for a while. It mostly depends on how fierce the wind is and how much snow falls. I promise we'll keep on if humanly possible, but we've got to be alert to possibilities for taking shelter. If it gets impossible to keep moving on the trail, we've got to be on the lookout for a place that offers some shelter to us and the horses. Trouble said there used to be several trapper's shacks above here. He is going to take to the higher ground at first opportunity and see if he can scout out some potential shelter. He might pick up prospects from an overview."

"Take the lead then. There's no time to waste."

An hour later, the snow began to fall, at first big flakes drifting slowly to the earth, but later the flakes turned into an indistinguishable mass like buckets of flour being dumped from the skies. Trouble peeled away from the others angling up a narrower path that forked off the main trail. His sorrel gelding, Tag, handled the steep incline like a mountain goat, Grant thought. He supposed the owner rider had given the critter plenty of experience.

Ethan Ramsey had guessed right, though. The juniper and cedar branches caught the snow, weighing down and bending over the trail and forming an arch of sorts through which the riders could pass and take a snow shower on their faces when they brushed against a dangling branch. The trees blunted the worst force of the increasing wind for some time, but after three hours on the deer path, Grant could see that time was running out. The trail had begun to fill with snow, nearly a foot deep now, slowing the party even more and causing the scattering of rocks just beneath the thin layer of sediment on the path to slicken and make the footing treacherous for the mounts.

He started at the sound of a gunshot from higher in the foothills. Ramsey signaled a halt, and Grant reined Blue up beside the lawyer-scout.

Ramsey said, "Trouble's found shelter. We just need to get to him." Ramsey pulled his Winchester from its scabbard, levered a cartridge into the chamber, pointed it skyward and fired an answering shot. "Let's move," he said.

Ten minutes later, Ramsey raised his hand again. He pointed to a narrow stream crossing the path and bouncing and splashing over rocks as it raced down the hillside on its journey across the grasslands below to the river. "There is a strip of ground along the stream that I think we can climb higher into the hills."

It was slow and tricky going but they reached the top of the plateau-like ground at the base of the mountain slopes farther up. The first thing Grant noticed was black smoke curling upward behind the curtain of snow to the north. "That's got to be Trouble," he said. "Let's give the horses a chance to drink and head that way."

Jeb said, "If we can find a place to shelter the critters, I've got two nights' grain, but there won't be any grass that ain't buried."

"That will be something anyhow," Grant said. "We just have got to get them out of this blasted wind."

They moved ahead toward the smoke, and Grant was relieved when they came upon a log cabin that had seen better days and a three-walled stable with a sagging roof not more than twenty feet distant from the cabin. At least the remaining walls would shield the animals from the worst of the bitter wind. Trouble's gelding was already hitched inside. Grant dismounted and hammered on the door, and Trouble appeared.

"You got room for visitors?" Grant asked.

"Darn right. I need more bodies to warm this place up. Put your critters up. Tag will be glad for company. Bring all your tack and gear inside. It'll be tight but a hell of a lot better than sleeping in a snow drift."

When they finished unpacking the mule and hauling all the supplies inside, along with personal gear and saddles, Grant and Jeb tended to feeding the horses that were tied to upright posts that supported what was left of the dilapidated stable. He hoped they did not pull the structure down.

Finally, with all gathered inside the single-room cabin, he had a chance to survey the accommodations. Nobody had shed their coats yet. A fire crackled in a fireplace with the mortar on many stones crumbling away, but cracks between uncaulked logs in the walls were admitting too much wind and snow to keep significant heat in.

Jeb said, "We can hang my canvas tarps on the wind sides of the walls. That should help. Get them on snug, and we should be able to keep most of the snow out."

Trouble nodded toward the dead wood stacked against one side of the little fireplace. "Got enough wood to get us at least through the night, but a lot of it's wet, and worse yet, half of it is cedar that you have to beg to burn. And then it smokes and doesn't put out much heat. I thought we could mix it with some dead oak limbs I came across and broke up."

Grant said, "You did fine. This is a palace compared to where we could have ended up."

"I'll get some coffee brewing," Jeb said, "and I can put some supper together later if some of you want to get started with the tarps."

During the daylight that remained, Grant was distracted by the chores that needed to be done to shelter the men and horses from the worst of the blizzard that had descended on the valley and surrounding mountains. Evening, however, brought his full focus to the mission and Hannah's dilemma. Time was precious. What if the snow did not cease for days?

He only half-listened to Bushwa's tale of his romance with Maggie White. "Pretty enough woman," Bushwa said. "Wouldn't go to the dance with me unless I made myself—what did she call it—'presentable.' Now there is a highfalutin word for you, especially for a woman who makes her living as a moonshiner. Anyhow, I went to the barber's, gave up my beard, cut my hair and even used the backroom tub. Got a new suit of clothes. All this for some expectations."

Trouble chimed in. "What were you expecting, Bushwa?"

"Well, what in the hell else would a man expect from a woman? I figured that was a ticket to her bed."

"Ain't that easy, Bushwa."

"You're just a shavetail kid. What would you know?"

Trouble shrugged.

Bushwa continued, "Anyhow, she said I cleaned up good, and she went to the dance with me. Danced with her some, but I had to play my banjo in the band. I even sung a tune or two with old Grant there. She seemed to think high of that. So I take her all the way home to her place, and I figured I had my ticket, maybe two or three. It was getting late, and I figured to stay over. Well, that notion died quick when we drove the buggy in to her place—one I'd paid good money to Trouble's livery to rent, I should add."

"You got a special rate," Trouble said.

"Special? You're damned thieves over there. You need some competition. Well, it don't matter none now, I guess. Anyhow, I helped her off the buggy, gentleman that I was, and I waited for her to invite me in for a drink. You know, it's good to start these things with a drink. She holds out her hand, and I take it, thinking she's going to lead me to her bed. You know what she does?"

Jeb said, "Tell us."

"She shakes my damned hand and thanks me for a nice evening. Shakes my hand like we was strangers just met up or something. She turns and heads for the door. And me, I'm hornier than an old bull elk by now. Been a coon's age since I had me a woman I didn't pay for."

Jeb said, "So that's when you decided you were done with her?"

"There's more. I just plain asked her if she was going to ask me in for a beer or something. She turns and says to me that she figured I wouldn't want to stop at that, and I says we could just see what happened. Figured my charm would get me home. You know what she says?"

"I'm waiting," Jeb said.

"She asks if I am intending to court her. And I says, 'If I say yes, does that get me in the door?' She says, 'Maybe, but don't try to go farther or you'll get your brains splattered against my clean wall. Nothing more unless we get married.' That was it. I hightailed for the buggy. I just ain't the marrying kind. Don't want to answer to no female. And why in the hell would she want to get married? She's tied that knot three times. Made herself a widow once, I heard. I ain't chancing that. And I gave up my beard with winter coming on."

Grant shook his head. He considered Bushwa a friend, but it annoyed him when the man blabbed on about things that would be better left private between a man and a woman. He figured Maggie was fortunate Bushwa had not bitten at the suggestion that he come courting. On the other hand, perhaps her words were chosen to chase him off. He pulled off his boots and crawled into the bedroll he had been sitting on.

Chapter 49

SHERIFF JIM TOLLIVER paced the floor of his office. The storm had swept in and dropped a good foot of snow on the town. The wind had died down, but at midmorning the shops were still closed as the merchants worked to clear snow from the boardwalks in front of their establishments. Ozzie White opened the door and stepped in, stomping the snow off his boots on a dirty towel Tolliver had dropped there for that purpose.

"Snowplow's starting to clear Main Street," Ozzie said. "Trouble saw to it that Birch Reagan was ready to step in while he was gone. Birch has got a couple of fellas he hired on at the sawmill working with shovels to help out. They'll do the boardwalks and such in front of the buildings for a fair price. You got to give Trouble credit. He's always ready to look after these things."

Ron Schwab

If there was a dollar to be made from it, the sheriff thought. Sometimes, he was a bit unsettled by his stepson's enterprise and ambition, but he realized that if not for people like Brady Yates, many tasks would be left undone. Brady, of course, could produce a dozen quotes from the philosopher Adam Smith on the subject.

Tolliver hated snow, wondering sometimes why he could not have fallen in love with a woman when he was on a U. S. Marshal's assignment in South Texas or Arizona. Last night, he had slept in a jail cell to avoid getting snowed in at home several miles from town, where his wife would be dealing with the storm consequences now. He knew that Sarah would have ample help, though. The Morris family lived directly across the river, and brothers Levi and Jacob would cross the bridge to see to chores and start clearing snow. If their older sister Samantha had not stayed in town, she would be there, too, and their mother, Millie Morris, would see that Sarah was looked after before the family went to work on their own place.

His nerves were on edge with concern about the men who had ridden out without him to pursue Hannah Locke's captors. He worried not only about Hannah but fretted about the unofficial posse that would have been hit by the blizzard out in the open range or foothills someplace. He reminded himself that these were seasoned men perfectly capable of looking after themselves. Trouble was twice his chronological age in experience and knowledge about things that counted—except women maybe.

The door opened again, and he was surprised to see Bobby Callaway walk in, an envelope in his gloved hand. "Good morning, sheriff. Got something you might be looking for."

"A message from Cletus Tate?"

"Yep. I'm danged jittery about this. I ain't ready to die."

"We'll see you are protected, Bobby. Let's sit down at my desk."

When they were seated, Tolliver extended his hand for the envelope, and Bobby surrendered it. Tolliver said, "I'm surprised Tate's in town. He must have stayed over."

"He mostly stays in town at any weather threat. Keeps an apartment in the upstairs of the Stock Growers building."

"I didn't know that."

"Yeah. I suppose I shouldn't say this, but he keeps a woman who's not his wife there, too. She works in the Stock Growers' office, and I guess the apartment's really supposed to be her place, part of her pay."

"Interesting." Tolliver opened his penknife and began slitting the envelope open. He pulled out a handwritten note and read it aloud: "Kill her now. Forget about hanging tree." It was unsigned.

Ozzie, who as usual had his ears on the alert from his own desk, said. "He is ordering Miss Locke kilt."

Tolliver said, "No doubt about it. He's obviously talking about Hannah Locke. This will help hang the son-of-a-bitch. Good job, Bobby."

"Now what? Joker will be looking for me to give him a message or tell him there ain't none. It's a Monday morning. He will have his eyes out for me."

"Are you sure he made it to town with the storm and all?"

"Yeah. I checked at Gaston's Stable. That's where I put my horse up, too, so I had an excuse to drop by before I went to see Tate. I've been staying at the Home Range boarding house myself the past few weeks, trying to stay clear of my pa. Tate told us to put up our mounts there, since your stepson owns Fletcher's and old Enos noses around too much."

He decided not to tell Bobby that Enos Fletcher had been his undoing—or savior, depending on perspective. "Where would we find Joker?"

"He would have stayed at the Lockwood Hotel last night. He lives on the high side when he gets to stay over. We don't have a set place to meet. Easier not to get noticed that way. He generally comes into The Salty Dog to see if I'm there. Then he'll go up to the bar and get a drink, look around and be sure I see him. When he leaves, that tells me I need to go in a half hour or so. He will be some distance away and follow me around till we have sort of an accidental meeting. If he don't find me there he will just mosey around Main Street till we bump into each other. Ain't that hard to meet up in a small town."

"I wonder if the Salty Dog has opened up yet."

Ozzie said, "I seen Porky open the front door just before I came in. He should be open for business by now."

Tolliver said, "Bobby go get yourself a drink and find a table in the back. You might be the only customer in the place, but that won't make any difference. I'll be in the walkway between buildings across the street. Ozzie will be outside our office shoveling snow. He can see the Salty Dog from here if I need more help. I understand this Joker is a tall, skinny fellow. I will see him go in and will be waiting just outside the door when he walks out. If he is already there, he will leave, and I'll stay on his tail till I make an arrest. Ozzie will come in and tell you when Joker is on his way to jail."

"What about Tate?"

"He will be our next stop. With Joker and Tate both in jail. I don't think you need to worry about your personal safety, but we'll talk after those two are locked up, and agree on whether you need something more."

An hour later, Tolliver saw a man fitting Joker's description slip into The Salty Dog. He walked out from between the buildings where he had been hiding behind a stack of empty crates and walked across the recently plowed street. He pressed his back to the front of the stone-fronted building that had windows set too high for passersby to peer in and waited some ten feet from the doorway.

Tolliver reached under his thigh-length deerskin coat and slipped his Colt from its holster, concealing it behind his back while he waited. He was glad the storm had left Main Street nearly deserted. He did not have to wait long before the man called Joker stepped out looking first to his left, then to his right where his eyes met with Tolliver's. His right hand moved instinctively to push his unbuttoned coat aside and draw his pistol.

Tolliver aimed his Colt at the man's chest. "You are a dead man if you pull your gun. Now raise your hands and step this way."

"What's this about? I didn't do nothing." He took several steps toward the sheriff.

"Stop and turn around, hands behind your back." By this time, Ozzie had arrived. "Take his pistol, Ozzie, then get the handcuffs on his wrists. We'll get him in a cell before we make our next visit."

Chapter 50

TOLLIVER AND OZZIE stepped into the tiny reception area of the Big River Stock Growers Association. They were greeted by a buxom, middle-aged woman with gray-streaked, black hair who offered a friendly smile. "May I help you?" she asked.

"I am Sheriff Jim Tolliver, and this is my deputy, Ozzie White. I would like to speak with Mister Tate."

"If you can wait a few minutes, I will check with him and see if he is available." She stood to go talk with her boss.

Tolliver said, "Please just stay put, ma'am. If you would just direct us to his office, we can find our way."

Her face had soured now. "There is only one office and a meeting room. Just go down the hallway. His office is the last one at the back. The other doors are for the storage and conference rooms."

They walked down the hallway that went straight from the reception room. Speaking softly, Tolliver said, "Ozzie, you wait in the hallway with your gun ready just in case things turn nasty. Keep your eyes on me. I am going to open the door and walk in without warning. I'll leave the door open wide."

"I'll be ready."

When they reached the office door, Tolliver turned the knob and stepped in, startling Tate, who had a coffee mug pressed to his lips and spilled half the contents down the front of his shirt. "What in the hell?" Tate said. "What are you doing, Tolliver, barging in here like this?"

"You are under arrest, Mister Tate, and you will accompany us to your new residence pending formal charges."

"You're crazy. I ain't done nothing wrong."

"We'll start with multiple charges of conspiracy to commit murder. I'm sure the prosecutor can find a nice collection of others. There should be some hanging offenses in there someplace. Now stand up and walk around the desk, and we will fix you up with some bracelets and take you for a little walk."

Tate started to rise from his chair, and suddenly a gun appeared in his hand. He leveled it at the sheriff who was reaching for his own. An ear-deafening blast echoed in the room. Tolliver expected to feel pain, but with his Colt clutched in his hand now, he started to squeeze the trigger, then stopped.

Tate's pistol had dropped on the desk and the man was sinking to the floor, his eyes widened in disbelief, blood trickling from his chest and soaking his white shirt. When he disappeared behind the desk, Tolliver turned and saw Ozzie standing in the doorway, holstering his old Peacemaker.

"I owe you, Ozzie," the sheriff said. He walked around the desk and saw the rancher motionless on the floor. He gave Tate's body a nudge with his boot toe. "Tate's dead," he said. "Why don't you hike over to the undertaker's and get somebody over here? I'll break the news to the lady up front."

Chapter 51

HANNAH'S SPIRITS WERE brightened some by sunrays sifting through the makeshift gunnysack window curtains when she awakened. That meant the snowfall had ended at least for a time. The snowstorms could be tricksters in this mountain country, seemingly disappearing before returning with a surprise encore.

Her mood dampened when her mind turned to her dilemma. Each second pulled her nearer to death. With luck, she had today, but tomorrow would likely bring the end. She had always wondered what it was like when a man was sentenced to die, and he waited hours or days for his death. Perhaps, like she did, he held tight to that sliver of hope that someone would rescue him from his fate—or that he was simply participating in a nightmare from which he would awaken.

She still clung to the hope of rescue, but she was a realist. Any posse organized to pursue her captors would have been hammered by the storm, too, and any trace of the Justice Riders would have been erased by the fresh snow. It was not her nature to endure the agony of waiting. She would attempt escape today no matter how slim her chances. Now she must identify the opportunity.

The privy was calling her, so she sat up on her floor mattress and pulled on her boots. She had not disrobed because she was not granted the privacy of a closed door. Of course, closure would have denied her heat drifting in from the fireplace. Without a changing of undergarments and shirt and britches since her capture, she figured she must smell like rotting carrion by now.

She stepped out of the room and into the parlor where she found Danek at his usual station. His back was to her, but he spoke. "George brought some plates up from the chuck house. Yours is on the table."

"I've got to make a trip to the privy before I eat. Is that okay?"

"Go ahead."

When she returned, she sat down at the table to eat the hotcakes and sausages on her tin plate and poured a mug of coffee from the pot on the stove. From his fireplace chair, Danek said, "When you are finished, sit down in here. We will talk."

The man had been silent and still as the mannequin in the general store most of her incarceration here. She could not imagine what they would talk about.

As she ate, she noticed that Danek got up and went to her room. Searching for something? He came out and dropped in his chair again without evidence of any trophy in his hands. When her plate was clean, she added a bit of coffee to that in her mug to warm it and took the mug with her into the parlor and sat down, waiting for Danek to initiate any conversation. She was not forced to wait long.

"Reaper left just before you got up. He is directing several of the men on a project."

"A project?"

"Yes. They are to cut a young tree down to make a crosspiece to lash between those two cedars downslope from the bunkhouse."

"Why is he doing that?"

"He is constructing crude gallows for your hanging this afternoon. Four o'clock to be precise."

A chill swept down her spine, and she would swear her heart skipped a few beats. She sensed her hands trembling and set her coffee cup on the tea table. She struggled to recompose herself before responding. "I see."

"I am sorry to be so blunt, ma'am, but we both must make decisions now."

"I don't understand. It sounds like a decision has been made for me."

"You don't seem like the kind who will accept a death decree and wait to meet your fate."

"That may be true, but I fail to see why you are telling me this."

"Because I want no part of it. I have always thought of myself as a soldier. I served as an officer in the Wojsko Polski, the Polish Army, and was educated in my former country's academy. Since I came to this valley with Reaper, I have watched while he strung up innocent people, and I remained silent. In the past we were mercenaries in range wars, and we tracked down and lynched men who were likely guilty of rustling."

"Likely?"

"Yes, likely. I told myself that, anyhow. But Reaper's mind snapped somewhere along the trail. He draws no lines now. I have drawn mine. I am departing late this afternoon before the scheduled hanging. You must decide if you want to ride out with me."

"Yes, of course, I've got nothing to lose."

"You should be at the stable shortly before three o'clock. If Reaper is here you will use the pretense of visiting the privy and then go behind the rise that angles toward the stable. Can you read the sun well enough to estimate the time?"

"Well enough, I think."

"Can you handle a strong stallion?"

"I was raised on horseback. Not to brag, but I have not met the horse I could not handle."

"You will ride the pale horse. He will be saddled and your Winchester in its scabbard, extra cartridges in the saddlebags. Can you use that rifle, kill a man if need be?"

"Damn right. I have killed before. But my buckskin . . . why must I ride the pale horse?"

"We will bring your buckskin as a spare mount if possible. The pale horse will be your shield. Reaper worships the animal. His soul would shrink and die if the horse should be killed. He will not order his men to shoot at you if you are astride that horse."

"It could be nightfall before we get far. It will be slow-going in the snow."

"The night will be our friend. Listen to me now. You were blindfolded when you were brought here. The canyon opening is narrow, no more than ten feet wide, and it is almost impossible to see from a distance. It appears like a mere crevice in the face of a sheer stone wall. If I am not with you, seek out a depression in the ground that angles downslope to the east. That is the wagon trail that has been seldom used. It will be snow-covered, but in the daylight, you should still be able to pick it out. That will lead to the wagon road that takes you to Lockwood. The trail through the trees will be too dangerous and snowed in. Once out of the trees and on the grassland, the snow will slow you, but you should not encounter much drifting."

"But you will be with me?"

"That is my hope, but just in case . . ."

"The porch. Reaper is back."

"Go to your room. Look under your pillow. We will not likely talk again till later."

She got to the room just before the door opened. She looked under the pillow and pulled out the Derringer secreted there. She moved out of sight and examined the weapon. She collected Derringers and often carried one. This one was a two-shot Remington model with pivoting barrels, one atop the other that shifted for reloading. Both were loaded and ready to fire. She slipped it into her boot.

She heard Danek and Reaper talking and joined them in the parlor. Danek was standing near the door, slipping into his coat and seemingly oblivious to her presence. "I am going to eat with the others at the chuck house at noon," he told Reaper. "I'll order two plates brought up here. I don't know what we've got in the way of drifts to break down. You can only do so much with shovels, but maybe we can get the worst of any drifting between here and the canyon entrance out of the way. It would be nice to be able to get a wagon out for supplies when we need to."

"Do what suits you. I was out early. I'm going to catch some shuteye for a spell. Busy day ahead."

Hannah knew now what the plans for a busy day entailed. She pondered shooting the monster while he slept.

Chapter 52

WHEN GRANT TOSSED his bedroll aside and grabbed his boots, he was surprised to see that Jeb Oaks had already built up the fire and had a big pot of coffee brewing near the fireplace's edge. Ramsey and Trouble instantly joined him, and only Bushwa, who was stretched out a few feet from Grant's own blankets, remained undisturbed, his loud snoring assuring all that he was still very much alive.

"Coffee's ready, boys. Grab your mugs. I got a bag of cold biscuits to gnaw on, but that's the best I can offer this morning."

Grant saw sunglow through the empty window space behind the tarp and was relieved to see that the snow had stopped. He stood and stretched before retrieving his coat from the floor near his blankets. "I'm going to water the rocks and then check on the horses. Then I'll have my coffee and one of the biscuits."

When he opened the door and stepped outside, he was pleased to find the wind had swept the snow away from the area outside the door. He walked away from the house and relieved his bladder and then went to check on the horses. Blue nickered when he approached, and a cursory inspection confirmed that the horses had endured the storm well. Thankfully, the cold against his cheeks told him that the temperature had not dropped nearly as low as he feared it might. Last night's wind, which had evidently blown itself out, had made it seem much colder.

"Horses look good," Grant announced when he returned to the shack. "We will need to get them to water before we pull out. They would likely appreciate a bit of grain if we can spare it."

Jeb said, "We can. I'll see to it as soon as I get my own things gathered up. I'm hoping we can find a patch of uncovered grass along the way to let them graze for a bit." He nodded at the sleeping Bushwa. "What about him?"

Grant sighed. "I guess he is my burden." He walked over to the snoring mass buried in the blankets and gave Bushwa's backside a push with his booted foot. "Hey, old man, time to meet the sunrise. We got work to do."

Bushwa poked his head out of the pile of blankets like a turtle popping its head from a shell. Eyes squinting against the light, "Who you calling an old man?"

"The guy who can't get out of bed on his own."

"Humph. I'll be up in my own time."

"Well, we're not waiting for you. The rest of us are packing up."

"What's for breakfast?"

"Coffee and a cold biscuit."

"Rather eat me a horse apple."

"There are plenty of those behind the horses. You might find a hot one if you get to moving."

The others began putting their bedrolls together and collecting their gear, and Bushwa rolled out and stumbled to the fireplace.

Grant said nothing further but noticed that Bushwa poured himself a tin cup of coffee and snatched up two biscuits, devouring them and sipping at his coffee as he stood with his back to the fire.

When Ramsey finished tying his bedroll, he stood and spoke. "I've been thinking, Grant. It's going to be a struggle on the trail today, and we still don't know exactly what we're looking for, but if we had Trouble stick to the high ground, he would have an overview that might pick something up. There ought to be smoke or some sign of a hideout with that many men holed up someplace. He can't be firing a gun to signal us, but he will probably be moving faster than we are, and he will be able to see where we're at. He could move downslope and head us off."

"That makes perfect sense. We can't plan our approach without having some idea of what the layout is." He turned to Trouble. "Will that work for you, Trouble?"

"Yeah, I'll see to Tag, and we'll head out and see what we can turn up."

By the time Grant and his party rode away from the trapper's shack, Trouble had been gone for nearly a half hour. They lost the better part of another half hour descending the slope to reunite with the trail they had been following prior to their retreat from the snowstorm. The slope along the creek's edge had been treacherous, and the riders were forced to dismount and lead the horses and pack mule over the slippery stones.

Grant found himself frustrated by the time that was wasting away and hoped the trail would allow them to increase the pace and close whatever gap remained between them and Hannah's captors. Ethan Ramsey took the lead again, searching out sign that was not concealed by snowfall. The assumption was that somewhere up ahead the riders would have veered off the trail and taken another route to the hideout.

The snow remained an obstacle, forcing the riders to dismount and lead the animals when a five-foot drift blocked the trail, or the path was slick with ice. The sun shone brightly by late morning, but hidden in the trees, they could not enjoy its warming rays.

Ramsey signaled a halt, and Grant led Blue up beside the lawyer. "Trouble is up ahead and coming our way—Trouble Yates, I should say."

Trouble approached leading his sorrel gelding. When he reached the searchers, he said, "Found them. All snuggled in a canyon that looks at first to have no way in or out. Walls are in the neighborhood of 150 feet on the upside where I was, maybe half that to the east. I got out my spyglass, though, and picked up a cut on the east wall, narrow at the top but widens as it drops to a width that would let a wagon squeeze through. I've heard such a place is called a slot canyon, but I've never seen one before. The entrance is tucked into a recess in the wall, so a man can't see it unless he's up close. Sort of like Mother Nature built a fort out here. There is a house near the dead-end side and other old ranch buildings that seem in fair repair."

Grant said, "And nobody knows about it?"

Ramsey said, "I've heard of a place in the valley like this, and I suppose others have been here. I've always thought it was just a story. Somebody said the Cheyenne, not the Sioux, chased the first ranching operation out because it was a holy place, but the Cheyenne disappeared from the area, and I've never heard it mentioned by the local Sioux."

"It doesn't matter," Grant said. "What we've got to do is get in that canyon, find out where Hannah is and get her out."

He asked Trouble, "Did you see any sign of where Hannah might be held?"

"No. There were men outside, though. Three were near a couple of trees working on some project there."

Ramsey said, "It would be easy enough to lay siege and pin them down in the canyon, but that doesn't get Hannah released—if she is still alive."

"She's alive," Grant said. "She's got to be. How long will it take us to get to the canyon entrance, Trouble?"

"Another half hour at the most, I'd guess. Good weather on horseback, and ten minutes would get us there."

"Let's move. We will make a final decision when we get there, but we will not be laying siege. Some of us will be entering that canyon."

He would get her out of that place. If he knew Hannah, she would already be plotting an escape. He just had to get there before she lost her life trying. He had come to realize last night that life without Hannah Locke was unimaginable.

Chapter 53

THE HOURS AFTER Danek's departure had passed slowly, agonizingly so. When Reaper awakened from his nap shortly before noon, one of the men brought bowls of stew to the door. Hannah had no appetite but forced herself to eat some of the stew. It looked like vomit and could have been the way it tasted. She did not want to know what was in the concoction. She sat at the kitchen table, and Reaper set his bowl on the counter and walked away. Perhaps the smell of it had killed his appetite, she thought.

He had not spoken a word and moved silently, trance-like about the house, apparently engaged in thought. She welcomed the quiet. It had given her time to think, so she could decide upon the opportune time to remove the Derringer from her boot and kill the man. She hesitated to move too quickly. Danek would not be ready at the stable for several hours, and someone might come to the house and learn of Reaper's death. She would wait till shortly before she was to slip out to rendezvous with Danek.

In her mind, the execution of Reaper made total sense. When she and Danek made their escape, once they exited the canyon, there would be no general to issue orders about pursuit. There was a good chance the little colony would descend to chaos. She had not noticed any structure that suggested a line of leadership succession, and Danek appeared to be an informal second in command. Strangely, she found herself not the least perturbed by the thought of placing a slug in the back of Reaper's head. It was more merciful than the death he had planned for her.

When she finished eating, she walked through the parlor to return to her room, but Reaper stopped her. "Sit down," he ordered, nodding toward the chair usually claimed by Danek.

She obeyed.

"We have decided to free you from this place," he said.

"Seriously?"

There was a rapping at the door. "Come in," Reaper hollered.

A bearish man wearing a coonskin cap and a scowl on his face stepped through the door. He was a menacing figure with a full beard and gnarled, shoulder-length hair. Reaper said, "This is Luther. He is going to keep you company. I must go and attend to final arrangements for your parting. He will take you to your horse when it is time and be your escort for the journey. Please understand that it is necessary that you be blindfolded again. We cannot risk you divulging our location."

"I understand." She understood that Reaper wanted to get her to the gallows with minimal fuss. Put her on the horse, lead it to the noose, slip it about her neck and slap the mount's rump, maybe fire a gun. Of course, once the rope was looped about her neck, Reaper would want the blindfold removed, so he could witness the surprise and fear on her face. But now what to do? Her odds of taking down both men with the little Derringer were little to none. She would be forced to let Reaper go about his business.

"How long before I leave?" she asked.

"Not long."

After Reaper left, she endured an awkward silence in the room with Luther. She had decided what she must do. "Will we make it back to Lockwood before dark?" she asked.

Luther squinted one eye and glared at her with the other. "Yeah, I suppose."

"Will I be able to ride my buckskin?"

"Not for me to say. Not my concern."

She determined that Luther had no interest in conversation, and the fire's heat appeared to be making him drowsy. She remained still in her chair and watched and waited a spell as he closed his eyes and nodded off. Every few minutes, he would jerk his head up, look at her and nod off again. She bent forward reaching her fingers to the calf of her britches as if scratching an itch. When his eyes closed again, she fished the Derringer from her boot, cocked the weapon and pointed it at Luther.

In Grant's dime novels, she thought, the adversary would be given the opportunity to draw his own pistol. She was not a character in a dime novel. His eyes opened for just a second before she squeezed the trigger and a slug drove between his astonished eyes. He slumped in his chair as blood rivulets rolled over his nose and cheeks before settling in his beard.

She got up and raced to the window, seeking out any indication that the gunshot had been heard by others near the buildings below the house. With the distance and the relatively feeble crack of Derringer fire, she thought it unlikely that the sound carried that far.

It was at least an hour before Danek would be expecting her appearance at the stable, but she could not remain in the house. She snatched up her coat, stuffed the Derringer in its deep pocket and went out the door toward the privy as planned, passed it by, and hurried down the slope into the shallow depression that angled in the direction of the stable.

When she reached the stable, she climbed over a board fence behind it as a half dozen horses watched her curiously. She caught her breath before easing as quietly as possible through the rear doorway, where she was greeted by a body stretched out on the floor.

She started when a voice from the shadows said, "I was hoping you would get here. It seems they have moved your hanging up some. I had no way to get word to you. Did you kill Reaper?" Danek stepped from an empty stall into the passageway that ran between the two rows of stalls.

She closed the door behind her. "No. I would have, but he left the house. Another man named Luther was left to watch me and be my escort for my return to town. He died in Reaper's place. You expected me to kill Reaper, didn't you?"

"I thought it possible. It was to be your decision."

"I decided but did not act quickly enough."

"The man in front of the door came in to saddle your buckskin. You were to ride him to your hanging. He said the time had been advanced. Reaper wants the deed done. Turk was not the worst of the lot. It gave me no pleasure to cut his throat. If he does not return with the horse in twenty minutes or so, someone will come to check. Also, Reaper will be sending someone to the house to tell Luther to bring you out."

"So what do we do now?" Hannah asked.

"We must leave your buckskin behind. I did not put a lead rope on him. Hopefully, the law can recover the horse for you when a posse returns to this place. The extra horse would slow us. Lucifer, the pale horse, and my mount are saddled. You do not know the best route to the entrance, so I will ride through the door first and you will follow. But we must ride like our lives depend on it, because they do. Do not stop for anything. If we can make it to the canyon opening, they will have a difficult time catching us."

"And if we don't?"

"There may be two hangings."

"Why are you taking this risk?"

He shrugged. "I did not come to America to be a killer of the innocent."

He led her to the two saddled horses hitched near the front of the stable. She stood by the pale horse, a huge, muscular animal, perhaps the finest stallion she had ever seen. Slowly she pressed her fingers to his muzzle. He did not flinch. She spoke to him softly. "You are a beautiful creature. I cannot help but love you. Can I ride you today?"

A few minutes later she slipped her booted foot into the stirrup and swung into the saddle. She clutched the reins and leaned forward and patted the stallion's neck, whispering words of affection meant only for him.

Danek nodded approvingly. "I think you have won him over. I have never seen anyone but Reaper astride this horse. It was forbidden, but Lucifer always seemed gentle enough. You obviously have a way with horses. I think he will respond to your reining. I am going to slide the door back just enough to allow us to pass. When I am in the saddle, I will immediately ride out the door, and you will follow."

He opened the door and was confronted by five men, two with rifles leveled at his chest. "Boss said you was up to something," a tall man with a black, brushy moustache said. "Plan on taking a vacation someplace?"

Hannah was suddenly weak. It was over.

"Hello, Curly. Take me, but let the lady go. You will live to regret it if you don't. If she doesn't get back to Lockwood safe, you will have every lawman in the territory swarming this place."

"Ain't my job to decide these things." He looked past Danek, and his eyes fixed on Hannah. "Get off that horse, woman. Take Lucifer's reins and follow me. You, too, Danek. Bring your horse. You can ride these critters on your road to hell." He turned to the other men, "Ted, grab their guns, and all of you keep them in your sights while we take us a little stroll." Curly started walking toward the twin cedar trees, where Hannah could see Reaper waited with several other Justice Riders.

When they reached the trees, she looked up at the single timber lashed between them about ten feet high. A rope with a hangman's noose was suspended from the timber with the other end anchored to a tree branch. She led the stallion up beside Danek. "I'm sorry, Danek. You didn't have to risk your own life."

"Yes, I did, ma'am. Not because of you, though. Because of me."

Reaper walked over to them. "Danek, as a traitor, you will die today. I have been uneasy about you ever since we arrived in Wyoming. You have been increasingly contrary. I have been watching you, suspected you might do something foolish. Did you kill Luther?"

Danek did not hesitate. "Yes, I did."

"You will watch Miss Locke hang, and then it will be your turn."

Danek's lie turned her mind to the Derringer in her coat pocket. One cartridge remained, hardly enough to take on this small army but sufficient to kill one man. She stuck her free hand in her coat pocket, readied the small pistol to fire. The hand was still in her pocket when Reaper turned to her.

"And you, Miss Locke. You thought you would ride out of here on my pale horse. Very foolish. But I will grant you one last ride. Curly, take one of those rawhide strips hanging from your belt and tie her hands behind her back. Then, you and Ted get her mounted on Lucifer."

She drew the Derringer from her coat pocket, knowing there would be no time to aim. The gun emerged, and she swung it outward and squeezed the trigger. The pale horse whinnied and backed a few steps at the pistol's crack, but otherwise remained steady. Reaper grunted and staggered backward but did not go down. A slug had obviously hit him, but the bulk of his coat hid the location of any wound.

An arm around her neck squeezed like a vice, and she dropped the now unloaded pistol, reaching back with her hands to fight off her attacker. Then, strong hands clasped around her wrists and pulled her hands behind her back. In a matter of minutes, her wrists were bound, and she was hoisted upon the pale horse's back.

She tossed a glance at Danek as the stallion was led to the suspended rope. He was held by two men but had not yet been bound.

A rider came up beside her, and the noose was slipped over her head and tightened about her neck. She was going to die. What would happen to the girls? And her father? She had never made peace with her father. She would never know what might have been with Grant. She was afraid, but not so much of death as for what she was leaving behind, the loss of a future.

Reaper walked up, bent over now, obviously in pain, hatred and contempt burning in his eyes. "Last words?"

And then all hell broke loose.

Chapter 54

GRANT, RAMSEY, AND Trouble crept through the slot in the canyon wall and studied the terrain in front of them, trying to identify the buildings across the snow-cloaked grassland. The faint sound of a gunshot caught their attention only minutes after they entered the canyon.

"Something going on down by the building and that pair of trees," Grant said. "Trouble, see what you can pick up with that spyglass of yours."

Trouble pressed the telescope to his eye briefly and handed it to Grant. "They're fixing to hang somebody, and one's got red hair dropping from under a hat.

"It's Hannah," Grant said and passed the telescope back. "We've got to move." He called back to Bushwa and Jeb, who were waiting just outside the slot opening. "Jeb. Bushwa. Bring up the horses."

When they were mounted, Grant said, "Spread out. Head for those two trees. Start shooting now. We need to draw their attention."

As they neared, some of the men at the trees began firing at them, but others were scattering for cover. He could make out Hannah astride the pale horse, a hangman's noose about her neck, but a stout man holding the horse steady with one hand and holding off the others with a six-gun in the other. A friend?

By the time he reached the trees, the Justice Riders were on the run, seeking cover where they could find it. All but one, who had to be the man called Reaper who was stumbling toward the pale horse with his pistol upraised. The man at the reins was trying to fire his pistol at Reaper, but his chamber was evidently empty. Grant was within twenty feet now and reined Blue in, raised his Colt and fired repeatedly at Reaper, sending slugs into his neck and torso and dropping him to the ground.

Grant dismounted and raced to the cedar tree where the rope was anchored and untied it. He went over and checked the man he had shot, noticing that the stout man was already freeing Hannah's hands.

Hannah nodded at the white-haired man crumpled on the ground. "He's dead?"

"Dead as a can of corned beef, as Bushwa always says. Is this Reaper?"

"It is, and I'm glad he's dead. An ugly thing to say, I guess."

Grant said, "I must go help the others. We're outnumbered, but I have a hunch the Justice Riders are on the run."

Hannah had dismounted now, and her friend was loosening the noose from her neck. She said, "This is Danek. I owe him. Danek, this is my friend, Grant."

The men each nodded warily at the other. "That your horse waiting nearby?" Grant asked.

"It is."

"Why don't you and Hannah meet up with us outside the canyon? We will talk when our work is done."

Chapter 55

Hannah mounted the pale horse and rode with Danek to the canyon entrance. She reined in just inside. She had been thinking about this man. The law would say he was a criminal, possibly an accessory to murder, although proving it might be a challenge to a prosecutor. She supposed it depended upon how many of the Justice Riders might point fingers at him.

Danek said, "You did not tell the man with the badge that I was one of the Justice Riders."

"No, I did not. Do you have money?"

"Yes."

"You ride on to Lockwood, take a room at the Lockwood Hotel—that is the last place anyone would look for a man on the run. Register as James Madison. Take a bath, get a shave and haircut first thing in the morning, buy some new clothes. There won't be many roaming the streets but stay close to the hotel and take your meals in their dining room. The storm may have stopped trains for a few days. When I find out the day and time for the first train leaving Lockwood for Cheyenne, I will see that a note with departure time and a ticket are slipped under the door to your room. Disappear. Start a new life. You will not be on a wanted poster, but I recommend a name change."

"Perhaps, I will become James Madison. Why are you doing this?"

"I believe in you, James. And I cannot ignore that you likely saved my life."

"Maybe I will become a sheriff or a marshal someplace, put my skills on the other side of the law—or become a lawyer."

"I've got a hunch you can do just about anything you set your mind to. Good luck and thanks, Danek—whoops, I mean James."

He smiled. She had never seen a smile on his face. It was a nice smile. "I thank you, ma'am. And I hope you marry that fellow named Grant. I saw the look on his face when he saw you were all right. That man had found his treasure."

Danek wheeled his horse and disappeared through the slot in the stone wall. "I will marry that man if he will have me," she whispered. And it was time to make some other things right in a life that was nearly cut short.

Chapter 56

HANNAH HAD SEEN Grant only briefly during the three days since they had returned from the slot canyon in a column that included a mule team and wagon loaded with six corpses along with seven prisoners, a few with minor wounds to be treated by Doctor Weintraub. The prisoners would be sent to Cheyenne for trial, and the territory attorney's office would handle prosecution since she was a potential witness. It was doubtful any would hang, but long prison sentences awaited.

She had sent a note with Gideon the previous night when Primrose accompanied the boy home from school after a snack at the Box L. It was an invitation to meet her at The Chowdown for lunch.

She had purposely set a late one o'clock lunch time, so the noon crowd would have thinned out and they could enjoy a bit more privacy, as well as not being pressed by other customers to move on. She had been sitting at her table for ten minutes now, but Grant was a few minutes late, not typical of the punctual novelist. No sooner had she thought it than he appeared in the doorway, spotted her, and headed for her table next to the far wall.

He took the chair across the table from her and sat down. "Ham's the menu today," she said. "The usual fried potatoes and beans. Raspberry pie is a change, too."

"I've never had ham here before. This is cattle country."

"Some folks like a little variety. I do. Trouble convinced Charlie to serve it to prove folks would like a change once in a while."

"Why does Trouble care?"

"He's thinking about getting into the hog business."

"I don't want to hear any more about it."

She laughed. "He's interested in your place, too, you know."

"My cabin?"

"Yes. If you decide you don't need it anymore, he would like to move in. I guess he's tired of sleeping in the stable hayloft. He wants a fireplace to sit by on the rare occasions he is sitting. A warm house to sleep in. His motives are not entirely pure. I think he wants to entertain

Sammy there. It will give him a different sort of challenge anyway."

"Hmm. Well, he can't live with me."

"What if you were living at the Box L?" She could not believe she said that. How would he take it?

He did not answer the question. "That reminds me. I was a few minutes late because I turned in my badge at the sheriff's office for the last time. Sheriff asked if I knew anything about a man named Danek. I lied and told him I never heard of the fella. Are you ever going to tell me about that man? He was with you that day at the canyon."

"I don't know any Danek, and you don't want to know him, either."

"Okay, that's the end of Danek. He's dead as far as I'm concerned. Anyway, while I was at the sheriff's office, I purchased a gift for you."

She looked at him suspiciously. "A gift from the sheriff's office?"

"I bought that nag you've been boarding out at your place for a generous contribution to the sheriff's contingency fund—you know, the pale horse."

"That magnificent stallion? I love him, and I think he is starting to love me back. How did you do it?"

"You might recall that I'm an expert at bad deals."

"But I couldn't get Jim to sell him to me."

"Confession. I asked him not to."

"Why did you do that?"

"I wanted to buy him for you. I'm trying to seduce you."

She laughed. "Seduce me. What makes you think you have to buy me a horse to seduce me?"

"Well, I am half joking. I thought it would be nice if we just got married."

She laughed again and started to speak when the waitress appeared with two plates of food. "I will be back with coffee and the pie," she said.

The two did not speak while they waited for the waitress to return, but their eyes were fixed on each other's. The warmth from those damned hazel eyes was enough to seduce her, she thought.

After the waitress left the coffee and pie, Hannah began to cut her ham. "Smells delicious," she said.

"Well?"

"Well, for a writer, your proposal—if that is what you just made—is not very creative."

"Yeah, I guess not." He reached across the table and took her hand. "Hannah Locke, will you marry me?"

She could not resist teasing him. "I will have to think about it."

"But . . ."

"I've thought about it. Yes, I will marry you, Grant Coolidge, P.J. Bowie, Jake West or whoever you are today. What woman could resist having so many husbands?"

He had seemed tense until now, but he relaxed and smiled. "I was thinking a week from tomorrow. That would be a Saturday. Early afternoon maybe. I cleared it with the Methodist preacher. He agreed on the condition we show up for church services once a month for the next six months. He says we have been a pair of heathens and should be better examples for the children."

"That doesn't give us any time to plan."

"You are wanting a big wedding? I've had two already and the marriages did not turn out well, as you know."

"No. I would only want a few guests, maybe Trouble and Sammy, the Ramseys, a few others. I can figure that out."

"Sammy says she can work up a simple wedding dress. She knows your . . . uh . . . measurements from other clothes they've made for you."

"I can't wear white, I'm afraid."

He chuckled. "I can't either."

"I guess the date is okay."

"I do have some out-of-town guests coming."

"You are serious? Your sister?"

"Not a chance. She would just sigh and say 'Here we go again.' Your father and brother Thad are coming if storms don't get in the way. My telegram just said it was a 'special' occasion. I didn't want to say why in case you said no."

"Oh, my God. How could you do this to me? I wanted them to come but . . . no, you are right. I shouldn't put it off. If I have learned one thing it's that we cannot count on a single day. Make peace, grab love, hold those who are dear to you before it is too late. I do not want to delay the wedding, and I want to see my father and brother."

Grant was eating now. "Your food is going to get cold."

"You were a confident devil about all this, weren't you? I just can't figure you out sometimes."

"Likely never will. I can't figure myself out. Better eat."

"I don't think I can." But she did, not leaving even a crumb of pie crust.

They talked for a time about living arrangements, agreeing that Grant's household members would move to the Box L, and Grant, of course, would share her bedroom, and Gideon's mattress would be laid out on the office floor for now. An addition of several bedrooms and another office would be constructed in the spring. Grant worried about Sarge accepting the new accommodations, and they agreed two dogs might add up to chaos till things settled down some, but they would make it work.

Finally, Hannah said, "I have an appointment at three o'clock. Maybe I can ride over this evening and talk to you some more about this. I thought Gideon could just stay over for the night when the girls bring him by after school. We would have some privacy."

He looked at her knowingly. "And you will tell the kids about our marriage plans?"

"Yes, of course, and not to stay up for me."

Chapter 57

HANNAH WALKED FROM her office to the railroad station. A dozen passengers were scattered about the boarding dock, waiting for the signal that they could board the train that had just pulled in. She cast her eyes over the passengers, split roughly even between women and men. Her search paused when she saw a man about Danek's size attired in a business suit and overcoat, his head topped with a derby hat and a small leather bag clutched in his hand. He was standing off from the others, and his back was turned in her direction.

She walked slowly toward him. When she was within a dozen feet, she said, "James Madison?"

He turned, doffed his hat and offered a sly smile. "Why, Miss Locke, this is a nice surprise."

"I just wanted to see you off."

"Thanks to you, I will be boarding soon."

"I hope you will write someday and tell me where you ended up."

"I shall do that when I have something positive to say about my life. Incidentally, I informed the old gentleman at the stable—Enos, I think his name is—that you are to have my horse and tack. The horse served me well. He was a good and loyal friend. You may sell him if you desire, but I know you love horses and will see he has a good home."

"There will be a place for him on my ranch."

"That puts my mind at rest."

"I am following your advice."

"Advice?"

"I am marrying Grant."

He smiled again. "That pleases me. I am glad for you both."

"They are starting to board," she said. She stepped up and hugged him. "May you always ride with the wind at your back. I will not forget you." She backed away.

He nodded, and she saw that his blue eyes glistened with tears. James Madison turned and walked toward the passenger car.

Hannah waited while he boarded, and James Madison looked back and waved when he reached the last step. She returned a small wave before turning away and heading back to her office, still uneasy about her decision to facilitate the escape of a possible accessory to murder. She hoped that she would hear from him one day with news that would validate the wisdom of her decision.

Chapter 58

SAMANTHA MORRIS WAS waiting for Trouble when he rode into the livery from an inspection visit at the sawmill. From the grim set of her mouth, he knew the visit would not be pleasant. His mind raced. What had he done now?

He dismounted, and Sammy marched up to him, her coat collar pulled about her neck and scarf covering most of her head. "Hi, Sammy. Didn't expect to find you here."

"No, I suppose not, but I expected to find you at Sarah's Fashion's office an hour ago. We were going to go over your sawmill books. When you did not show up, I decided to walk over here a bit ago to see if you were here."

"Dang. I forgot. I got busy at the sawmill. The building is down now, and Birch Reagan and his hires are getting the lumber sorted and trimmed up."

"Keeping me waiting doesn't bother you a bit, does it? You don't think my time is worth a nickel. Well, I am charging you for the hour you should have been there—at my full rate. No discount."

"Aw, why would you do that?"

"Because if money is involved, you will remember next time."

He decided a change of subject was in order. "You heard that Grant and Hannah are getting hitched?"

"I've heard rumors."

"I am going to be best man."

"You, a sixteen-year-old?"

"Closing in on seventeen. And you are invited to the wedding. There won't be formal invitations. It's a small affair." She seemed to soften a bit.

"Well, I suppose that could be fun."

"Yeah. And I'm going to buy Grant's cabin and twenty acres, too. Have me a real home, where we can meet up sometimes. Maybe you can help me fix it up some."

"I don't know about that. It's not proper for a lady to go to a man's house unchaperoned. I suppose my mother could come with me."

"That ain't what I had in mind."

"Ain't?"

He sighed. "That is not what I had in mind."

"I know exactly what you had in mind. And it is not going to happen until we get married, if that ever happens."

"I'd marry you tomorrow, but you said you won't till we're both eighteen."

"That's right."

"Well, we can talk about this later. At least, we will have a place all ready for you to move into. Room for chickens, and I was thinking, maybe some hogs."

"Hogs?"

"Yep. I thought maybe you could tend to them while I'm off working. Lots of money to be made in hogs out here. Not near enough of them to satisfy the market."

"You are going to be off working, and I am going to stay home and take care of hogs? Brady Yates, do you think I am crazy?"

"Well, you will have house chores and cooking and the babies, too. I'd like lots of them. And you can do the bookkeeping for the businesses at home. It will save some money, since you would be off payroll then."

"What about my work at the fashion company. I am part owner, you know."

"I hadn't given that much thought, I guess."

"We've both got a lot of thinking and talking to do before we get more serious about marriage. It's starting to seem to me like you are looking for a slave, more than a wife."

"You're mad, aren't you?"

"You are so sensitive to have noticed." She turned and walked away.

Trouble called after her, "Are you going to the wedding with me?"

She did not reply.

Chapter 59

HANNAH FELT LIKE her stomach was rebelling when she heard the distinctive whistle from up the tracks signaling that the train from Cheyenne would be arriving soon. As if sensing her apprehension, Grant wrapped his arm about her shoulders and pulled her close.

"It will be fine," he assured her.

She was not so confident. She was rarely at a loss for words. Three days. She would be forced to carry on conversations with her father for almost three days. She had no idea what to say, how to close the gap of all these years of separation and estrangement, and she could barely recall what it was all about. Something about her notion that he abandoned her after her mother's death following childbirth, when he had surrendered the twins to her aunt to be raised. She realized now such a decision would not have been that simple for a bereaved father.

How foolish she had been. He had always remained a presence in her life. They had even resided at his Manhattan residence during their high school years when school was in session, returning to their aunt's and uncle's Flint Hills ranch weekends and vacation time. As a lawyer, how many times had she shaken her head in disbelief at the foolish, often imaginary, grievances folks, especially families, fought over? And her own quarrel had not been with her father but with herself.

The engine chugged into the station, pulling two passenger coaches and a string of empty coal cars that would be filled when the engine pulled them onto the spur that branched off to the vicinity of the mines. The train creaked to a stop, and now she found herself trembling. Grant gave her a squeeze.

Minutes later Thaddeus Locke stepped off the train, followed by a rail-thin, white-haired man. Oh, my God. Her father had become an old man. Thad stood on the platform, looking for his greeters, and Myles Locke stepped up beside his six-foot son, shorter now than the son whose adult height he had once exceed by an inch.

She had lost these years because of her wretched stubbornness, and she began to sob, clutching Grant's hand

and pulling him with her through the throng. When he saw her headed their way, Thad stepped out to embrace her, but she passed him by and went to her father falling into his arms and almost knocking him over. "Oh, Daddy, welcome to Lockwood. Forgive me. I've been such a fool. I love you. I love you. I'm so glad you are here."

Myles Locke kissed her forehead. "And I love you, my dear. More than you can imagine. I am a very happy man today." He held her tightly for a bit and then released her. "I did bring your brother with me if you hadn't noticed."

She turned to her smiling brother, still the cheerful, fit rogue with the twinkle in his gray eyes, and moved quickly to his embrace. "Hello, Little Sis," Thad said. He had always called her that. Family lore said that he was ten minutes older, although both were born on the fourth of July just over thirty years earlier.

From the corner of her eye, she saw that Grant was shaking hands with her father. "Oh, I must introduce you to Grant."

"He has introduced himself, but Ian has already told me a lot about this brave man. He told me that the young Grant Coolidge was the most fearless man he ever fought beside. This comes from a Medal of Honor recipient."

"I knew Grant received a terrible bayonet wound, but he never talks about the war beyond his friendship with Ian."

"And he may never talk about it." He tossed a look over his shoulder. "Our bags will be here shortly. What next?"

She stepped away from him and took her father's arm. "A friend of ours, Brady Yates, is waiting with a carriage to take us to the Lockwood Hotel. We will show you to your reserved rooms and give you an hour to settle in. Then we will return and take you for a late lunch at The Chowdown. You cannot experience our culture here without eating at the Chowdown. Oh, I forgot to tell you. Tomorrow, you will be attending a wedding."

Her father and brother both looked at Grant. "I guess I forgot to tell you," Grant said, "I sent another telegram to your father."

She sighed, "Why am I not surprised? I suppose I will need to get accustomed to somebody always being a step ahead of me."

Later, during a roasted beef lunch, Hannah was pleasantly surprised to find that her frail-looking father had a voracious appetite and a keen mind that was quicker than most. She could not recall his precise age, but he would be a year or two past seventy, ancient to her. But she was coming to realize that age was often a matter of perspective.

"Tell us about the wedding tomorrow," Myles said.

Hannah said, "A very simple affair. No more than fifteen guests. I hope you will be willing to walk me down the aisle. My girls will both be bridesmaids. Our boy, Gideon, will be ring bearer, and Grant's best man will be Brady Yates, also known as Trouble. Music is to be provided by our friends, pianist Winifred Beard and Bushwa Sparks, a banjo player."

"I would be honored to escort you down the aisle."

Hannah fought back tears when she saw the wetness glaze her father's eyes. "We have rented the carriage for the day, and this afternoon, we will give you a quick tour of Lockwood and make a brief stop at Grant's cabin before going to the Box L, where the girls will have a light supper ready, and you can get acquainted with the kids. Sunday, your last full day here, will be a family day at the ranch and time for talking. We have a lot of catching up to do."

"You aren't taking a honeymoon?" Thad said.

She smiled and looked at Grant. "My moments with Grant are all the honeymoon I need for now. We hope to take a week or two to travel this summer. We can't leave the ranch behind in winter, and Grant has publisher deadlines to meet. I thought a stop in Manhattan, Kansas would be nice and then maybe on to Ohio to see Grant's sister and her family."

"A proposal," Myles said.

"Yes?" Hannah replied.

Myles said, "A Locke family reunion on July Fourth. If we start planning, perhaps we can get everybody back."

She looked at Grant who nodded approval. "We will be there. It is time for the Lockes to gather again."

About the Author

Ron Schwab is the author of the popular
Western series, *The Blood Hounds, The Law
Wranglers*, *The Coyote Saga*, and *The Lockes*. His
novels *Grit* and *Old Dogs* were both awarded the
Western Fictioneers Peacemaker Award for Best
Western Novel, and *Cut Nose* was a finalist for the
Western Writers of America Best Western Historical
Novel.

Ron and his wife, Bev, divide their time
between their home in Fairbury, Nebraska and their
cabin in the Kansas Flint Hills.

For more information about Ron Schwab and
his books, you may visit the author's website at
www.RonSchwabBooks.com.

Made in the USA
Coppell, TX
15 March 2023

14287176R00249